PRAISE FOR RON WALTERS

"If extremely fast-paced, sci-fi tech thrillers are your thing, then Ron Walters' debut, *Deep Dive*, is a must get. It's Blake Crouch's *Dark Matter*, filled with Tal Klein's *The Punch Escrow*, rolled up and lightly dusted with *Mythic Quest*. This was a tightly crafted, super fun, and original take on the virtual reality rabbit hole, and I couldn't turn the pages quickly enough."

– Chris Panatier, author of *The Phlebotomist*

"Walters finds gold in the VR trope in this techno thriller about a man who wants to be a better Dad but is no longer sure if his children ever existed. The story is quiet and loud, slow and fast, in all the right places."

– R.W.W. Greene, author of *Twenty-five to Life* and *The Light Years*

"A neat little slice of military-industrial paranoia that messes with reality – both virtual and actual – to good purpose. Liked it a lot."

– Dave Hutchinson, author of the *Fractured Europe* sequence and *The Return of the Incredible Exploding Man*

"Ron Walters' sci-fi debut, *Deep Dive*, packs an emotional punch while delivering believable, seamless world-building. For a parent, there's nothing more cold-sweat-inducing than imagining a world where your kids are erased from existence; just a blip on your mind, and absent from everyone else's. But that's exactly the horror facing Peter, who must find a way to reclaim a life only he seems to remember. A brilliant, quick-paced read."

– Gabriela Houston, author of *The Second Bell*

"Simultaneously, a heartwarming story of a father on a mission to get back to his family and a twisty technothriller, *Deep Dive* offers a mindbending peak into the frightening future of VR while asking the question: in a multiverse of possibilities, which reality do you fight to keep? A sci-fi treat!"

– Hayley Stone, author of *Machinations*

"A blistering, page-turning debut that's equal parts *Inception* and *The Matrix*, with a brilliantly heartbreaking concept at its core. You won't be able to put this book down."

– Dan Hanks, author of *Captain Moxley and the Embers of the Empire*

"*Deep Dive* is an imaginative, pulse-pounding sci-fi thriller with a poignantly relatable emotional core. The story is drawn so deftly and believably that I had a few goosebumps moments of 'What if this could really happen?' I couldn't read it fast enough!"

– Elly Blake, New York Times bestselling author of the *Frostblood* series

"*Deep Dive*, a fast-paced story about a man who tries out a virtual reality headset and emerges to find his actual reality – and what matters most – has melted away, will keep you turning pages until late into the night. Ron Walters is an author to watch!"

– Kristin Wright, author of *The Darkest Flower*

Ron Walters

DEEP DIVE

ANGRY
ROBOT

ANGRY ROBOT
An imprint of Watkins Media Ltd

Unit 11, Shepperton House
89 Shepperton Road
London N1 3DF
UK

angryrobotbooks.com
twitter.com/angryrobotbooks
Big dreams fall apart at the seams

An Angry Robot paperback original, 2022

Cover by Kieryn Tyler
Edited by Eleanor Teasdale and Paul Simpson
Set in Meridien

ISBN 978 0 85766 926 1
Ebook ISBN 978 0 85766 927 8

Printed and bound in the United Kingdom by TJ Books Ltd.

9 8 7 6 5 4 3 2 1

To Liz, Charlotte, and Caroline

CHAPTER ONE

I don't remember what it's like not to work.

First thing I do when I wake up is check my messages. Last thing I do before I go to sleep is check my messages. Even when I'm not at Omega Studios fielding gameplay bugs, frazzled employees, and blown deadlines, my days are bookended by the siren song of my phone pinging with one incoming notification after another.

Take today. It's Sunday morning. I should still be in bed with Alana, waiting for Cassie and Evie to come charging into our room demanding breakfast.

Instead, I'm sitting at the kitchen table, nursing a lukewarm cup of coffee while I alternate between feeling overwhelmed by the production schedule and staring frozenly at dozens of unanswered emails, all the while trying to convince myself that we're not falling behind, that *Starflung*, our latest video game project, won't crash and burn like *Scorchfell* did.

Recent history suggests otherwise.

I sigh, shaking my head at the prospect of dumping another five years down the digital drain, and force myself to pick an email at random. The moment I thumb it open and start reading, a throat clears in front of me.

Blinking, I look up from my phone and see Alana standing in the doorway. Her arms are crossed, hazel eyes narrowed, shoulder-length brown hair pulled back into a loose ponytail.

"You forgot?"

I scrunch my face, confused. But then I hear Evie calling out from upstairs, "Are they ready?"

"Shit." I toss my phone on the table and start to get up, but Alana waves me off.

"It's fine. I'll make them."

I can tell by the stiff, methodical way she moves around the kitchen gathering ingredients and mixing chocolate crepe batter from memory that it's the polar opposite of fine.

"I'm sorry," I say. "I totally spaced."

Alana smacks the pancake pan on the cast iron stovetop. "It's her goddamn birthday, Peter."

"I know. It's just–"

Right on cue my messenger app dings. I glance at the screen, unable to stop myself from scanning the preview.

It's from Bradley. All it says is, *You up for a test run?*

A nervous thrill races through my body as I tap out a quick reply. *It's finished?*

Get your ass over here and see for yourself.

The metal ladle cracks sharply against the pancake pan. "Seriously, Peter?"

I send a thumbs up emoji and put the phone on silent. "Bradley says the new headset's ready."

Alana's shoulders tense. "You're going into work."

I know I should say no. This can absolutely wait until tomorrow. But we're beyond behind, and if he's done what he claimed he could do, I've got to see it. "Only for a little while."

Alana jabs a spatula under the crepe and tosses the steaming pancake onto a plate. "So when you said Meg was going to start handling more of the workload, what you really meant was, 'Get off my back'."

"What? No! It's just, she's already doing, like, ten things, so I..." My voice trails off. Alana's heard this excuse before. "You're right. I'll tell Bradley I'll see him tomorrow."

As I pick up my phone, Alana pours more batter into the pan and pivots to face me, dark goop dripping down the length of the ladle like she's just brained a zombie.

"Please," she says. "You'll act all put out for the rest of the day if you don't go in." She thrusts the ladle at me. "But so help me God, if you don't get home in time to make Evie's birthday dinner, I will end you. Got it?"

My brain's coldcocked by a second forgotten promise: I'm supposed to cook Evie her favorite meal, fried chicken fingers and gooey mac and cheese.

I am such an asshole.

I can tell by Alana's raised eyebrows and pursed lips that she's well aware of just how much of an asshole I am, but she has the grace not to say anything before turning back to flip the crepe.

As if our conversation has summoned her, Evie bounds down the stairs, skates sock-footed into the kitchen, and plops into the chair next to me, her ever-present pink blanket tightly in hand.

"I'm hungry," she announces.

Alana slides the plate of crepes onto the table. "Good morning, birthday girl. Get something to drink."

Evie pours apple juice into a glass, miraculously not spilling any, and takes a big gulp. "Can I open presents?"

"I told you last night," Alana says, "you have to wait until we have cake."

My youngest child goes imp-grin and puppy-dog eyes. "Can we have cake now?"

I chuckle, lean over, and plant one kiss on the side of Evie's head, getting a mouthful of unruly curls that smell like half a bottle of strawberry shampoo. "Nice try, kiddo. Where's your sister?"

Evie rolls her eyes. "Reading."

"Wow, she's, like, *so* boring."

"Right?" Evie tugs her blanket over her shoulders like

a makeshift cape. "Since it's my birthday can I play *Animal Crossing*?"

I lift a crepe onto her plate. "I thought you said you were hungry."

"I am." Evie shakes cinnamon sugar onto the pancake, rolls it into a tight tube, and takes a bite out of the middle. "So can I?"

Alana drops another crepe onto the pile. "No screen time before breakfast."

Evie purses her lips, a mini version of Alana. "But Daddy's got his phone and he's not eating."

"That's different," I say.

"How?"

Because your mother might brain me if I even think about reaching for a crepe.

"I'm not playing on my phone, I'm working."

"What's the difference?" Evie asks.

"A paycheck," Alana mutters.

The dig hits hard. Omega Studios is our main source of income. Alana quit teaching to stay home with the girls and has been subbing part-time ever since Evie started kindergarten, but there's no way we could survive on her paycheck alone. If Omega goes belly-up, which is a distinct possibility, it will take my family with it.

Another message from Bradley pops up. *You left yet, dickweed?*

Evie leans over. "What's a dickweed?"

I nearly choke. "Nothing, sweetie," I say, swiping the message closed. "Just something Daddy's friend thinks is funny but isn't."

"Then why'd he say it?"

"Because Daddy and his friend still think they're ten," Alana says.

"Cassie's ten and she doesn't say dickweed."

Alana nods sagely. "She's got a point, Peter."

I kiss Evie again. "I'll tell Bradley to stop saying bad words, OK?"

"OK."

I ruffle Evie's curls, then walk over to Alana and wrap my arms around her. "Have I mentioned how much I adore you?"

"Too soon, buddy." She shrugs me off. "Go tell Cassie you're leaving."

Evie looks up from her crepe, lips sandy with sugar. "Where are you going?"

"Daddy's friend needs him to look at something for work."

"But it's my birthday!"

My chest constricts at the distraught expression on her face. *God, I really am the worst.* "I know, kiddo. I'm sorry. I'll be back before you know it, OK?"

She frowns. "We're still having mac and cheese tonight, right?"

"I'll make it extra gooey."

She nods. "Good."

Feeling more awful than ever, I ruffle her hair again, then risk approaching Alana again. When she doesn't duck away I kiss the side of her neck, savoring the faint floral scent of yesterday's perfume lingering on her skin. "I love you."

"I know," she says, "and I love you, too, even if you are a giant pain in the ass."

I've been married to Alana long enough to know that all is not forgiven, that her joking tone of voice is nothing more than an offer to temporarily cease hostilities in order to avoid the mutually assured destruction of an actual fight. I take the olive branch, praying it doesn't break before I get home.

"Cassie," I call upstairs as I tug on my shoes, "I've got to go into work for a little while. You're in charge."

Floorboards creak, and my oldest child appears at the top of the stairs, a *Babysitter's Club* book in one hand and a concerned look on her face. "Do you have to?"

I nod. "Take care of Mommy for me, OK? And be nice to your sister."

Trailed by a mane of long black hair in desperate need of

trimming, she flies down the stairs and launches herself at me. I catch her just in time, letting out an *oof* as the corner of her paperback digs into my spine.

"I miss you already," she whispers, willowy arms clasping me tightly.

I inhale the scent of coconut shampoo, trying to ignore the pangs of guilt that cling to me as fiercely as my daughter. Routine is important to Cassie. Any change to an established plan – like, say, me telling her I'd be home all weekend – is enough to throw her into a tailspin.

"It's only for a few hours. When I get back you can help me bread the chicken fingers."

Cassie loves cooking almost as much as she loves reading. She pulls back, examines my face for any sign of deceit. "Promise?"

I kiss her forehead, set her down, and hold out my hand, pinky finger sticking up. "I'll even let you fry some of them."

She smiles, curls her pinky around mine, and squeezes. Content with our pact, she sweeps past Alana, who's moved to stand in the doorway, and sits in the chair across from Evie.

"That's Mommy's seat," Evie says as though Cassie's committed some cardinal sin.

Cassie sets down her book, claiming the spot. "But I want to sit here."

"Mommy already put her water glass there." Evie jabs a forkful of crepe at the chair diagonal from her. "You have to sit over *there*."

"It's fine, Evie." Alana shakes her head. "I'll sit next to you."

"But I want you to sit next to *me*," Cassie pouts.

I pull Alana into one more embrace. "Good luck."

This time she hugs me tightly. "Don't forget about your family, Peter."

"Never." The girls are still arguing about where Mommy's going to sit as I close the front door and walk to my truck, every step heavy with regret.

After the *Scorchfell* debacle, when the negative reviews came rolling in like a flurry of unblockable finishing moves, I promised Alana I'd figure out how to manage my time better. And I did, for a couple of months, until the doubt grew too much to keep at bay. I started adding an hour here, an hour there, and before I knew it I was back to my old habits. Call it selfish pride, call it financial anxiety – either way, it's led me here, to a Sunday morning meeting with my business partner in lieu of celebrating my kid's seventh birthday.

Sitting in the driver's seat staring at my house, I almost message Bradley and tell him to hold off on the beta test. Alana and the girls are more important than the VR game we're collaborating on.

Problem is, this isn't just any game. Virtual reality is risky, but if the headset Bradley designed really is next-level immersive, it'll not only usher in a new era of gaming, it will also save my career. I have to see the headset for myself. Have to know I'm not wasting my time. If *Starflung* tanks like *Scorchfell*, I'm done. Creatively. Professionally. Personally. All the time I spent building Omega Studios from the ground up, all the time I've spent away from Alana and the girls, it'll all have been for nothing.

Firing up the truck, I back out of the driveway, ease into the road, and watch my house shrink in the rearview mirror until I round the corner at the end of the street and it disappears from view.

Halfway to Bradley's office I get a message from Meg, my senior developer.

Hypothetically speaking, if I murder Gary because he's fucking around with the fast travel system AGAIN, would you be my alibi?

"On a scale of one to *God of War*," I say, the truck's hands-free microphone translating my words to text, "how likely is it that Gary will still be alive tomorrow if I ignore you?"

Meg responds with a gif of Kratos ripping apart a draugr with his bare hands.

Dammit. This is the last thing I need to deal with, especially today, but Meg and Gary are notorious for their creative disagreements, which usually culminate in one of them threatening to quit if the other isn't fired. At this point I can't afford to lose either of them. Thankfully, Omega Studios isn't too far out of the way.

"Be there in ten," I say.

Unsurprisingly, there are only a few cars in the parking lot. Eighteen months ago, half a year out from *Scorchfell*'s release, it would've been full, but that was back when I thought crunch time was necessary to make a good game. Since then I'd established a blanket rule that extra hours were strictly voluntary, and would absolutely be compensated. If I had any sense I'd follow my own dictate, especially considering how upset Alana is with me. But I can't slow down, not yet. We need a win. Otherwise…

No. There's not going to be an otherwise. We've got this.

Fixing a bright-eyed smile on my face, I stride through the front door.

My mood shifts the instant I set foot inside Omega Studios. It's not a drastic change; I don't feel better, necessarily. But there's an energy here, a sense of purpose and possibility. It's far less intense than it used to be, but it's still there, waiting to be rekindled like a dormant *Dark Souls* bonfire.

For a moment I believe there's a chance we're going to pull this off, that *Starflung* really could be our comeback. But then a loud, incensed, "Fuck physics!" kills the moment, and I remember why I'm here.

I weave my way past empty workstations until I reach Gary's desk. He and Meg are too engrossed in their argument to notice my arrival, so I keep my distance, getting the lay of the battlefield before I throw myself into the fray.

Gary Stapleton, lead graphics coordinator, jabs a finger at one of the two flat-screen monitors on his desk, where the three-dimensional inverted cone of a wormhole pulses with silver light inside the cobalt and magenta remnants of a supernova. "Here. Right here. This location is all wrong."

"For the hundred-thousandth fucking time," snaps Megan Kuang, senior head of development, "the wormhole is fine where it is."

"And for the hundred-*millionth* time," Gary retorts, "if you park it inside a supernova, all the energy leftover from when the star collapsed will be sucked into the wormhole the instant it opens."

Meg crosses her tattooed arms, the Triforce on the left mashing into Sephiroth's face on the right. "So?"

"Do you *want* the ship to get flash-baked by radiation?"

"I wish you'd get flash-baked by radiation," Meg mutters. "Dude, you know this is all *fictional*, right?"

Starflung is a semi-open world action RPG about a father searching for his family after they get separated en route to a new home planet. Early on in the game, he uncovers alien wormhole technology that not only allows him to instantaneously traverse vast distances of interstellar space but also exposes the conspiracy behind the alien attack that split his family apart.

Gary grits his teeth, pale cheeks flushing an unhealthy shade of purple above his black Dream Theater T-shirt. "That doesn't mean we can circumvent the laws of astrophysics."

"Actually, that's exactly what it means." Meg waggles her fingers up and down like a birthday party magician. "It's not real, it's an *illusion*. We can do whatever we want. Except change the wormhole location, because that will totally fuck up the fast-travel system. Also, it looks pretty there."

"Pretty? *Pretty*?" Gary's voice rises an incensed octave.

And there's my cue. "Hey, you two. Destroy any star systems today?"

Gary swivels toward me. "Peter. Thank God. Will you please tell Meg she's being completely unreasonable?"

"Excuse me?" Meg drops her arms, hands balling into fists. "Do you know how long I've spent mapping out the wormhole network? Three months, Gary. Three months! No fucking way am I scrapping all that work."

Gary glares at her. "When the physicist nerds put our game on blast, you'll only have yourself to blame."

It takes everything in me not to groan. There will no doubt be a contingent of trolls who tear apart every scientific inaccuracy in our game, but Meg's not wrong. This is our project. We can do whatever we want with it. And right now, that means ensuring the gameplay mechanics not only work properly but make sense in the context of the story, as opposed to the kitchen sink approach we went with for *Scorchfell*.

While Gary and Meg bicker about the intelligence levels of trolls, my eyes drift to the poster tacked to the wall behind my desk. I've thought about taking it down more than once, but haven't been able to bring myself to get rid of it. I can still remember how excited we were during concept meetings, how innovative *Scorchfell*'s graphics, narrative, and customization options seemed. Biblical plagues, desert labyrinths, mythical creatures, and an anti-hero main character robbed of his rightful inheritance methodically exacting revenge on those who'd done him wrong – it was massive, it was daring. It was going to be our *Horizon Zero Dawn*, the game that took us from a respected studio of twenty-seven employees with one small adventure project under their belt to a AAA powerhouse capable of competing in the big leagues.

It didn't.

"Look," I say, interrupting Gary's dissertation on Lagrange points. "I get your issue with the supernova, but finding that first wormhole by that particular star is a super important plot point. Can't we just add some sort of special shielding to the ship, like something players have to find during an earlier quest?"

Meg scowls. "I literally suggested that, like, two minutes before you got here."

Gary tilts his head. "I'm sorry, was that before or after you threatened to stab me in the eye with my stylus?"

"I'm just saying," she shrugs, "don't mess with my shit."

"Oh my God, you two." I dig the heels of my hands into my eyes. "Gary, can you design the shield or not?"

Gary reaches out and adjusts the position of the Master Chief figurine situated next to his mousepad. "Hi, have we met?"

I'm starting to understand Meg's homicidal impulses.

"Just let me know when it's done." I look at Meg. "We good?"

She shoots me an overly exuberant thumbs up worthy of any JRPG. "A-OK, boss man."

"Great. Then I'm heading to Bradley's."

"Oh shit, the headset's done?" she asks excitedly.

"Enough for a beta test, yeah."

Gary doesn't bother to hide his frown as he turns back to his monitor, but he at least refrains from voicing his displeasure. Unlike Meg and me, he's been against taking Omega Studios down the virtual reality road since day one. Admittedly, his concerns are somewhat valid. VR games are cool in concept, but most of them suffer from less than stellar headsets which, on top of being expensive and never quite as immersive as players expect, often cause nausea, anxiety, and eyestrain after prolonged use.

Bradley swears the headset he's designed will have none of those issues, but I'd be lying if I said I wasn't as worried as Gary. That's part of the reason I didn't say no when Bradley messaged. I need to see the headset in action, to know for certain that it's truly next-gen. If it is, and if we can make *Starflung* as good a game as I think it can be, then we won't just save Omega Studios, we might very well find our names keeping company with all the other video game greats.

Meg pats me on the shoulder. "Remember, dude, if you die in the Matrix, you die in real life."

"Thanks so much for that."

She grins, pops a two-fingered salute off her forehead. "Anytime."

On the way back to the parking lot my phone rings. Alana's name glows on the touchscreen.

I answer the video call. "Hey, honey. Look, I really am sorry about–"

"Hi Daddy!" Evie grins and waves excitedly.

I grin, wave back. "Does Mommy know you have her phone?"

"She said I could call to tell you thank you for the present!" Evie holds up a doll in a pink and green tartan dress that bears a remarkable resemblance to her. "Her name's Amelia. She has hair like mine! See?" She presses Amelia's plastic cheek to hers, their tawny curls tangling together.

"You two look beautiful," I say, forcing my smile to hold steady in spite of the barb lodged firmly in my heart. Logically, I know I have no right to be upset that Alana caved and let Evie open a gift now instead of waiting for me to get home. After all, I left, ditched my kid on her birthday. Not to mention, my track record for coming home when I say I'm coming home is abysmal. But I am upset, and the thing that stings the most outside of missing yet another family moment is that I had no idea Alana had gotten Evie a doll.

Bradley's headset better be worth it.

I drag my heavy heart into the truck and prop the phone so I can still see Evie. "Did you and Cassie help Mommy clean up after breakfast?"

"I put my plate in the sink."

Admittedly, that's a big step. "Is Mommy there?"

Evie shakes her head. "She's upstairs. Are you almost done working?"

The question splinters me. "Not yet." I start the truck. "But I'll be home as soon as I can, OK? I've got some serious mac and cheese to goopify."

Evie puts the doll in front of the camera and bobs it from side to side. "Amelia wants to know if you'll make it extra extra extra cheesy."

"So cheesy," I say, pulling back onto the main road, "every mouse in the house will try to steal it."

"Daddy!" Evie giggles. "We don't have mouses in our house."

I squint against the sudden glare of sunlight bouncing off the hood. "Look under Cassie's bed."

"Cassie!" Evie yells. "Daddy says there's a mouse under your bed and you have to start taking it on walks!"

"That's not true!" Cassie screeches in the background. A second later I hear her infuriated feet stomping up the stairs in search of the rumored rodent roommate.

"I had a bad dream last night," Evie says apropos of nothing. "It gave me a stomachache."

"I'm sorry, sweetie." I ease around a slow-moving sedan, the family inside singing along to a song only they can hear. "Do you want to talk about it?"

"You went sailing on this weird ocean. It was all gray and black like those old-timey movies you and Mommy watch. You got lost and I was sad."

My grin slips. Atlas's burden is nothing compared to the weight of Evie's words.

I am such a horrible father.

"I promise I'll be home as soon as I can, OK?"

"OK. I love you, Daddy. Bye bye."

"I love you, too, Evie," I say, but the phone's already gone dead.

CHAPTER TWO

Bradley's cutting edge tech company, Boundless, is housed in a twenty-story building that looks like something out of a futuristic sci-fi movie, all glass and chrome and angles sharp enough to slice your retinas if you stare at them for too long.

I pull up into a queue of cars waiting to be let through the security gate. Boundless takes up most of the building's real estate, but rumor has it that at least one semi-clandestine government agency rents sublevel office space. No matter how many times I've gotten him drunk, though, Bradley refuses to neither confirm nor deny it.

After five minutes I reach the front of the line. The gate guard checks my name against the guest list on his tablet, then hands me a pass, lifts the checkered security arm, and points me toward the visitor's garage. Inside the building, a second guard at the lobby checkpoint compares my pass to my driver's license, after which I make for the elevator.

The great glass box whisks me silently up to the sixteenth floor, where Bradley's research and development teams spend their days dreaming up tomorrow's tech. The hallway walls are covered in floor-to-ceiling photographs of Boundless' many triumphs: kids playing games on Bradley's console, now in its third generation; adults wearing Bradley's first virtual reality headset and marveling at unseen wonders; and, most astonishing of all, a paraplegic veteran, electrodes attached to her head and legs, walking for the first time in years with the assistance of a neuro-cranial device that circumvents her damaged spinal cord and allows her thoughts to control her legs.

It's all impressive as hell, and more than a little intimidating. But Bradley and I have known each other for a long time, so I'm only moderately jealous of his corporate riches and global fame.

Before he became Bradley Moss, tech mogul, he was simply Bradley Moss, innovative hardware nerd busting his ass alongside yours truly. But Bradley was always more interested in the gadgetry than the games. When he left Omega Studios, shortly after *Anna's Tears*, our first project, released, it was with a prototype console he'd built in his garage workshop. That console now claims as much of the market as the PlayStation, Switch, and Xbox combined.

It means a lot that he came to me with his prototype headset and convinced me to take *Starflung* virtual. I might still be wallowing in *Scorchfell*'s atrocious Metacritic score if he hadn't. I'm not sure Alana or the kids see it in such a positive light, but hopefully, with Bradley's brain on my side, I'll be able to make up for my chronic absenteeism by showing my family I've got what it takes to be a success.

A white kid with carefully styled messy brown hair and an artfully crafted beard sits behind the reception desk at the end of the hallway, playing on his phone. I say kid. He's probably in his mid-twenties, but to my thirty-eight year-old eyes, anyone under twenty-five qualifies as a child.

He glances up at my approach, holds up one manicured finger, taps his ear with another, and whispers something into a thin headset. An ID card hanging from a lanyard around his neck says his name is Christopher Doran. Based on the smell of cologne wafting off him, he clearly subscribes to the more is better approach.

"Can I help you?" Doran finally says.

"I'm Peter Banuk. I'm here to see Bradley – Mr Moss."

Doran makes a big show of studying his phone. "You don't have an appointment."

"He messaged me an hour ago and asked me to come by."

"I'm sorry, Mr Banuk, but if you don't have–"

I show him Bradley's last DM, the *dickweed* front and center. "My daughter thinks he's hilarious."

Doran sighs. "And this is why we keep a PR firm on retainer." He puts his back to me, whispers into his headset again, nods, then swivels around and points to the door on his right. "Third conference room on the left."

"Thanks."

On the other side of the door is a warren of offices, laboratories, and open, sky-lit greenspaces. My skin prickles as I walk past a lab where two blue-coated technicians have attached one set of electrodes to a mouse and another to a man not much older than Doran. In the next room down, two women with VR visors are engaged in some sort of battle involving either swords or gun-chucks.

"Peter!"

I crane my head to the left, and there he is, legs kicked up on a conference room table that gleams as brightly as his teeth.

Bradley Moss, tech guru extraordinaire.

He looks exactly like his *Time* magazine Person of the Year profile picture. Close-cropped black hair, warm brown cheeks, chiseled jaw, tight-fitting black T-shirt, torn jeans, and a pair of tattered green low-top Converse that are older than my kids.

He points at the phone pressed to his ear, holds up a finger, and mouths, *One second.* I get the impression this is a private conversation, so I hang in the hallway, hyperaware of my dad bod, patchy facial scruff, and the Florida-shaped coffee stain on my right thigh that I've only just noticed.

Bradley's *one second* lasts another five minutes. He keeps his voice low, and I do my best not to eavesdrop while I debate messaging Alana just to say hi, but at one point Bradley sits up all outraged and says loudly, "I don't give a shit what those dickbrains say, tell General Shepard I won't do it for less than fifteen million dollars a pop. Got it?" He listens intently for a moment. "Good. Call me when it's done."

He tosses his phone onto the conference table, exhales loudly, and waves me in. "The next time I decide to go after a government contract," he says, "feel free to punch me in the fucking throat."

"My heart bleeds for you, buddy."

Bradley grins and drops his feet to the floor. "You want a coffee or something? I had some Jamaican Blue Mountain flown in fresh yesterday. Shit is amazing."

"I'm good, thanks."

"Suit yourself. How's Alana?"

I shrug. "Kind of pissed that I'm here."

This clearly confuses Bradley, but then he's on his fourth marriage, so that's not surprising. "You told her what we're doing, right?" Because as every good spouse knows, next-gen tech can smooth over all manner of marital woes.

"Let's just say she's less than impressed."

"That's because she hasn't used my headset." He grabs his phone and hops up. "Speaking of, follow me."

I used to believe the sort of stuff Bradley's company designs was created in mysterious underground bunkers controlled by strange cabals of military-industrial tycoons. Truth is, the heart and soul of Boundless is the fleet of laughing twenty-somethings drinking smoothies and munching chips while they input code or manipulate esoteric three-dimensional models on their computers. Some of them look up as we pass and wave at Bradley, who returns their greetings with a smile and a chin nod.

"Oh, I almost forgot." He hands me his phone. "Sign this."

I squint at the document on the screen. "A user agreement?"

"Lame, right? This just covers my ass in case you have a stroke or something."

That stops me in my tracks. "I thought you said you'd worked out all the kinks."

"Relax, Pete. It's just a technicality. I sign shit like this a dozen times a day."

Not entirely reassured, I draw my finger across the screen, etching out a scribble that Alana still doesn't believe gets accepted as a legitimate signature.

"Awesome. Thanks, man."

Several corridors later, a riveted steel door bars our way. Bradley presses his hand against a glowing biometric pad set into the wall, then leans forward and allows his eyes to be scanned.

There's a series of dull metallic clunks, a soda can hiss of cold compressed air, and the door trundles open.

Goosebumps terraform my arms as Bradley ushers me inside.

On the other side of the door is a woman, a computer, and a chair.

The woman sits at the computer, typing away. The rapid clicks of her keystrokes echo faintly around the spacious but otherwise empty room. The flat screen monitor in front of her is segmented into six sections. Code fills one, the text scrolling up at a solid clip in tandem with her typing. Inside another, the image of a brain like you'd see on an MRI pulses quietly. The other four sections contain various readouts, which all display flat lines.

"How's my baby, Reggie?" Bradley says.

"About ready to pop," she responds without spinning around. Her typing grows faster, the code spooling on the monitor at a blinding rate as her tight black braids bounce above her shoulders.

Bradley nudges me toward the leather gaming chair, which sits on a slightly upraised section of floor about fifteen feet from Reggie's computer. A bundle of cables snakes out from the base of the chair and across the floor, connecting it to the computer.

As gaming rigs go it's a bit over the top, as is the way he picks up something off the chair and, bowing his head, presents it to me like a holy relic. "Your helmet, squire."

In his palms is the headset, which at first glance looks like a pair of oversized ski goggles that someone forgot to fit with transparent eyeholes. Not exactly the stuff of technological legend, aesthetically speaking, and yet I can't help but feel like a kid at Christmas as I take it from Bradley and put it on.

The headset fits perfectly, not too snug, not too loose, and blocks all external light. The weight is noticeable but not unpleasantly so. I could wear it comfortably for hours.

"So," Bradley says. "What do you think?"

I turn toward his voice. "I'm not gonna lie, I kind of feel like hunting cyborgs."

Bradley laughs, and for a moment my brain flashes back to when we used to work together. We'd stay up late, chatting like college kids about everything from aliens to other dimensions until we were drunk on theory and sleeplessness.

The jealousy from being left behind is still there, but I can't help feeling eternally grateful that Bradley agreed to partner up with me.

This is going to work.

I remove the headset, blinking the room back into focus. Reggie taps the enter button on her keyboard, then spins and smiles at me. Soft LED light pops off the silver ring piercing her right nostril. Dark brown freckles form constellations on her light brown cheeks.

"So you're the guinea pig, huh?"

"According to the user agreement. Although I think I accidentally agreed to change my legal name to Test Subject Alpha."

"Been there." She links her fingers, flips her hands around, and cracks her knuckles. "You've done VR, right?"

"Yeah."

"Then you should be fine."

"Should be?"

Reggie grins. "It's pretty intense the first time."

"Relax, Test Subject Alpha," Bradley says. "What Reggie meant to say was, do you have any questions before we get started? No? Awesome. Then let me ask you something. Outside of physical complications like eyestrain and nausea, what's the biggest drawback to VR games?"

I want to get on with this, but I can tell Bradley's enjoying holding court, so I play along. "People expect them to be a lot more immersive than they are. VR's supposed to feel as real as actual reality, but every game I've ever played still feels like a game."

"And why is that?"

I think about it for a second. "Partly because the games themselves haven't been that impressive, partly because of haptics."

Bradley snaps his fingers and points at me. "Precisely. Up to this point, every single VR unit has required players to not only wear a headset, but to use haptic controllers like gloves or handheld devices that, through kinesthetic technology, produce forces, vibrations, or motions that mimic the experience of touch."

I look around but don't see any extra gear. "OK, I'll bite."

For a moment it seems as though every light in the room has focused their beams on Bradley. "My lawyers will sue me if I say too much, but the compressed version is that, through a combination of focused ultrasound and electroencephalogram technology, we've developed a headset that, by stimulating specific parts of the brain, actually delivers the world's first true full dive virtual reality experience."

I laugh. "Bullshit."

Bradley's good, but full dive virtual reality – in other words, full sensory immersion where the virtual world is indistinguishable from the real world – is, like the wormholes in *Starflung*, the stuff of science fiction.

Bradley, however, is not laughing. Neither is Reggie. They both stare at me with stoic, expectant expressions like a pair of professors patiently waiting for their dim-witted student to catch up.

My hands tremble slightly as I study the headset. "You're telling me this thing–"

"–is a legit BCI," Reggie finishes for me. "The first fully immersive Brain Computer Interface, codenamed Deep Dive. You don't have haptic controllers because you don't need them. So long as you've got a functioning brain, the electrodes we built into that headset will literally read your mind and translate your thoughts into actions. For all intents and purposes, you will truly be the character in the game."

My entire face scrunches with incredulousness. Bradley, ever attuned to his audience, spreads his hands to either side like Morpheus welcoming Neo to the Matrix.

"Is it really so unbelievable, Pete? EEGs track and record brain activity. Sound waves from ultrasound machines have been used to treat everything from musculoskeletal issues to depression and anxiety. People have been talking about incorporating noninvasive biofeedback into virtual reality rigs for years. We actually did it." He crosses his arms. "So, McFly, are you ready to see the future?"

Despite any latent skepticism, my response is instantaneous. "Hell, yes."

He pats the chair. "Then hop on board."

The chair is as comfortable as it looks. I sink into its embrace, relishing the cloud-soft cushioning, the way its curves and angles hug my body.

"What now?"

"Just put on Deep Dive and lie back. Reggie will take care of the rest."

The world goes dark as I adjust the headset. My entire body is tense with excitement, but I do my best to relax.

"What do you think?" Bradley asks. "Twenty minutes?"

"Maybe ten," Reggie says. "We don't want to melt his brain."

"True. Can you hear me, Pete?"

"Unfortunately."

"Good. Here's how this is going to work. Reggie's going to activate the training simulation we designed. It's not exactly what your game will be like, but it will give you a feel for the virtual environment. We're setting the timer for ten minutes. Assuming all goes well, we'll increase the duration of the dive the next time around. You shouldn't experience any discomfort, but if you do, just raise your hand and we'll pull you out. Got it?"

At the mention of discomfort, I remember the user agreement I signed. Part of my excitement gives way to nervousness, but I swallow it down and give Bradley a thumbs up. "Let's do this."

He squeezes my shoulder. "Get ready to have your reality rocked, buddy."

I hear the whisper of conversation, but whatever he and Reggie are saying now is blocked by the headset. I resist the urge to fidget, focusing instead on keeping my breathing slow and steady.

If Bradley's not bullshitting me – if he's really cracked full immersion – then this headset is, pun totally intended, a complete game changer. This is the sort of thing nerds like me have been dreaming about ever since we watched *Tron*.

"All right, Pete," Bradley says. "I'm going to count down from five. You ready?"

Overwhelmed by an abrupt spike of anxiety that renders my mouth dry and speechless, I give him another thumbs up.

"Fantastic. Here we go. Five."

I exhale slowly.

"Four."

Resist the urge to scratch my nose.

"Three."

Lick my lips.

"Two."

Blink rapidly.

"One."

For a split second, a riot of colors play across the inside of the visor. It's like staring at a rainbow from the inside out. Almost immediately it folds in on itself, creating a dizzying, kaleidoscopic tunnel. My brain knows that my body isn't moving, but it feels like I'm flying forward at unimaginable speeds until, without warning, the panoply of colors disappears and I'm standing on the edge of a cliff overlooking a wide, desert valley surrounded by craggy mountains.

The transition is so abrupt, so disorientating, that I nearly topple over, not so much from arrested motion but from the shock and awe of finding myself in another world.

And not just any world.

This is a desert world that haunts my dreams almost every night. A desert world I devoted years of my life to creating.

It's the desert from *Scorchfell*.

And it is astonishing.

The noonday sun is hot on my face. Sweat drips down my brow and into my eyes. It feels so natural, so normal for this kind of environment that at first I don't really register what's happening. But then I reach up to wipe away the sweat and realize I can *feel* the perspiration clinging to my fingertips. I lick my lips and can *taste* the dust coating them. A warm breeze curls around me like an unseen cat, filling my nose with the *smell* of dirt and sunbaked vegetation.

If I didn't know I was wearing a headset, I'd swear I was actually here.

And that's when it hits me.

Holy shit. He actually did it.

As I gawp at my surroundings, trying to decide where to go first, I spy a sandstone labyrinth far down in the valley, and that's when I realize something else.

This isn't *my Scorchfell.*

I mean, it is, but the labyrinth was only used in the demo we previewed at E3. The crowd at the game expo loved it, and I always regretted not incorporating it into the final version of the game, but changes we made to the story necessitated cutting it.

How Bradley got his hands on the demo I have no idea, but digital thievery or not, I'm beyond flattered he used it for Deep Dive. I'm dying to see the labyrinth up close. I start to take a walk, but my foot's only halfway through the first step when the world blurs around me, and all of a sudden I'm standing *inside* the labyrinth.

The laugh that escapes my digitized mouth is beyond joyous. It's pure, rapturous, a childlike exaltation of unbridled delight. I raise my arms in the air and release a barbaric yawp, dancing in place as I shout to the blue-skied heavens.

There's no disconnect between deciding to perform an action and having to press a button on a controller or move my hands so the haptics in a glove register what I want my character to do. Action here is as instantaneous as it is when I'm in the real world in my real body.

I don't just feel like I'm playing the character in the demo.

I *am* the character.

I start to run, shadow-boxing the air and yelping as I dash down one corridor after another, not caring whether I encounter a dead-end.

"This is amazing!"

Bradley's voice booms from everywhere and nowhere. "FOR THIRTY MILLION DOLLARS IT FUCKING BETTER BE."

The sound of his voice is so startling I trip over an uneven stone and stumble into a wall. Pain shoots down my arm. Wincing in delight, I look around, searching for Bradley, but I don't see him anywhere.

"Where are you? Holy shit, did you build a *second* headset?"

His words reverberate like thunder. "DID YOU NOT JUST HEAR ME SAY HOW MUCH THIS DAMN THING COST?"

I press my hands over my ears, scrunching my face. "Dude, why are you yelling at me?"

"OH, SHIT, SORRY. REGGIE, TURN DOWN THE VOLUME ON THE VOICE-OVER, WILL YOU? OK, how's this?"

"Much better. So you're not here?"

"Nope. There's a real-time mirror of the labyrinth on Reggie's screen. Think of me as your own personal god looking down from on high. Bow, puny mortal!" He chuckles. "So, you like it?"

I run my hand along the rough surface of the sandstone wall, inhale the warm scent of sun-kissed sand, wipe more sweat off my brow. "No joke, this is the most incredible thing I've ever experienced."

"Damn right it is."

I can hear the pride in his voice, and for a second I'm back to feeling jealous that he's scored another resounding success while I'm barely treading water. But then I remember that this won't solely be Bradley's accomplishment. *Starflung* is going to be the flagship game when Deep Dive releases.

For the first time in a long, long while, my future as a developer doesn't seem so dismal. I feel, dare I say it, optimistic, like anything is possible. I can't wait to show this to Alana and the girls.

"Five minutes, Test Subject Alpha!" Reggie yells.

Five minutes? I could spend hours in here. Days, even.

I wander around the maze, imagining the metallic interior of a spaceship in place of the sandstone walls, the light of a billion stars sparkling in the interstellar distance instead of the endless blue sky arcing high above me.

"Three minutes!"

I reach a T-junction. To the right, the passageway continues for about twenty yards before branching right again. To the left ten yards down lies a door.

"Two minutes!"

Left it is.

Spurred by visions of hidden treasure, I speed-walk down the passageway, more excited to explore this world than any other game I've ever played.

"Sixty seconds, Peter," Bradley says right as I reach the door. "Just to warn you, you'll probably feel a little weird when you surface and take the headset off, but it'll wear off quickly."

"Got it." As much as I can't wait to get back to the real world so I can tell everyone I know how amazing this is, a large part of me is bummed that I can't explore longer.

I reach the door. It's made of dark red metal. There's no handle, so I push on it.

At first, it doesn't budge. The metal is cool beneath my hands, a welcome break from the hot desert air. I squat down, searching fruitlessly for a keyhole or a handle. The back of my neck prickles, and I whirl around, fully expecting to see the manticore boss we included in the demo bearing down on me.

Save for a passing, ghost-like shadow, there's nothing there.

"Five seconds, Peter."

Shaking off the chill, I stand and push on the door again. This time it moves. Not much, maybe a centimeter or two. I dig my feet into the sandy floor, striving for purchase, and push harder.

"Four seconds."

The door swings silently open.

"Three."

I peer inside, see nothing but a bright silvery blur filling the space on the other side.

"Two."

Shadows appear, swimming through the opaque air like globular black motes floating behind a pair of closed eyelids.

"One. All right, take off the headset."

"Hold on a second."

I step over the threshold, and the labyrinth disappears.

For a moment, it feels like I'm swimming in the middle of an endless silver sea.

But then one of the black motes floats toward me, and the sea explodes.

The pressure is so intense I feel like my entire body is being crushed into a tiny cube. I cry out, but my voice is drowned by a buzzing like a thousand bees have invaded my ears. I reach up to tear off the headset, but my uncooperative arms spasm like they're being manipulated by a drunken puppeteer.

The pain is so knife-in-the-guts intense I can barely think beyond the fact that something has gone very, very wrong.

Unbidden, images of my family flash through my mind. Of Alana, the forced smile on her face as she said goodbye to me this morning. Of Cassie, the way she clung to me like she thought she'd never see me again. Of Evie's elvish pout when I told her she couldn't use my tablet.

I try to anchor myself to one of these memories, but they slip through my mind like vapor. A void like a miniature black hole opens up inside my head and drags me down into a dark, bottomless pit populated only by the frenzied buzz of invisible bees and a deep-hearted pang of guilty remorse that Cassie and I might not be cooking chicken fingers and mac and cheese for Evie's birthday after all.

The gravity of it all is too much. I feel myself giving in, letting go. Time loses all meaning. A second passes, an hour, a year, an eon.

But then everything comes to an abrupt, silent stop, leaving my limbs limp and my lungs gasping for air and my brain so confused it's all it can do to keep functioning.

A moment passes, then another, until finally I manage to blink. That tiny movement becomes the most painful thing I've ever experienced, a sudden onset migraine of epic proportions throbbing behind my right eyebrow.

Somehow I fight my way through it, and, groaning, ever so slowly force open my eyes.

The world has gone prismatic, lit by an ungodly orange glow. It takes a few seconds for my vision to clear.

When it does, and I can mostly see again, I look around for Bradley, fully intent on beating the ever-loving crap out of him once I have my strength back.

Only Bradley's not there.

Neither is Reggie, nor the chair, nor the room.

In their place is a rain-spattered windshield framing a nearby streetlight that glimmers prismatically in the stormy darkness.

I'm no longer inside Bradley's building.

I'm sitting in the passenger seat of my truck.

And I have no idea how I got here.

CHAPTER THREE

Totally perplexed and more than a little freaked out, I try to sit up, but the migraine attacks my head with a series of double-tracked rim shots, battering my brain with drumbeat after relentless drumbeat. The urge to throw up hits me like Mjölnir, and before I can stop myself I spew bile all over the floor.

Groaning, I wipe my mouth on the back of my hand, squeeze my eyes shut, and gently rest my pounding head against the window. Rain patters against the roof. My clothes are wet, and my skin feels oddly sticky. The faint, sharp scent of rubbing alcohol drifts around the interior of the truck. My mouth tastes earthy, fishy, like I've guzzled overly chlorinated water.

It's next to impossible to reason my way through the pain, to figure out how I wound up in my truck, but one thing's abundantly clear.

Something went horribly, horribly wrong with the headset.

After a couple of minutes I'm able to open my eyes again. I squint out the windshield, but between the migraine and the glare of the streetlamp I can't tell where I'm parked. What's more unsettling, though, is the fact that it was morning when I walked into Bradley's office but it's decidedly nighttime now.

I glance at the clock display above my head. It's two o'clock in the morning.

How the *hell* is it two o'clock in the morning?

My brain hurls out possibilities, each more outrageous than the last. Most of them involve Bradley ordering some low-level lackey to get rid of my body before word gets out that his headset makes brains implode.

I immediately dismiss this scenario as patently ridiculous. Bradley's a cutthroat businessman for sure, and I wouldn't put it past him to pull a little light corporate espionage. But we're friends. Maybe not as close as we once were, but I'd hope our personal history and professional partnership would prevent him from dumping me in the proverbial ditch.

Problem is, if I'm right about the headset malfunctioning, why didn't he take me to a hospital when things went haywire?

The coolness of the window soothes my aching head, easing the intensity of the migraine, and I realize I'm approaching this all wrong.

The most logical explanation is the simplest.

Also the most extraordinary.

I'm not really in my truck.

I'm in a simulation.

And if I am in a simulation, that means I never took off the headset, which also means I'm still wearing it.

Praying I'm not about to short-circuit my brain, I sit up, lift my hands, and reach for the headset.

It's not there.

All I feel is bumpy scalp and damp hair.

"What the fuck?" I whisper.

All the fear I've been desperately keeping at bay comes crashing in, flooding my mind with a terror no survival horror game could ever duplicate.

I prod my head, but it's no use.

The headset's still not there.

Which means I'm not in a simulation.

I really am inside my truck.

Frantic fingers dig my phone out of my pocket. I open the

contacts list, mash my thumb onto Bradley's name, and lift the phone to my ear, ready to excoriate my friend.

"We're sorry," an automated voice responds, "but that number is no longer in service."

I lower my phone, staring at the screen to make sure I haven't misdialed someone else or accidentally edited the number.

I haven't.

Where are you? I text.

The message bounces back as undeliverable.

More confused than ever, I thumb open all my social media and email apps.

Every single one of them has been logged off, and for the life of me I can't remember any of the damn passwords.

Hands trembling, I go back to the contacts list and bring up Alana's name. Mercifully, her number works, but the call goes straight to voicemail. I text her, but that also goes unread. Either her phone's dead or she left it downstairs. Neither option makes sense, though. Ever since we had Cassie and Evie, Alana's been borderline neurotic about keeping her phone fully charged and by her side at all times.

Cassie and Evie.

Oh shit.

If the truck clock isn't wrong, if it really is after two am, then not only did I not make it home to cook Evie's dinner, I missed her birthday entirely.

"No no no no no."

I press my head to the dashboard. In my mind, Alana hugs Evie, tells her Daddy got stuck at work, and offers to make dinner for her. They eat, watching a movie of Evie's choice. Maybe the girls temporarily forget about what a terrible father they have. Alana, however, does not. She thinks about texting me, decides not to because I lose track of time more often than not and she's tired of having to remind me that my family matters more than some stupid game. Eventually she tucks the girls in bed, promising Daddy will kiss them goodnight when he gets home.

And the award for Worst Father of the Year goes to...

I've already missed so many important moments: Cassie winning the school spelling bee by correctly spelling encyclopedia, Evie scoring her first of many trips to the emergency room by taking a header into the wine rack, the girls burying their beloved guinea pig TumTum in the backyard. A birthday is a small thing until it's not, and right now it is very much not.

Dude, get it together. Yes, you're an asshole, but that's nothing new. Right now you need to get home. You can figure out what the hell happened with the headset later.

Right.

I unlock my phone again and open the map app. This, thankfully, still works, and quickly pings my location. I don't recognize the street name, but as I zoom out I see that I'm at least in my city. I type in my address. The GPS plots a route, telling me it will take thirty-six minutes to get home from my current location.

That done, I slide over into the driver's seat. The keys are still in the ignition, which is both good and bad. Good because it means I can head home. Bad because it triggers another onslaught of questions, each and every one of them circling back to the likelihood that Bradley, or someone who works for him, had to have driven me here.

Unless I'm really *not* inside my truck.

I shake my head, grip the steering wheel tightly.

No, no way. I can't still be inside a simulation. I'd know it.

Wouldn't I?

I would.

Except.

Shit.

Bradley was right about one thing: Deep Dive worked. The desert labyrinth felt as real as anything I've experienced in, well, real life. And because it *felt* real, I have to at least entertain the possibility, however farfetched, that I'm so deep in a simulation my brain can no longer discern between what's virtual and what's real.

The problem with that line of thought, however, is that in order for me to be trapped inside this particular simulation, Bradley's stupid fancy headset would've had to not only map my brain down to the last neuron, it would've also had to convert that information into data it then used to create a digital world based entirely on my memories.

No. Stop it. This isn't some mashup of Total Recall *and* The Matrix. *This is real. For whatever reason, you are in your truck. Go home, kiss the girls, and spend the next ten weeks apologizing to Alana. Worry about Bradley and the headset later.*

Right. OK.

The truck growls to life, and I carefully accelerate off the shoulder. It takes everything in me not to race home, but the last thing I need is to get pulled over for speeding or a suspected DUI. Even so, between the migraine and the rain it's hard to fully focus on the road. More than once I veer into the other lane without meaning to, but the streets are fortunately, albeit strangely, free of other cars.

All around me are buildings I don't recognize, unlit warehouses and half-finished construction projects that soon give way to office complexes and apartment blocks. Eventually I reach familiar terrain, and mentally tick off landmarks as I pass them. The mediocre Italian place Alana and I endure because Cassie loves the tiramisu. The shoe store where Evie started crying because they didn't have the pair she liked in pink and we committed the egregious sin of suggesting she settle for green, Cassie's favorite color. The movie theater where we've lost countless hours to banal, soulless films that treat kids like imbeciles instead of thinking human beings.

My chest eases a little at the familiarity of it all. My fingers relax their grip on the wheel, and my headache goes from a full percussion section to a lone, nervous drummer.

Everything's going to be fine.

I repeat that mantra for the rest of the ride. Thirty-eight minutes after waking up in my truck I arrive at my house.

As I park next to Alana's minivan, the front porch motion light kicks on. I fully expect to see the bike we got Evie for her birthday – the present I knew about – lying on its side along with all the other yard toys the girls never remember to put away.

Shockingly, the porch is free of clutter.

Shit. That means Alana spent the evening angry-cleaning.

I climb out of the truck, duck my head against the rain, and hurry into the house.

Inside, all the lights are off, including the one above the stove that Alana always leaves on for me no matter how pissed she is.

Sighing, I kick off my shoes, toss my keys in the basket on the kitchen counter, retrace my steps to make sure I locked the front door, and then tiptoe up the stairs.

I'm groggy enough that I forget to skip over the creaky spot on the landing. It lets out a woody moan. I tense, freezing like a burglar caught in the act, but no one wakes up.

The hallway at the top of the stairs is darker than normal. It's not until I reach Evie's bedroom that I realize why.

Her door is closed.

Evie's door is never closed.

She's afraid of the dark, always has been. Even as a baby we had to leave a nightlight on. Nowadays she's graduated from a nightlight to this spinning globe contraption that projects green and purple stars all over the walls and ceiling. A couple of weeks ago she did something to the mechanism that rotates it so now it does this stuttering double-click halfway around. The noise doesn't seem to bother her, but Cassie, whose room is directly across the hall, complains it keeps her up at night.

All I hear is silence. All I see is darkness. There's no hint of broken gears, no ambient glow painting the quarter-inch of space between the floor and the bottom of the door.

Wondering worriedly if I've somehow wandered into the wrong house, I open the door, step hesitantly into the bedroom, and turn on my phone's flashlight, adjusting the brightness to the dimmest setting so I don't wake Evie.

My heart stutters like the missing globe light.

Normally, Evie's floor is a deadly obstacle course of rumpled clothes, stuffed animals, and disassembled Legos.

Tonight, it's completely, bewilderingly, horrifyingly free of clutter.

Hand trembling, I aim my phone at the corner where Evie's bed has been since we rearranged her room a few months back.

The bed isn't there.

My stuttering heart comes to an abrupt, chest-constricting stop.

In place of the bed is a leather couch. A leather couch I've never seen.

I frantically sweep my phone left and right, scanning the room for any hint of Evie, but all I see is an unfamiliar roll-top desk, a fancier gaming chair than any I've ever owned, and a potted, long-leafed plant that, unlike every other plant we've ever owned, looks like it's well watered.

There's no sign a child has ever inhabited this room.

The world as I know it drops out from underneath me. My paralyzed heart shrivels to half its size, the air vacates my lungs.

This can't be real.

It can't.

There is no fucking *way* this is real.

But my brain can only process what my eyes can see, and what they see is a complete and total lack of Evie.

This is a simulation. A demented, inexplicable, hellish facsimile of my life. It has to be. A simulation has an exit. The nightmarish alternative…

"No."

I stumble backwards, bounce off the doorframe, and lurch across the hallway to Cassie's door, shouldering it violently open because at this point I'm beyond caring if I scare her awake. No amount of fright she might experience at the sight of her manic father can compare to the gut-wrenching terror gripping my entire body.

This time I flip on the light switch. As I blink away the glare I utter the most needful, heartfelt prayer I've ever uttered, pleading to any higher power on duty tonight that my oldest daughter is in the process of sitting up in bed, rubbing confused, sleep-crusted eyes as she opens her mouth to ask what I'm doing.

My prayer goes unanswered.

Like Evie's room, Cassie's shows no evidence that a kid has slept here, ever played here, ever set foot here. No drawings adorn the walls, no toys lie in wait for unsuspecting feet, no dresser drawers hang half-open because they're so overstuffed with pajamas they've become impossible to close.

In place of everything Cassie is a treadmill, an elliptical machine, and a wall-mounted television.

"Alana!"

The echo of my scream chases me down the hallway as I race to my bedroom, one hundred percent certain I'm about to discover that my wife, like my daughters, has mysteriously disappeared.

"What the hell?" Alana's sitting up in bed, the comforter kicked halfway down her legs, her face mottled with shadows and bafflement. "Were you just running?"

The sight of my wife halts my feverish charge as effectively as the dusty walls of my digital labyrinth.

I stand in the middle of our room, swaying in place, gasping for air. Diffuse orange light from the streetlamp outside the window creeps in between the slats of the venetian blinds, creating a geometric mess of the bedsheets.

"You... You're..." I can't seem to form proper words. Can't seem to think. All I can do is stare at my wife, afraid that if I take one more step she'll up and vanish like Cassie and Evie.

Alana knuckles sleep from her eyes, pulls her hair over one shoulder. "Use your words, Pete. I'm what?"

"I..." My throat bobs with the weight of words I can't bring myself to speak. My body shakes so much I'm surprised my bones haven't disarticulated themselves. All I seem capable of doing is drinking in the shape of my wife as though she's the only source of water in a world made of desert.

Alana draws the comforter up to her midriff. "OK, now you're officially starting to freak me out. Why are you standing there like that? Did you just get home or something?"

"Where..." Again, I can't quite make my mouth form the question I desperately need answered. I've seen the empty rooms, but there's part of my brain that's convinced if I can hold out a little bit longer, if I can refrain from asking what happened to the girls, I'll hear the pitter patter of tiny little feet, feel two pairs of spindly little arms wrap themselves around me, and this nightmare will all be over.

Alana reaches over to the nightstand and taps her phone. "Christ, it's late."

I swallow. Cough. Clear my throat. "Where are the girls?"

My wife scrunches her face. "Girls? What girls?" She sniffs the air, wrinkles her nose. "Oh, I get it. Meg got you high again, didn't she?" Alana shakes her head. "You know that high-octane blend messes with your head."

I frown, only wishing this were the product of too much weed. "I'm not... what do you mean, what girls? Our daughters, Alana! Where the hell are our daughters?"

Alana's expression goes from puzzled concern to outright alarm. She swings her legs off the bed, tugs the strap of her nightgown back onto her shoulder. "I don't know if this is your idea of some weird stoner joke, but I am not amused."

"Where are Cassie and Evie, Alana? What happened to all their stuff?"

Even in the darkness I can see Alana's eyes widening with alarm. "Cassie and Evie? You're kidding, right? Please tell me you're kidding."

The way she says their names, it's like I've brought up

former acquaintances, two people we used to know but are no longer a part of our life.

"Alana. Please." I gulp, clench my jaw and do my best to remain calm even though all I want to do is scream. "Where are our kids?"

My wife stands and cautiously approaches me like I'm some rabid animal. The light from the streetlamp clings to her nightgown, lending it a fiery, ghostly shimmer. "Holy shit, you're serious, aren't you?"

I nod, tears streaming down my cheeks, the migraine taking a backseat to the greater pain of realizing that Alana clearly has no idea who I'm talking about.

Alana cups my face, her eyes brimming with fear. "Pete, we don't have kids. Cassie and Evie are the names of the girls in *Scorchfell*."

CHAPTER FOUR

I don't remember falling.

One second I'm standing, struggling to process what Alana's just told me. The next I'm horizontal on the floor, legs curled into my chest, head cradled in my wife's lap while she brushes rain-damp hair off my forehead and begs me to tell her what's wrong, to tell her what she can do to help me.

But I can't speak. All I can do is listen over and over and over to the playback of her words.

Pete, we don't have kids. Cassie and Evie are the names of the girls in Scorchfell.

This isn't happening. It can't be happening. I touch my head, desperately trying to convince myself that the headset's there, I'm just not looking hard enough.

"You're scaring me, Pete," Alana says, her voice cracking with unrestrained anxiety, her fingertips brushing mine away before gently prodding my scalp in search of an injury I know isn't there. "Say something, please."

I open my mouth. Close it. Dig my fingernails into my palms. I don't know what to say. Don't know what to think. My mind runs rampant with random memories of our daughters. The delight on Cassie's face one family vacation when we said she could get her ears pierced. Evie gleefully allowing Alana to pull out her first loose tooth because I, it turned out, didn't have the stomach for it.

Alana lowers her head, her hair cocooning my face. "Honey, I don't mean to dismiss whatever it is you're going through right now, but I am really freaking the fuck out here. If you don't start talking I'm calling 911."

More images of my kids play through my mind, the edges fuzzy with time but no less distinct for it. Images that, according to Alana, aren't real.

But they *are* real. How could they not be? I have two daughters. *We* have two daughters.

A tiny voice from the deepest, darkest depths of my head asks, *Don't we?*

"OK, that's it." Alana shifts beneath me.

"W—Wait." I may have no idea what the hell is going on, but talking to Alana, even if she does think I've suffered some sort of head wound or, worse, a complete mental breakdown, is infinitely more preferable than the prospect of explaining myself to a pair of paramedics.

Besides, if I'm right that my mind really is trapped inside a simulation, the most rational thing for me to do is play this out like I would any other game.

That said, if I'm wrong about this being a simulation…

Nope. Not pursuing that questline. No way no how.

Taking a deep, steadying breath that's anything but, I lift my head off Alana's thigh, press my hands to the rug, and push myself upright.

The room goes off-kilter for a moment. I squeeze my eyes shut, willing the world to quit spinning. When I'm mostly certain I'm not going to fall over, I open my eyes, meet Alana's, and immediately look away.

"Hey." She stretches her legs to either side of me, places her hands on my knees, and says softly, "Whatever this is, we'll figure it out, OK? No judgement. Just you and me."

Just you and me.

Chest tight, I stare at Alana's left hand, at the soft gleam of the white-gold wedding band encircling her finger, then glance at my own. I remember picking them out, how we both wanted something simple that wouldn't break the bank, how a year after we had Cassie Alana's ring slipped off and disappeared.

Alana's fingers tighten around my knees. "Hello?"

I need to start talking before Alana really does call 911. Prolonging the inevitable is tantamount to hiding inside a castle with no supplies while a well-supplied army lobs explosive cannonballs at the walls. But if I don't establish some sort of foundational truth I'll risk everything crumbling apart before I can even begin to figure out how to win this fucked up game.

If it even is a game.

Without looking up I ask, "Do you remember losing your ring?"

Alana's clearly taken aback by the question but has the grace and understanding to roll with it. "I was planting tulip bulbs. It must've slipped loose when I took off my gloves." She twists the replacement band on her finger. "I keep hoping I'll find it some spring from now, but I'm pretty sure it's gone for good."

"My old one's in your jewelry box, right?" We both got new ones because I wanted mine to match hers. Figured I could link my old one on a chain and let one of the girls wear it as a necklace.

Without warning her hands release my knees. I force myself to look up again and wish I hadn't. There's deep, feral fear in Alana's eyes. Accusation, too. "Jesus Christ," she says, "did you have an affair? Is that what this is all about?"

"What? No!"

Her voice goes up an octave. "Then why the fuck are you asking about our wedding rings?"

Because somehow, we both remember that, *but only I remember Cassie and Evie. Because I'm either stuck inside a computer simulation that's turned my life into some insane domestic suspense thriller or I've lost my fucking mind, and at the moment I don't know which scenario is worse.*

Alana puts a finger under my chin and insistently lifts my head. "Peter."

Our eyes meet. I start to turn away again. She traps my chin and leans forward, dark wavy hair cascading over her shoulders and halfway down her arms.

"I need you to listen very carefully," she says. "I love you with all my heart, but I'm about two seconds away from losing my goddamned mind. You come charging into our room in the middle of the night like a fucking psychopath screaming about children we don't have and then you just fucking sit there? Uh uh. No way. Not happening, Pete. Get the fuck out of your head and *talk* to me. Now."

"I don't know what to say."

Alana releases my chin and clasps her hands in her lap. "Start with something simple."

Nothing about this is simple. "Like what?"

"Like, why were you out so late?"

"I was at work."

"It's almost three o'clock in the morning."

"I know."

"Did you and Meg get high?"

"No."

"Did you fall asleep in your office?"

Shortly before *Scorchfell* went gold, when everyone on the dev team was stupidly crunching sixteen-hour days to get the game finished, I dragged a couch into my office. I napped on it every once in a while, but mostly it was a place I could stretch out and detox from staring at computer screens for hours on end instead of doing the sensible thing and going home.

Alana drags her fingers through her hair. "I'm running out of patience, Pete."

"I told you, I–"

Her hair.

I don't know why it's taken me this long to see it. Her hair is one of the first things I noticed about her before I mustered the courage to ask her out. Most people think it's black, but when the sun hits it you realize it's more of a chocolatey brown.

The color's not what's causing my breath to hitch and my heart to thud painfully against my ribcage, though.

It's the length.

When I left the house this morning, her hair hung to her shoulders.

Now, it falls halfway down past her elbows.

I close my eyes, damn near hyperventilating to stave off the panic attack I can feel lurking in the rafters of my beleaguered brain, fully prepared to pounce the moment I lower my guard. It takes everything in me not to tear at my head in search of that fucking headset, but that would only add to Alana's belief that I need to be hospitalized.

Simulation or not, a straitjacket is definitely not the route I want to go. I can't lie, though. One of Alana's many superpowers is sussing out untruths. If I operate on the assumption that this really is a simulation created in part by my own mind – and right now, that's about all I can handle – then lying is antithetical to the dialogue mechanics that lead to a positive outcome in this purgatory of a game.

Always the paragon, never the renegade.

"When I left the house this morning," I say, "you were making crepes and the girls were arguing about where you were going to sit."

Alana's expression is one of helpless terror, the kind reserved for unavoidable car crashes. "Stop it."

I can't. Not now. "We have two daughters. Their names are Cassandra and Evangeline. Cassie is ten and loves reading. She's always nervous, always worried about everything. But she loves being in school plays and just won the spelling bee. Evie turned seven today. She climbs trees and puts rocks in her backpack and swears she hates books but the other afternoon I caught her reading graphic novels to her stuffed animals. Both girls absolutely adore you. They–"

"I said *stop it*!" Alana shouts. She shoves her hands into my chest, knocking me onto my back, and flings out her arms.

"Look around, Pete. Do you see anything in this house, any *fucking* thing at all, that indicates we have kids?"

I've already seen the porch. The living room. The bedrooms. I glance impotently around our room, see the barren wall behind our bed where Evie taped a bunch of misshapen hearts last Valentine's Day.

"No," I whisper, even though the girls' voices continue to torment my mind like I'm Senua standing at the gates of Helheim.

Alana's crying freely now, tears running down her cheeks in ghostly rivulets. "I swear we'll get you whatever help you need, OK? Just, stop talking about the girls from your video game like they're real people. Because they're not, Pete. They're not. You understand that, right?"

"I..."

She sniffs, wipes her nose on the back of her hand, and stands. "Get up."

I let her pull me off the floor and lead me out of our room. Down the hallway, the other bedrooms gape silent and dark like the entrances to tiny tombs.

Her grip firm, Alana leads me down the stairs and into the living room.

Normally there are half a dozen Barbies scattered across the floor, piled on the sofa, arranged on the mantel above the fireplace which we've told the girls time and again is off limits.

Now, there's nothing. The living room is bereft of toys, the furniture as spotless as showroom models.

My gut betrays me, flip-flopping from the absolute certainty that this is a simulation to the unswerving conviction that this is all very, very real. It's my own version of Schrodinger's Cat, only in this case my brain is the cat.

Alana stops in the middle of the living room and points at the entertainment center. "Open it."

I stare uncomprehendingly. "What?"

She remains statue-still. "The drawer under the consoles. Open it."

Understanding dawns, rakes sharp, frigid claws down my spine. Opening that drawer, giving in to the inevitability of this moment, is the last thing I want to do.

But part of me needs to know. Needs to see.

So I move to the entertainment center, drop into a crouch, and pull out the drawer.

"It should be right up front," Alana says, flipping on the light next to the couch.

She doesn't say what *it* is, but I know. I peer into the drawer. Scan the spines.

"See it?"

Trembling, I reach in and remove a game case.

"Bring it here."

Step by hesitant step, I join Alana on the couch.

"Look at the cover," she says.

I already know what I'm going to see, but now that the moment's here I can't bring myself to look.

Once I look, there's no going back.

"Alana. Please."

"Peter, so help me God, if you don't look at that cover…"

I lower my head.

The top half of the cover art is the title of the game. *Scorchfell.* Each letter of the word surrounded by flames.

Below the title are the words GAME OF THE YEAR EDITION.

On its own, that phrase is more than enough to stagger me. *Scorchfell* flopped. It was on precisely no one's list for game of the year. But it's what's below that phrase that delivers the killing blow.

"What are their names?" Alana says gently.

I don't want to answer. Answering means admitting the unthinkable.

"I asked you a question, Peter." Alana taps the faces on the cover. "What. Are. Their. Names?"

I would give anything for the option to reload a previous save, specifically right before I put on that fucking headset, but this is it. The point of no return. Because no matter what argument my brain makes to explain why I'm seeing what I'm seeing, there's no denying the identity of the two girls depicted below the fiery title.

They're standing inside a sandstone labyrinth. The older girl is crouched in front of a red metal door. The younger girl is tugging at the older girl's shirt, trying to get her attention. Behind the younger girl, farther down the passageway, is a menacing shadow.

I'd recognize their faces anywhere. I've lived with those faces for a decade. Watched both of those faces emerge wailing into the world. Woken up to those faces crawling into my bed at ungodly early hours demanding pancakes. Kissed both of those faces goodbye knowing full well I wouldn't be home on time. Broken promises to those faces more times than I can count.

Alana shifts next to me, waiting for my answer.

I point shakily to the older girl studying the door. "Th–That's Cassie." I move my finger slightly to the right. "And that's–" I gulp "–that's Evie."

The game case falls from my suddenly limp hand onto the carpeted floor.

I sit there, shattered, silent, a broken-hearted husk of a man who believes with every fiber of his being that he is the father of two beautiful, amazing little girls. Two beautiful, amazing little girls who apparently only exist inside a video game.

It almost doesn't matter whether I've gotten stuck inside the most elaborate simulation ever devised or experienced some sort of psychological break. At this point they're one and the same: an interminable waking nightmare.

Time passes. Minutes, hours, it's hard to tell anymore.

It's still dark outside. The only source of light is the lamp next to the couch, and even that's not strong enough to banish the shadows that have gathered around us.

My head's back in Alana's lap, knees curled up to my chest.

Her finger traces nervous lines on my shoulder. The game is out of sight on the floor. Neither of us has spoken in a while. She's probably wondering whether I'm going to freak out again.

"I'm sorry," I say.

Alana's voice is falsely steady, the carbon copy of someone doing her best to remain calm. "For what?"

"Yelling at you earlier. When I, you know–"

"–all but accused me of hiding children who don't exist?"

A nauseating chill passes through me. "Yeah."

Alana nudges me. I sit up, cross my legs, and face her from the opposite end of the couch.

She reaches out and grasps my hands. "I'm your wife, Peter. I adore you. But right now I am really fucking scared there's something seriously wrong with you. Like, psych ward wrong."

"Me too." Admitting that out loud doesn't provide any sort of relief; if anything it makes me feel even worse. But I'm determined to play the game no matter how painful it is, because if I don't, if I listen to that nagging doubt that insists this is real, then I'd have to admit I'm not a father. I'd have to admit my daughters don't exist.

I can't do that. I won't do that.

"Tell me the truth," Alana says. "Did something happen today?"

So many details are fuzzy, there's so much I don't understand, but I attempt to explain the basics. "I think it has something to do with the new VR headset Bradley just finished designing. I don't know what the hell went wrong, but it definitely malfunctioned because it knocked me the fuck out. When I came to I was inside my truck. Bradley was nowhere in sight. I tried to call him to find out what happened, but his number wouldn't work for some reason. So I drove home, which is when I, you know…"

My voice trails off as I realize Alana's expression mirrors the one she wore when I first freaked out about Cassie and Evie.

"Why are you doing this?" she whispers, removing her hands from mine and hugging her knees to her chest.

"Doing what?"

"Lying. Making up more stories."

"I'm not... I don't... Alana, I swear to you, I'm telling you the truth. That headset fried my brain. Either that or..." I hesitate, but I'm committed to this now, so I force myself to go on, "or this is a simulation. Which I know sounds crazy! Like, what? It doesn't feel like a simulation, though." I reach out to touch her foot. "*You* don't feel like a simulation."

My intention was to simply reassure her, but as I admit that, a fairly large crack appears in the cornerstone on which I've built my theory that this is all some virtual mind-game.

A headset that can sync my brain with a computer in order to play a video game is one thing. A headset that either by design or malfunction can instantly map the one hundred billion neurons in my brain while simultaneously mining my memories to create and maintain a persistent virtual prison?

Another fissure destabilizes my cornerstone.

God help me, what if this really is real?

Alana jerks her foot away before I can fully fall down that rabbit hole, shaking her head as though she's attempting to dislodge the insult of being told she might be nothing more than a figment of my imagination.

"I knew you shouldn't have quit therapy."

That knocks me out of my mental tailspin.

"Quit therapy? Alana, I've never–" I stop myself there. After the day I've had, *never* feels like too bold a reach. "I'm sorry. It's just–"

"I mean, I get it," she continues, ignoring me. "Grief counseling sucks. But you swore you were over it, and the insurance was about to cut out, so I let you stop going. Clearly that was a mistake."

The room drops a hundred degrees. "I was in grief counseling?" It comes out before I can stop myself.

"For fuck's sake, Pete, you're seriously going to sit there and tell me you don't remember your best friend dying?"

"My best–"

Oh no. No, no, no, no, no.

She's wrong. Has to be. Because if he's dead, if this is real, then that means I couldn't have used the headset. And if I didn't use the headset…

"When?" I say quietly.

Alana throws up her hands and slides off the couch. "I'm out. I can't do this anymore."

"Alana, please. Just tell me when Bradley died."

She stares down at me as though I'm the most wretched, helpless mess of a human being she's ever laid eyes on. At first I don't think she's going to answer, she really is done with me, but she mutters something indecipherable and then says, "A year and a half ago, six months before *Scorchfell* came out."

CHAPTER FIVE

People say the truth will set you free, but they're wrong.

The truth fucking sucks. The truth will tear your heart out of your chest and crush your soul and splinter your mind until your body is nothing more than a hollow shell.

I wish I still had faith that all of this was taking place inside a computer program, but the truth is, I don't. Yes, *Scorchfell*'s desert felt real, but I designed it. My house? My wife? Those things have always existed and continue to exist outside of me. I only have to open my eyes and heart to see proof of that. So for good or ill, I choose the reality of Alana, because right now I very much need something solid to cling to, otherwise my head might explode.

What this means then is that something has screwed up my brain so completely that an entire fictional life has apparently overwritten my actual life. A fictional life where I have daughters and a wife understandably frustrated by my work habits and a career that's nearly over before it ever had a chance to begin. An actual life where I do not have daughters, my wife is extremely worried about my mental well-being, and my career is by all verifiable measurements a success.

I want to scream. I want to break something. I want a reset button.

Instead, I wander around the house in a daze, searching for signs of a life I know I won't find.

The worn, oblong smudge on the wall beneath the stairwell landing window where I did my best to erase the family portrait two year-old Evie drew with a permanent black Sharpie.

The crack in the tile by the oven where nine year-old Cassie dropped the cast iron frying pan when it got too hot after she fried a dozen eggs as a surprise breakfast in bed for me and Alana.

Gone are the alphabet refrigerator magnets, the crafting supplies, the stacks of picture books, the stuffed animals, the piles of sodden towels bunched on the bathroom floor because the girls still haven't figured out that the bathtub isn't a swimming pool.

Gone, just like my girls.

Gone, just like Bradley.

Everything I remember, everything that was dear to me, everything I ever took for granted.

Gone, gone, gone.

The only constant is Alana, who leaves me to my fruitless pacing while she sits at the kitchen table, ignoring me in favor of researching mental health disorders while gnawing on the left side of her bottom lip, something I don't remember ever seeing her do.

Eventually I complete my aimless circuit of the house and make my way back to my wife. She wordlessly holds out her phone. I take it, fully expecting to see an article about grief-induced psychosis.

It's a photo.

In it, Meg is handing me a gold disc. It's the master copy of *Scorchfell*. Behind Meg, Gary and the rest of the Omega Studios staff are frozen in the act of applauding.

I flip to another photo. In this one, I'm standing on the stage at the Game Awards, accepting the trophy for Game of the Year. Meg and Gary and the rest of the dev team are by my

side, the flaming *Scorchfell* logo emblazoned on the massive
screen behind us.

"I'm guessing you don't remember any of that, do you?" The
anger in Alana's voice has been replaced by tired resignation.

I shake my head.

"You were so convinced someone else was going to win,"
Alana says. "I kept telling you it was your year, but you refused
to believe me."

She goes quiet then, the obvious follow-up to her statement
hovering in the air above us like an invisible guillotine.

Just like you won't believe me now.

This is awful. This is everything I've wanted, everything I've
spent years pursuing. Tangible proof of the success I've craved
since the day I decided to make video games for a living.
Tangible proof that all the effort I put into it, all the time I
spent away from my family pursuing my passion, was worth it.

It didn't happen, though. *Scorchfell* flopped.

Alana's picture and the game case that's still lying on the
living room floor say otherwise.

I grit my teeth, once again vacillating between accepting
what I see and holding tight to what I know. Giving up the
simulation theory hasn't made this any easier. If anything it's
opened up an infinite regression of possibilities. But for the
moment, my memories win out. Cassie and Evie remain real
no matter their physical absence. No picture, no amount of
accolades, can tell me otherwise.

Whether I can make it through this dungeon without dying
and starting over from scratch, however, is up for serious
debate.

"Do you want coffee?" Alana says.

"Sure." I don't, but at least it's something to do, something
to focus on.

She puts the kettle on the stove to boil, grinds fresh beans,
and scoops them into a stainless steel French press pot.

I don't remember buying a French press. I don't remember

either of us ever grinding coffee beans. We always just bought pre-ground coffee for the drip machine. But there's no drip machine in sight.

The water boils. Alana moves the kettle off the burner, gives it a few seconds, then pours water into the French press. After four minutes of me trying to think of something to say and Alana keeping her back to me while she stares at the coffee pot, she presses down the plunger, pours two cups, and sets them on the kitchen table.

"Sit."

I sit, pull the cup of coffee toward me, and inhale the rising steam.

It smells wonderful. I hate that it smells wonderful but I drink it anyway. It tastes like orange and cocoa and burns the roof of my mouth.

"So." Alana eyes me over the rim of her cup. Steam wafts in front of her face, turning her hazel eyes milky. "For starters, I think you need to go see Dr Blake."

"He's my therapist."

"Yes. I've already emailed his office. I'll call when they open at eight."

I take another sip of coffee, biting back the urge to argue against what is clearly not a suggestion but a mandate. My circuit around the house, useless though it was in terms of uncovering evidence of Cassie and Evie, made me understand even more that I was alienating Alana, the one person I can currently count on to anchor me. For now, I need to go along with whatever she suggests, to tone down the kid rhetoric even though it's killing me to keep it bottled up. Because even if I have suffered some sort of nervous breakdown, I really, really don't want to be admitted to a psychiatric hospital.

"You started seeing Dr Blake about two years into making *Scorchfell*," Alana continues, having apparently reached enough of an internal compromise that she's willing to fill in the blanks of my unremembered life for the time being. "You were getting angry over the slightest things and having trouble sleeping. He put you on anti-anxiety meds."

"Oh."

That at least sounds accurate. I've never been a good sleeper. The slightest noise wakes me. It only got worse once we had Cassie and Evie. The first year with Cassie I was up every half an hour, constantly checking to make sure she was still breathing. I was a little better once Evie came around, but the little turd proved to be a night owl and would babble to herself at all hours of the night. She still talks in her sleep and gets all "Daddy, stop, I do not!" whenever I bring it up.

Kids get embarrassed about the weirdest things.

"From what I've read online," Alana says, "there are loads of things that can affect your memory – stress, a virus, stuff like that. You seemed to like Dr Blake, but if you'd rather go to someone else, we can look into that, too."

"It's fine," I say. "I'll talk to him."

"Today."

I blink, remember it's Monday now. I've lost half a weekend. "Are you sure he can see me on such short notice?"

"If he can't, we'll hit up every shrink in the city until we find one who can fit you in." Alana pours more coffee into her cup, then tops mine off with the last couple of ounces. "I'm going to do everything I can to help you get through whatever this is, but only if you're willing to put in the work."

Truth be told, I'm not entirely sure I want to get through this. I mean, yes, I want to know that I'm not unstable. I want to know that my mind is my own. And I certainly don't want Alana to constantly wonder when – not if, but when – I'm going to forget who she is. But in my head, her version of getting through this and mine end in very different ways.

"I love you, Peter," Alana says, reaching out her hand. "No matter what, I'm here for you, forever and always. Got it?"

I watch a ripple of ceiling light dance along the curve of her wedding band, then take hold of her slender hand – her nails done in a rich cabernet that's as unfamiliar as her long hair – and say, "Got it."

Alana's snoring next to me.

Despite the coffee, she started yawning around four-thirty. She normally doesn't get up until six-thirty on school days, and two hours of sleep is better than none. The second she laid down she was out. This at least is a habit I recognize, an intimate landmark in an increasingly foreign world where everything seems to have gone completely off-kilter.

I haven't slept a wink. My eyes burn with insomnia, but every sleep exercise I try – deep breathing, muscle relaxation, counting Marios – is quickly overwhelmed by memories of Cassie and Evie.

I consider getting up and losing myself in a video game. Alana says games get her brain too riled up, but they've always helped calm and center me. Problem is, the very thought of gaming makes me think about *Scorchfell*, about the fiction of Cassie's and Evie's faces gracing the copy sitting in our living room like some booby-trapped loot box.

So I lie here next to my wife, listening to the mixtape of her snores and the soft ocean roar of her white noise app while my mind spirals everywhere and nowhere.

Alana mumbles something indecipherable, then rolls over, tugging the sheets halfway off me. Goosebumps prickle my bare skin. Outside, dawn is lightening the sky.

The need to do *something* to distract myself finally wins out. Quiet as can be, I slide out of bed and head downstairs, pretending to ignore the deafening silence emanating from Cassie's and Evie's bedrooms.

It takes me a few minutes to locate my work laptop. I half-expect it to be a different brand, but it's the same I've always had, though the lid is noticeably free of tiny fingerprints.

I start with my social media accounts. Thankfully, all the

passwords are saved, so each site opens without issue. I scan through photos at a feverish rate. Some I recognize. Others show me and Alana vacationing in places like Costa Rica, Bali, and Paris that I have no memory of visiting.

It's the same everywhere. Me and Alana. Alana and me. Me and Alana.

Online and off, there's not a single shred of evidence indicating we have children.

Cut that shit out, I tell myself. *It's up to you to remember them. If you let them go, then they're truly gone.*

I realize how delusional I sound, wavering between knowing in my heart that the girls exist and believing in Alana and what I can see with my own two eyes.

But why the rest of it? Why, on top of my daughters, do I have these ostensibly false memories of *Scorchfell*'s dismal reception, of Bradley being alive?

Knowing exactly what I'll find, I nonetheless Google my friend's name.

Article after painful article confirms exactly what Alana told me.

Bradley Moss, Tech Mogul, Dead at 39.

Tech Pioneer Suffers Sudden Fatal Heart Attack, Leaves Behind Legacy of Innovation.

I skim a few of them, looking for anything that mentions virtual reality or gaming. For the most part, his career trajectory jibes with what I remember: co-founded Omega Studios with me, sold me his half of the company, and founded his tech startup.

So far as I can tell, there's nothing to indicate Bradley ever delved into virtual reality.

Still, on a frustrated whim I search for virtual reality and false memories.

Lo and behold, I get a solid hit.

The first result is a scholarly article about a Stanford University study conducted with preschool and elementary school students who were introduced to various virtual stimuli including swimming with whales. The results varied depending on the age and type of virtual stimuli each child experienced, but the gist of the research seemed to be that it's possible for children to develop false memories of the events they witnessed or participated in while immersed in a virtual environment.

Problem is, believing a single virtual event actually occurred is one thing. I don't only remember one thing. I remember *everything*. An entire fucking life. My brief time in virtual reality involved the *Scorchfell* labyrinth, which, based on the game's cover, apparently made the final cut after all. But again, that's one thing. Nothing about my experience could have generated a life's worth of memories.

A couple more minutes down the wiki rabbit hole unearths a disorder called False Memory Syndrome. Sadly, most of the information surrounding the syndrome has to do with discredited recovered memory therapy. Despite the fact that most scientists agree that memories can be altered by external factors, False Memory Syndrome itself is not accepted as a valid psychological condition, at least among official psychiatric circles, and other than the study I read, nothing links it to virtual reality.

"Well that's just fucking great," I mutter.

"What's fucking great?"

I practically fall out of the chair at the sound of Alana's voice. I spin around, cheeks and ears flushed like I've been caught watching porn.

"Nothing. I…" My voice trails off as she peers over my shoulder and sees what I'm reading. A strand of her hair tickles my ear. The faint scent of orange and mint wafts into my nose.

"Maybe don't use the internet to self-diagnose yourself?" She kisses my cheek. "I'm not sure I can handle a mental breakdown *and* cancer."

There's a lightheartedness to her tone that someone else might mistake as authentic. I know her, though. Her entire aura drips with stress. That ostensible tranquility in her voice is one hundred percent tactical, a temporary buff to the emotional armor she's donned in order to prevent anything – in other words, me – from knocking her off her feet again.

"Come on," she says, squeezing my shoulder. "I don't know about you, but I'm starving. Crêpes Suzette sound good?"

She's already heading toward the kitchen so she doesn't see my face go bloodless.

Crêpes Suzette is one of my favorite breakfast dishes. I suggest it all the time, but Alana isn't a fan of all that syrup. The girls, on the other hand, would bathe in maple syrup if we let them, but orange syrup is akin to poison.

"Hey, could you bring me the Grand Marnier?" Alana calls out.

I can't do this. I can't.

"H– Hold on a sec," I croak.

Alana sticks her head out of the kitchen. "You OK?"

I compose myself as best I can and stumble up before Alana can get a good look at me. "Be right there. Just need to go to the bathroom."

The moment I sit on the toilet, the tears I've been blocking burst out of me with all the pent-up force of a frozen water pipe.

Sobs rack my body, shaking me so hard it's all I can do to keep from falling onto the floor. Nausea crashes into me a few seconds later. Lurching up, I barely manage to pivot all the way around before I throw up all the coffee I drank a few hours ago.

Throat raw, nose snotty, I hover above the toilet until the dry heaves pass. Ever so gingerly I move over to the sink, wash my face, and rinse out my mouth. The reflection in the mirror returns my stare like an animated corpse regarding its past self.

When I feel like I'm presentable enough to pass emotional muster, I flush the toilet, wipe down the sink, and open the door.

Alana doesn't say a word, simply slips her arms around me and holds me tight. I hesitate, then wrap my arms around her and rest my chin on top of her head.

For a solid minute we stay locked together, me desperate for a tether to keep myself from spinning off into madness, Alana doing her best to hold us both in place. Her body fits against mine the same as it always has.

"I'm OK," I finally say, though we both know I'm far from it.

"Dr Blake's office opens in forty minutes," she replies, her words warm against my chest. "Tell me the truth. Can you make it until then or do we need to go to the ER?"

My mind fills with Hollywood images of patients staring empty-eyed out second-floor windows covered in wire-mesh screens. "I'm fine. Seriously. I think the late-night coffee on an empty stomach caught up with me, that's all."

Alana tightens her embrace. "Don't bullshit me."

"I'm not, I swear." I kiss the top of her head. "Look, I don't know why I have all these memories swirling around inside my head, but that's why I'm going to see Dr Blake, right? And if for some reason he can't help, he'll refer us to someone who can."

"You're just saying that so I'll shut up."

"Alana." She tilts back her head and meets my gaze. "I'm OK, honest. Emotionally hungover and tired as hell, but OK."

She side-eyes me with a hefty dose of skepticism. "I want to believe you."

"Then believe me, Scully."

Scowling, she smacks my arm. "Too soon, Pete. Too soon."

The tension's mostly broken, though. I plant a quick kiss on her lips. They're as soft as I remember, slightly sweet and sticky from the honey lip balm she applies religiously. She hesitates, then returns the kiss. For an all too brief moment, I give myself permission to sink into it, to pretend like nothing's changed, to believe I'm simply a husband kissing his wife in the middle of their house.

Our lips linger, but then my stomach grumbles, ruining the moment. Much to my surprise, Alana snorts. It's the first time I've heard her come remotely close to laughing since yesterday morning, when Evie asked what dickweed meant.

I pull away, smiling to hide my heartache, and say, "So about those crepes."

For the next half hour I ignore the fact that my wife not only makes but eats a meal she's always professed to dislike. Stress does funny things to our brains and bodies, after all. Most likely she simply wanted to do something nice for me in my fragile state. I also ignore the longer hair and the spattering of freckles flanking her nose which I only notice when she shifts in her seat and the morning sun slips through the kitchen window and falls on her cheeks.

When we're done with breakfast, I clean the dishes while she disappears into the living room to call Dr Blake's office. I strain my ears, worried about what she's saying, but she keeps her voice too low to hear.

The phone call seems to take forever, to the point where I start panicking that Alana's vanished like Cassie and Evie, that I've been talking to myself this whole time. I start to walk toward the living room, but then she reappears, and I heave a sigh of paranoid relief.

"They had a cancellation," she says. "He can see you at ten thirty."

The relief on her face is palpable. I glance at the clock above the stove. It's after eight.

Wait. It's after eight. On a Monday.

"Don't you have school?" I say.

Alana tosses her phone on the table and refills her coffee. "I called in sick. They got me a sub."

"Oh."

She takes a long sip, regarding me over the rim of the cup. "Do you not want me to go with you?"

"What? No! I mean, yes. I do want you to come."

Don't I?

The muscles in my forearms suddenly tense like I've been lifting weights. I glance down, realize I'm wringing the life out of the towel I used to dry the dishes.

"Good," Alana says. "Because you are in no state to drive yourself."

I opt not to mention that I also have no idea where Dr Blake's office is.

Freshly nervous about talking to a stranger, I pick up a dish I've already dried and dry it again. Alana comes up behind me and wraps her arms around my torso.

"I'm going to suggest something you might not like," she says.

Oh good God, what now?

"Um, OK."

"I think we should cancel the trip to LA. I know you're excited about showing off *Starflung*, but it's only a few weeks away and I'm not entirely sure you'll be up to it by then."

It takes me a second to put the pieces together. "Are you talking about E3?"

The Electronic Entertainment Expo is the biggest gaming event of the year. Developers, publishers, and tech manufacturers announce new projects, show off gameplay from upcoming releases, and promote everything from the latest haptic controllers to next-gen consoles. We premiered *Scorchfell* there, way back when. I'd been thinking about showing off some of the early gameplay for *Starflung*. It would make for good exposure, a way to let the industry and the fans know that we were still out there. But I was nervous about the reception it might receive – people are quick to take a failure like *Scorchfell* and assume the next game will be just as bad, or worse. If the crowd booed when the curtains parted to reveal Omega Studios' logo, there was a very good chance I'd up and quit right then.

"What else would I be...?" Alana sighs into the space between my shoulder blades. "You forgot about E3, didn't you?" Her arms go limp, falling free as she backs away from me.

I force myself to turn around, the flush warming my cheeks answer enough. "I'm sorry." It's the only thing I can think to say even though I am so, so tired of apologizing for things I don't remember. For being the source of the distress playing across my wife's face as she listens to her husband explain once again that he has no recollection of the life they've built together.

She shrugs. "I'll call the airline later. You should probably be the one to tell Meg, though."

Fantastic. Another awkward conversation to look forward to.

"Anyway," Alana says. "I need to take a shower. Will you be OK by yourself for a little while?"

I nod. "Maybe I'll play a game or something." The very thought makes me want to throw up all over again.

"Good." She acts like she's going to say something else, then gives me a half-hearted smile and goes upstairs.

I stand in the kitchen, lost in a fractured mess of memories as motes of dust float in the golden river of sunlight pouring in through the kitchen window. Eventually the childless silence becomes too much to bear. I grab a roll of paper towels and the Windex from underneath the sink, then head outside to clean up the vomit I left inside the truck.

CHAPTER SIX

The weather is warm, the sky blue. All around the neighborhood, cars are backing out of driveways. A few people wave when they catch sight of me. I return their waves to be polite, but the truth is, I don't recognize any of them.

A white two-door hatchback with heavily tinted windows slows as it passes my house. I squint at the darkened driver's side window, unable to make out the person inside. Sunlight refracts off raindrops clinging to its hood. The hatchback comes to a near stop before suddenly revving its engine and tearing off down the street like some *Gran Turismo* cosplayer, narrowly avoiding clipping a maroon minivan packed to bursting with kids.

Jerk.

I step off the front porch and make my way to the truck. When I open the driver's side door I nearly keel over from the stench of hours-old puke. Holding my breath, I unroll a wad of paper towels and lay them on the rubber floor mats. When the wad's soaked through I use another bundle of sheets to pick it up and toss it onto the driveway, then spray a hefty dose of Windex and repeat the process until the mats are as clean as I can make them.

As I lean against the side of the truck gulping fresh air, I glance down at the mess of soggy paper towels, wishing I'd thought to grab a pair of gloves.

My fingers tighten around the bottle of Windex, the sound of crunching plastic crackling in my ears.

The paper towels are stained bright pink.

Bright pink, like stomach antacid.

Bright pink, like diluted blood.

Dizzy with fear, I cast my exhausted mind back to when I woke in the truck and threw up. I don't remember tasting blood, but then I was pretty out of it.

My vision sparkles. I close my eyes, thumbing my right eyebrow in a vain effort to stave off the approaching headache.

If the pink liquid is blood, maybe it was just a one-time deal, some sort of side effect of whatever happened to me.

Right, because that would make this better.

Whatever the case, I feel fine, relatively speaking, and there was no sign of pink when I spewed coffee all over the bathroom sink. One thing's for certain, though: I don't want Alana to see it.

"You all right, Peter?" a voice calls out.

My eyes pop open. A white woman I don't know is running in place at the end of the driveway, a massive chocolate lab tugging at the leash clasped in her right hand.

I push off the truck, forcing a friendly smile. "I'm fine. Just got a little woozy for a second."

"What'd you have for breakfast?" Her tennis shoes slap concrete as she continues to jog in place while the lab licks something off the ground.

"Crepes. Why?"

She nods sagely. "There you go. Too much sugar. You need more protein in your life."

"I'll, ah, make sure I eat some eggs when I go inside."

She makes a finger-gun at me. "Sounds like a plan. Later, Peter. Tell Alana I haven't forgotten about girl's night."

"Will do." *Whoever you are.*

With a wave, the apparent busybody sprints off, dragging the lab behind her. Down the street, a small white car abruptly jets away from the curb, tires squealing as it whips around the corner.

My skin prickles as though the temperature has suddenly dropped fifty degrees.

Yes, there are plenty of white cars in the world, but that one looked suspiciously like the hatchback that went all *Speed Racer* a few minutes ago. The fact that it sped off right when the woman stopped talking to me is highly disconcerting.

You're being crazy. She wasn't some undercover cop. The driver of that car wasn't surveilling you. These things are called coincidences.

"Just because you're paranoid doesn't mean they're not after you," I mutter, moderately certain there's no legitimate reason for anyone to actually be after me.

Casting one last suspicious glance down the street, I toss the soaked paper towels into the trash bin and head into the house to get ready for my therapy session with Dr Blake.

An hour later, Alana takes one sniff of my truck and insists on driving her car to the appointment. It's a bright red VW Beetle, something I remember her always talking about wanting but could never bring herself to buy because it's in no way conducive to toting around a family of four. The sight of it inside the garage is beyond jarring, and for the first time in my life I miss the minivan and the splatter pattern of food and permanent marker stains the backseat's accumulated over the years.

Unlike the minivan, the Beetle has leather seats and still has that pungent new car smell. I settle in awkwardly, unused to being relegated to the passenger seat, and drum my fingers on my knees as Alana gets us on the road.

"Yes?" she says.

I blink, realize I've been staring at the hoop earrings she put in. I've never seen her rock hoops. She hardly ever wears earrings. It's unnerving, as is the styled ponytail, the sleeveless black blouse, the fitted gray slacks.

"You look nice," I say.

She smiles, reaches out, and pats my knee. "You're sweet. How are you feeling?"

"I don't know. Nervous, I guess."

"We'll be there soon. Try to relax, OK? Here." She hands me her phone. "Pick something."

I scan her music selection, happy to see that this at least is mostly the same. Lots of Americana, a spattering of Motown, the random rock band. I put on a Jason Isbell album and rest my head on the seatback, watching the city slide by as Alana sings along to the songs. I come close to relaxing, but every few seconds my brain reminds me about where we're going.

Dr Blake's office is across town, in the opposite direction of where I woke up in my truck. I'm expecting a sterile shopping center-type complex and am pleasantly surprised when Alana steers us into one of the city's older neighborhoods where stately Victorian homes line the street, all of them set back from the road and protected by carefully manicured hedgerows or wrought iron gates.

We pull into a gravel driveway bordered by topiary trimmed into geometric shapes. Alana puts the Beetle in park. We both sit staring at the house. Its wraparound porch is painted a soothing shade of sea green, the shutters on the windows a bright shade of white, the front door a deep sapphire blue.

"I'll be right here when you're done," Alana says, reaching into the backseat and picking up a stack of papers.

"You're not coming in?"

"Dr Blake said I should sit this first session out." She pats the papers. "Besides, I've got a crap-ton of end of the year essays to grade."

"Oh."

She leans over and kisses my cheek. "You can tell me all about it when you're done. Now get going. And," she hesitates for a moment, "be honest."

Feeling summarily dismissed, I climb out of the Beetle and

walk slowly toward the house. Gravel crunches under my feet, the sound eerily similar to the noise Evie makes when she's going to town on a bowl of cereal.

Dr Blake is going to have a field day with me.

The blue door swings open right as I'm about to knock.

"Peter! It's so good to see you again. Do come in."

A dark-haired man I'm assuming is Dr Blake steps to the side, ushering me into the house with wide brown eyes that gleam above a black-bearded smile. He's wearing tan linen pants and a white button-down shirt fashionably untucked with the sleeves rolled up to his elbows.

"I've been meaning to send you a thank you card for the game," he says, closing the door behind me. "Patrick absolutely loves *Scorchfell*. I think he's on his third playthrough."

I wince, still unable to reconcile the game's success with the spectacular mess I distinctly remember making of it. Dr Blake nods as though he mentioned the game simply to judge my reaction, then gestures for me to follow him.

He leads me down a hallway of varnished dark wood flooring, the walls hung with paintings depicting pastoral farm scenes, and into his office at the end of the hall.

"Please, sit." He indicates two huge green leather armchairs in front of his desk.

I take the one on the left. Dr Blake nods again as he slides into a well-worn brown leather chair behind his desk, making me wonder if the seat I chose has some psychological significance. Behind him, a shelf displays local awards and a row of professional books. The only one I recognize is the DSM 5, the *Diagnostic and Statistical Manual of Mental Disorders*.

"So," he says, steepling his fingers. "Alana says you're experiencing memory issues?"

I shift position in the chair. It's ridiculously comfortable and smells faintly of citrus leather oil, all of which makes me want to be anywhere but here. Dr Blake seems nice enough, and the décor is certainly soothing, but I have no memory of this office, no memory of past conversations with this man. He, however, clearly knows me, knows my wife well enough to call her by her first name. There's a history here that I'm not privy to. It makes me feel like I'm playing an online game against someone using cheat codes.

But I did agree to see him, and he's very deliberately waiting for me to respond to his question, so I sigh and say, "I'm forgetting things."

He quirks an inquisitive eyebrow. "Such as?"

I explain about the trip to E3 and Bradley's death.

"I consulted my notes from our previous sessions before you arrived," Dr Blake says. "We spent several months discussing how your friend's untimely passing affected you."

So you say. I just nod.

"But this morning you told Alana you were unaware Bradley had died."

Again, I nod. Dr Blake leans forward and writes something on a pad of paper, then re-steeples his index fingers and presses them against his chin. "Are the coping strategies I prescribed no longer working?"

"Maybe?"

"I see." He jots down another note. "Well, we can certainly talk about other methods to manage your grief. However, what concerns me more is the fact that Alana says you're not only forgetting things, you're also remembering things that never happened."

I feel like throwing up. I want to bolt. I open my mouth. Close it. Look down at my hands. A simulation would be so much easier than this.

"Peter."

"Our daughters," I say, still unable to meet his eyes.

"But you don't have children."

I shrug. "That's what Alana keeps telling me."

"Have you recently discussed having children?" he asks.

"No." *Because I already have them.* "Why?"

"When did you first begin to believe you have children?"

You mean outside of the last ten years? "Yesterday, I guess."

"And what happened yesterday?"

I steel myself. *Here we go.* I start with the crepes and work my way up to using Bradley's headset.

Dr Blake interrupts me. "But Bradley died. So you couldn't have used the headset."

"And yet here we are." It comes out more snappishly than I intended. "Sorry. It's been a long day of rationalizing the irrational."

"There's absolutely no need to apologize," Dr Blake says. "I understand you're feeling agitated and a little bit attacked. I'm only clarifying things in order to get a clear idea of your situation. I am in no way judging you."

I'm not entirely convinced that's true – therapists are people, and people love to judge – but I pretend like I believe him. "OK."

"For the sake of narrative cohesion, however, what happened after you used the headset?"

"I honestly don't know. I was about to take it off when it malfunctioned. One second I was sitting in Bradley's lab, the next I was inside my truck with no memory of how I got there."

"At which point you drove home and discovered that the daughters you thought you had did not in fact exist."

I clench my fists. The way he says it, all clinical and to the point, makes me want to punch something.

"Again, I'm not judging you," Dr Blake says. "The brain is a very complicated thing. Memories are subject to so many internal and external factors. Take a crime scene: ask four witnesses to describe what occurred, and none of their stories will fully match up. In fact, one witness may recount seeing something that completely contradicts what the others have reported."

"That's different, though," I say.

"How so?"

"For starters, no one's questioning whether a crime occurred. There's a body. Proof. Not to mention, you're talking about one singular event. I'm talking about an entire life that ostensibly never happened."

My chest constricts as the words leave my mouth. I tell myself I'm phrasing it that way for the benefit of Dr Blake, that internally I still believe Cassie and Evie are real. But every time I allow for the possibility that they aren't, I feel the thread connecting me to them unraveling strand by tenuous strand.

"As I said," Dr Blake replies, "the mind is a complicated thing, and often responds to trauma in unpredictable ways."

"You think something traumatic happened to me?"

Dr Blake takes a moment to respond. My eyes stray to the DSM 5 on the shelf behind his desk. I wonder how many of the neurological conditions inside that book apply to me right now.

"I think," he finally says, "that you've been under a lot of stress lately. Putting aside your memories for a moment, *Scorchfell* has been a massive success. Even so, you spent several years of your life developing that game. When I first saw you after Bradley passed away, you were having trouble sleeping."

He says it like he's dropping a bombshell he's been keeping on the backburner, waiting for just the right moment to deploy it.

"What does Bradley have to do with anything?" I say.

"Quite a bit, in fact." Dr Blake rests his forearms on his desk, fingers interlaced atop his notepad. "Would you say that Bradley was a healthy person?"

I laughed. "Dude's jacked. He spends–" I pause, clear my throat "–he *spent* as much time at the gym as he did inventing shit."

"You two were the same age?"

"He's… He was a year older."

"So you're the same age now as he was when he died."

Understanding dawns as I realize where Dr Blake's led me. "You think I'm having some sort of relapse?"

"In a manner of speaking. Losing someone close to you is never easy. I'm assuming you've heard of post-traumatic stress disorder?"

My brow crinkles. "I thought that only happened to people who went to war or got assaulted."

Dr Blake drums his fingers on his desk, a staccato four-four beat on repeat. "On the contrary, PTSD can occur for myriad reasons in a variety of scenarios. For example, you lost Bradley while you were under an immense amount of pressure to finish *Scorchfell*. If I recall, you once described the game as all-consuming, a make or break situation. It was so stressful, in fact, that you developed extreme insomnia. Add to that Bradley dying, and, well…"

He spreads his hands to either side as if he's just won a debate. Quite frankly, he very well might have, because all of this sounds very convincing. But the counterargument to his win is that I'm not having trouble sleeping, I'm having trouble believing my entire life is a lie.

I say, "People with PTSD don't suddenly start remembering things that never happened."

"PTSD can have many symptoms. Have you ever heard of dissociative amnesia?"

"I mean, I know what amnesia is, yeah."

"Dissociative amnesia occurs when a person endures a traumatic event or intense levels of stress and begins to experience memory loss. The brain, in order to cope with said event or stressor, becomes unable to recall certain autobiographical information typically related to that event or stressor."

I give myself a few seconds to wade through his explanation. "But I didn't just forget one event. According to Alana I've forgotten our entire life and replaced it with another."

For the first time, Dr Blake frowns. "You raise a fair point. However, we all handle stress differently. What might be a minor aggravation for one person can cause another to go catatonic. Some of it has to do with brain chemistry, some of it with personal temperament." He leans back and crosses one leg over the other. "Let me ask you another question. Do *you* believe you invented the life you imagine you've had?"

I almost lie, but then figure, *Fuck it.* "No."

"And why not?"

"Because every fiber of my being tells me my daughters exist. I know what their shampoo smells like. I know that Cassie has trouble adapting to change. I know that Evie has started to repeat everything her sister says because she knows it annoys the piss out of Cassie. I know that Alana is beyond frustrated with me for always being at work even though I swore I was going to spend more time at home. I know that *Scorchfell* flopped and if my next game doesn't do well my career is pretty much over."

"But *Scorchfell* was a success."

I can't argue with that, so I don't respond, simply do my best to maintain eye contact with him.

He leans back, steeples his fingers again, and stares at me, saying nothing.

"Can I ask you a question?" I say.

"Of course."

"Have you ever heard of False Memory Syndrome?"

"Ah. You went Googling." He says this with a smile, but I can tell he's annoyed that I tried to self-diagnose myself.

"If it helps," I say, "I'm pretty sure the internet told me I have brain cancer. Either that or lupus."

Dr Blake chuckles. "Yes, I've heard of False Memory Syndrome. If, pardon the pun, memory serves, it's been linked to widely disproven studies involving memory recovery therapy."

"Right, I read that, too." I gesture at the *Diagnostic and Statistical Manual of Mental Disorders* on the shelf behind him. "I'm pretty sure that book doesn't list it as a legitimate psychological condition."

"Based on its dubious history, I would imagine not."

I lean forward. "But here's the thing. The syndrome itself may be crap, but scientists have been able to cause people to have false memories."

I recount as much as I can from the study I read about the children and the virtual whales.

When I finish, Dr Blake counters my claim with the exact argument I made to myself a few hours ago. "What you're talking about is an example of an unformed mind convincing itself that a single event occurred, when in fact it did not. You claim to have experienced an entire life. Hundreds upon thousands of memories. Not to mention, you yourself looked into Bradley's death. The internet confirmed it, yes?"

I nod.

"Then how could you possibly have used a virtual reality headset twenty-four hours ago and, in turn, incur an entire lifetime's worth of false memories because of that virtual experience, when the very man who invented that headset has been dead for over a year, rendering it impossible for him to have given you the headset in the first place?"

Well, fuck.

I open my mouth. Close it. Stare at Dr Blake, who doesn't even have the common fucking decency to look like a smug asshat for having not only completely demolished my entire false memory theory in about five seconds flat, but went and plagiarized my own damn hypothesis to do so.

Dr Blake taps his teeth with his pen. "You seem quite focused on the virtual reality aspect of all this. To dive off the conspiracy theory board for a moment, have you considered the possibility that you are still wearing this headset you claim Bradley gave you?"

My eyes widen. "Are you seriously telling me you think I'm stuck in a simulation? " My mental elevator rockets all the way up to the thirteenth floor.

"Of course not. What I'm telling you is that, from my point

of view, it's quite plausible that *you* think you're stuck in a simulation."

"If I did, would that make things worse?"

"It depends."

"For what it's worth," I say, "I don't think I'm stuck in a simulation." Not anymore, anyway.

"That's progress, at least." Dr Blake takes half a minute to scrawl more notes. "That said, all of this begs the question of whether it is actually important if an event truly happened."

"You don't think it is?"

Dr Blake shakes his head. "Whatever the underlying cause – and we will not only discover it, but help you find ways to cope with it and move past it – you firmly believe you are a father to two girls. The memories you have of them are as real to you as the breakfast you had this morning, are they not?"

"One hundred fucking percent."

"You see what the problem is, though, don't you?"

I hate myself for saying it, but I say it anyway. "They're not." I swallow the lump in my throat. "Real."

"Precisely," Dr Blake says. "For the moment, your delusion only appears to be affecting your relationship with your wife. Which, obviously, is something you need to work on. My concern is that, if not addressed now, it will infiltrate other aspects of your life. Granted, many people practice what others view as delusional thinking and get along just fine. All you have to do is look to religion and its reliance on faith for proof of that. Your situation, however, is a bit more delicate than that."

"No one thinks people are crazy for believing in God when there's no tangible proof God exists."

"True," he says. "But billions of people believe in some form of higher power. If it is a mass delusion, it's too entrenched in our psyches to ever pull off a hard reset. You, however, are a different story."

I slouch deep into the chair. "So I've got sudden onset PTSD."

Dr Blake leans back in his chair. "The jury's still out."

I roll my eyes. "That's super helpful, thanks."

"Look, you're a writer, right?"

"I mean, not exactly. I wrote the treatment for *Scorchfell*, but we hired scriptwriters to actually craft the narrative."

"Now you're just being pedantic. Putting semantics aside, *Scorchfell* was your idea. You wrote what was essentially the instruction manual for how the game's story should play out."

"I had help, but for the most part, yes."

"And part of that instruction manual was crafting the world of *Scorchfell*. The setting, the cultures, the monsters, those sorts of things."

"Yes."

"In essence, you created an entire world from scratch. Including the main characters."

"It sounds much more impressive than it actually is. Honestly, I… Oh."

Dr Blake nods as the point he's making hits home. "You see where I'm going with this. Your brain is naturally hardwired to invent fictions. By all accounts you're very good at it. I can personally attest that *Scorchfell* is an inspiring example of what the video game medium can accomplish, primarily because of the core relationship between the two sisters and how they're forced to survive in a world that wants nothing more than to devour them whole. The narrative is really quite something, especially the dynamic between the girls and how it reflects the challenges within each subsequent level. I never knew something like a video game could generate such an emotional response. The problem is, the success you achieved with it has been tainted."

"It has?"

"Don't be obtuse. You and Bradley were close." Dr Blake holds up a hand to forestall my correction. "I'm not talking about how you remember Bradley. I'm talking about how you yourself described your relationship with him. You were as close as brothers, and then he died. A healthy guy, right about your age, also at the height of success, who likely suffered a heart attack due to the immense amount of pressure his work required. So there you are, grieving your friend after enduring several years of your own intensely stressful job, everyone wondering *What's next for Peter Banuk*? while you're sitting at work wondering how in the hell you're going to pull off an even more impressive follow-up without killing yourself like Bradley did."

Well, shit.

"Where were you before you woke up in your truck last night?" Dr Blake asks.

"Bradley's office," I say in a quiet voice.

"Which we've both agreed is impossible, seeing as Bradley passed away more than a year ago. So what's the more rational explanation? That you are the father of two daughters your own wife does not recall giving birth to, let alone raising, who were somehow wiped off the face of the earth after you used a virtual reality headset given to you by a man twelve months in his grave? Or that your own desire for children, as evidenced by your insightful portrayal of Cassandra and Evangeline in *Scorchfell*, coupled with the pressure of creating a follow-up game combined with the knowledge that your friend quite literally died because he worked himself to death, all finally came to a head yesterday, resulting in some form of dissociative episode that has rendered you unable to tell certain facts from certain fictions?"

Fuck. Fuck fuck fuck.

I want to refute his argument, call bullshit on his logic. "I–"

Without warning, a chime rings.

"Well, I don't know about you," Dr Blake says, "but I feel like this has been a very productive beginning."

"Wait, that's it?"

"Not at all. Our session is simply over." He pulls out his appointment book. "I'd like to see you again in two days. Does Wednesday at two thirty work for you?"

"Um." I don't really know how to feel about more appointments. To be honest, part of me was hoping this was a one-time deal. "I guess it's OK."

"Good. Then I'll pencil you in." He pushes the book aside and removes a small pad of paper from his desk. "In the meantime, I'm going to write you a prescription for sleeping pills and something to take the edge off your anxiety."

"I'm good, thanks." I rarely take medication for headaches. No way am I adding anti-anxiety meds, let alone sleeping pills. "I'll be fine."

The scritch and swirl of Dr Blake's pen as he signs his signature to the bottom of the prescription are signal enough that he thinks I'll be anything but fine.

He rips off the paper and hands it to me. I don't reach for it. His arm remains solid and steady above the desk.

"I really don't need anything," I say.

"Did you sleep at all last night?"

My non-answer is answer enough.

"Exactly. I'd rather you not have a repeat of last year's insomnia on top of everything else."

Considering I don't remember last year – or at least, the last year he's talking about – his concern for my sleeping habits doesn't hold much water. But I can tell he's going to hold his arm in place until his muscles lock and he's unable to lower the limb.

Sighing, I reach out and take the piece of paper. I make a point of letting him see me fold it and slip it into my pocket. "Happy?"

"If this puts you on the path to recovery, then yes, I'm happy. What matters more though is whether you're happy." He raises both eyebrows this time. "Are you?"

I hesitate, then say, "No. But I want to be."

"That might be the most honest thing you've said all session. More importantly, it means you recognize there's a problem and you're willing to put in the work to fix it." Dr Blake escorts me back down the hallway. At the front door he holds out his hand. "You might consider taking some time off," he says. "Just to clear your head, give your mind a chance to relax."

Shit. I've been so worried about the girls I completely forgot about the fact that I'm supposed to be at work. "I'll think about it."

"I'm serious, Peter. Self-care is as important as productive therapy sessions."

I wouldn't go so far as to say that this session was productive, and I'm certainly not looking forward to spending more time in his office. But I'm not so far gone that I don't appreciate what he's trying to do. At this point I'm willing to try anything if it helps me.

I shake his hand. "See you Wednesday."

"Go home and get some rest. Doctor's orders."

"I will."

I don't, though.

As soon as I'm back in the car, I ask Alana to drive me to Omega Studios.

CHAPTER SEVEN

From the outside, Omega Studios looks exactly how I remember it. Same boxy Lego shape, same stormy sky paintjob. The perfect unassuming place for a small, independent gaming company to make its mark.

It's Monday, so the parking lot's full. Alana pulls into my spot, which is marked by a fancy nameplate bolted onto the sidewalk curb, but keeps the Beetle in idle.

"I'm still not sure this is a good idea," she says.

"It'll only be for, like, half an hour," I respond. "I just want to check in with everyone and tell Meg about E3."

This is only partly true. I'm not really worried about asking Meg to take point on unveiling *Starflung*. Not only is she a spotlight junkie, she also knows as much about the game as I do. More, probably. She's also the better gamer, especially when it comes to debuting live footage.

The real reason I want to go into work, however, has to do with reconnaissance. Non-existent children aside, I need to see how *Scorchfell*'s success has affected the studio. A quick chat with Meg should at least let me get a cursory lay of the land so I don't make a complete ass of myself when I do come back full-time.

"Maybe I should go in with you," Alana says, tucking a strand of loose hair behind her ear.

"I'm perfectly capable of talking to Meg on my own."

"What if something triggers you?"

Pretty sure that ship has sailed. "Isn't the whole point of therapy to face your fears?"

Alana purses her lips. "You literally had a breakdown, like, five hours ago."

"What are you talking about?"

"Your little episode in the bathroom before breakfast?"

Oh, that. "I told you, the coffee upset my stomach."

"Right." She reaches for the gearshift.

I lay my hand on top of hers. "Look, how about this. You take my prescription to the pharmacy while I talk to Meg. As soon as you're back, we'll go home and watch a movie or, you know, something." I trace her knuckle with my fingertip.

Alana narrows her eyes. "Peter Banuk, are you propositioning me?"

"Maybe?"

My stomach does this sort of nervous flip-flop at the thought of being intimate with her. Sex has always been relaxed with Alana, plenty passionate before the girls came along, not quite as amorous afterward, but we still make time for it, and after nearly twenty years together I absolutely relish seeing my wife naked. Of course, with Cassie and Evie in the picture, there's always the very real possibility that one of them will barge into our room at the wrong moment, so there's a level of haste that wasn't there pre-kids.

Now, though, I have no idea what our sex life is like. In fact, I have no idea what our married life is like at all.

"How are you horny?" Alana says. "You just got diagnosed with PTSD."

I bat my eyes. "Dr Blake said sex is a proven stress reliever."

"Liar." She shakes her head, squeezes my hand. "Fine. I'll run to the pharmacy. But you better be outside the second I get back or I'm coming in guns blazing."

"Deal." I lean over and kiss her cheek, then make my escape before she can reconsider.

As Alana's car disappears from view, a flash of white from the far side of the parking lot catches my eye. I squint, raising my hand to block the sun, and see a small white hatchback with tinted windows slinking between the rows of cars.

I react on instinct, throwing myself into a dead sprint as I make a beeline for the hatchback, well aware that attempting to chase down a car on foot isn't the sort of thing someone of sound mind would do. But there's no way this third sighting is a coincidence. It's probably just some creeper, which in itself is highly unsettling, although as I dash through the rows of parked cars I wonder if maybe whoever it is knows something about my memory issues. It's highly improbable, but after the past twenty-four hours I'm pretty much open to any possibility no matter how unlikely it seems. Whatever the case, I'll be damned if I'm going to sit around twiddling my thumbs while some rando stalks me.

Sadly, the driver has no intention of letting me catch him. The engine revs, growling like some souped-up Mario Kart stock car. My heart redlines, legs pumping like overworked pistons, but it's too late.

The hatchback peels out and launches itself into oncoming traffic, narrowly avoiding clipping a delivery van. A blue sedan screeches to a halt, horn blaring. The hatchback carves a controlled sine wave between cars before being swallowed up by lunchtime traffic.

Cheeks flushed, chest heaving, I give up the pursuit and collapse against the side of a Land Rover, trying to catch my breath as the reality of what I just did wallops me upside my head. Yesterday I would've never dreamed about confronting a potential stalker. Now I'm chasing their car in a public parking lot?

Who are you, dude?

The midday sun is hot on my sweating face. Part of me

wants to call the cops, but that would open me up to questions I'm not ready, able, or willing to answer.

So I rest there, composing myself while the adrenaline drains from my body. When I'm steadier, I make my way into Omega Studios.

Like the outside, the inside of the building is mostly how I remember it. Same scent of burnt coffee, same labyrinthine arrangement of workstations. The din of conversation fills the air. It's a familiar sound that immediately grounds me.

Unlike yesterday, though, Gary and Meg aren't arguing about spaceship design. In fact, they're in Meg's office, laughing. Together. On purpose. And not, as far as I can tell, at each other.

That sight alone is enough to remind me that all is not well in my personal Denmark.

And then I see the trophy case.

Omega Studios doesn't have a trophy case. Yes, we won a couple of honorable mentions for *Anna's Tears*, but those awards are in my office.

Almost like I'm sleepwalking, I stride over to the trophy case, enamored by the shine of so many plaques.

The trophy from the Game Awards, a silver armless angel with up-thrust chest and back-thrust wings standing on a pedestal, holds pride of place.

Mesmerized, I gawp at the metal angel, studying the play of lamplight across its angular body, the way each letter in *Scorchfell*'s name seems to glow with radiant, white-hot fire.

Alana was right to be worried, because the emotions raging through me are damn near debilitating.

It can't be real.

I pinch myself, close my eyes and count to ten.

When I open them, the trophy's still there.

It's real.

I want to throw up.

This is it. The thing I've been striving for since I started out in this business. Tangible, incontrovertible proof that I have what it takes, that I won't burn out and fade away, forgotten, like so many other creatives desperately striving for recognition. But all I can think about is the quiet house I woke up to this morning. About the Legos I'll never step on. About the late nights I'll never spend comforting one sick kid while Alana comforts the other and we do our best not to gag as we shove puke-stained bedsheets into the washing machine at two o'clock in the morning.

Being a parent is messy and stressful and a giant pain in the ass a lot of the time, but staring at this trophy and all it represents makes me realize even more how much I love being a father. Yes, I haven't been a particularly good one these past few years, but the fact remains that I love my kids with all my heart and soul, and no trophy will ever make me feel the way I felt when Cassie grabbed my finger for the first time or when Evie woke up from her first nightmare and called out for me.

I cannot imagine my life without my girls. But that's exactly what the universe seems to be asking me to do. And it's utter fucking bullshit. Losing Cassie and Evie isn't worth any amount of accolades.

"It never gets old, does it?" a voice says from behind me.

The voice startles me so much I damn near jump out of my shoes. I spin around. "Meg. Jesus, you scared me."

"My diminutive size often has that effect on unassuming men." Megan Kuang frowns up at me. "Dude, you look like shit. I thought Alana said you were sick."

"Alana called?"

"Duh. She said you were puking your guts out all night. You don't need to bring that shit in here." Covering her mouth with her hand, she points at the front door. "Go. The Fuck. Home."

I raise my hands to ward her off. "Fine, fine, I'm going." I turn to leave, then stop and pivot back toward Meg. "Wait, I have a question."

Her thin eyebrows narrow. She pulls out her phone and

shakes it at me. "Among this thing's many uses is the ability of its operator to pose a question without spreading his nasty man-cold germs everywhere."

"You know I can fire you, right?"

An uproarious laugh escapes Meg's mouth. "There are at least three other studios that would be more than happy to hire me *and* give me a massive bump in pay. Plus, Gary's next in line. Do you really want him in charge of the troops?"

We both turn as one and watch Gary trundling toward his workstation, a donut in one hand and a tablet in the other. A sizeable crumb falls to the floor. Gary either doesn't notice or doesn't care, just keeps on walking.

I shudder. "They'd mutiny by the end of the day."

"Dude, this place would be empty by lunchtime." Meg flaps her hand dismissively. "Ask your question and scram."

"This is going to sound weird, but–" I scoot closer, earning stink eyes from Meg "–have I ever talked about wanting kids?"

Her eyes widen to the size of game discs. "Holy shit, dude, is Alana *pregnant*?" She punches my shoulder, apparently no longer worried she'll contract my man-cold. "I always knew you had it in you." She grins mischievously. "Actually, I guess it's Alana who had it in her."

"Oh my God, Meg, would you lower your voice?" I glance around to see if anyone overheard. Gary's head pops up like a spooked groundhog, twitching this way and that until he sees me. He waves, donut still in hand and losing more crumbs, then retreats back to his workstation. The rest of the team is thankfully too engrossed in their screens to care that Meg's breaking about half a dozen sexual harassment policies.

"In all seriousness," she says, "congrats. You're gonna make a good papa."

I wince at the sting of her words. "Alana's not pregnant."

"I thought you said you knocked her up."

I sigh. "I asked if I've ever talked about wanting kids."

"Oh. Right. That's way less interesting." She scrunches her

face, then shrugs. "I don't know. Maybe? You say a lot of things I don't always listen to, but I guess there's a chance we've talked about our respective desires to add to overpopulation?"

"Thanks so much, that's super helpful."

Her cheeks puff with a closed-mouth smile. "Anytime. Now amscray."

"One more question and I swear I'll leave." I might as well go all-in. "Have we ever talked about getting into virtual reality?"

The look she gives me has me questioning my own sanity all over again. "Um, why?" She squints. "You aren't experiencing sudden onset dementia, are you?"

"Humor me, OK? My brain's been foggy lately." I cough loudly.

She backs away a few feet. "I swear to God, if I get sick…"

"Meg, please. It's important."

"Yes," she says. "We've talked about it." She cocks her head. "You really don't remember?"

"Why did we decide not to pursue it?"

"That's the thing. We did pursue it."

"What happened?"

"You seriously don't remember any of this?"

"Meg."

She and I have been coworkers for a while, and friends for nearly that long. I know that she realizes something's off with me. Hell, a kindergartner could tell I'm acting strange. Problem is, I can't tell her the truth. Not because I don't trust her, but having my wife and therapist think I'm crazy is bad enough. Meg's as protective of Omega Studies as I am. I don't want to give her any reason to think I'm not capable of doing my job.

"At the risk of sounding like an asshole," Meg says, "we were in talks to start working on a virtual reality game, but then your buddy at Boundless died and the negotiations fell through. After that we decided to focus our energy on other projects like *Starflung*."

I damn near stagger into the wall. If what she's saying is true, then that means Bradley – this Bradley – might've been working on a headset like the one my Bradley developed. And if that's the case…

I do my best to keep my voice all casual and steady. "Did we ever try out a prototype?"

She shakes her head. "They showed us some mockups, but that's about it. Why, are you thinking we should take another look at it? There are loads of tech companies that would jump at the chance to work with us."

"No, it's not that. It's just…" Dammit, this is getting too complicated. I want to ask if there's another point of contact at Bradley's that I can talk to, but the more I speak, the nuttier I sound.

"See, this is what happens when you work on too many things at once." My face must display confusion, because Meg holds up her hands and makes air quotes. "Your 'secret project'? The one you've been designing on the sly for, like, the last year? What, you think I didn't notice how weird and distant you've been acting lately?"

Secret project?

"Honestly, I have no idea what you're talking about."

Meg winks at me. "Right. OK. Whatever you say, boss. Promise me one thing, though. If you decide to jump ship for a bigger studio, take me with you, because I might actually murder Gary if I have to handle him by myself."

"I'm not working on a secret project, and I'm definitely not leaving Omega. I just…" I can tell by her face that nothing I'm saying is dissuading her. "Look, my brain's been out of whack lately, that's all."

Meg's expression immediately softens. Despite believing I'm contagious, she closes in on me, looks around to see if anyone's nearby, and says quietly, "Hey, I've been there. It's OK."

Now I'm the one who's confused. "What's OK?"

She taps a finger to her temple. "Having issues with your

brain pan. Depression sucks, man. You taking any meds?"

I almost say no, but then I remember the prescription Alana's getting filled. "The doctor wants me to."

"Good. No shame in that at all."

I can't decide whether or not it's good that she thinks I'm depressed. Guaranteed half the people at Omega Studios are on one form of anti-anxiety medication or another.

She bestows one of her rare smiles. "Go home. Relax. Take the rest of the week off. Fuck knows you've earned it. The game will be here when you come back. Until then–" she mimes cracking a whip "–I've got you covered."

"Thanks."

"Now scram, I've got shit to do. This game isn't gonna develop itself."

I tell Meg goodbye, exit Omega Studios, and speed-walk to Alana's car, all the while keeping an eye out for my automotive shadow, which of course I don't see.

"How'd Meg take the news?" Alana says as I duck into the Beetle.

"News?"

"About E3?"

Shit, I completely spaced and never told Meg about E3. "Um, she was cool with it. Excited, actually. Said she's way better on stage than I am."

The lie comes easy. Too easy.

Alana nods sagely as she merges into afternoon traffic. "I mean, she's not wrong. I love you with all my heart, but public speaking is not your forte."

I suppose it's comforting to know at least that hasn't changed. "Did you, ah, get the prescription filled?"

Alana jabs her thumb at the backseat. "Pharmacist had to call the sleeping pills into another branch. It should be ready later this afternoon."

I force a smile and lean back in my seat. I'm not excited about popping pills – as much as they'll theoretically help balance me out, they won't actually solve my problems. That's on me. It helps, though, that I know Bradley and I planned on working together. That alone is enough to make me think there's a chance, impossibly thin though it might be, that I might finally figure out what the hell has happened.

Alana still has papers to grade, so when we get home I'm free to hop on my laptop and run a search for correspondence between myself and Bradley or one of his company's reps.

The messages I dig up are from well over a year or two ago, which explains why I didn't stumble across them last night when I cyber-stalked myself.

I go through them one by one, reading the first few in full before resorting to skimming, my ears primed for any hint of noise. So far as I can tell, though, Alana's firmly ensconced upstairs. I dislike being secretive, but I don't want her to think I'm dwelling on whatever mental sidestep my brain's taken. That's not to say I'm not dwelling. I'm totally dwelling. But it's for a good reason.

It's not until the third page of emails that I finally come across something interesting. It's a message dated about six months before Bradley died.

Pete–

I talked to Jerry, my executive VP. He's tentatively on board but is being a dickweed about using the headset for something as "pedestrian" as a game. Asshole wants to go straight to the military. I'm like, dude, we've got plenty of contracts with the Man. I wanna do something fun. Apparently he's allergic to fun because then he got on me about the game not being developed in-house. I tried to explain that there's a difference between hammering out a cool piece of tech versus crafting a quality video game. (Loved Scorchfell, *by the way. Best thing you've done yet. I might've shed a tear when it ended but if you tell anyone that I'll pull your nuts out through your navel). Anyway.*

I'll get Jerry straightened out soon enough, so go ahead and
start coming up with pitches to wow me.
Later, turd.
—B

I re-read the message, searching for any hidden subtext, but Bradley's infamous for saying what he thinks and calling out people for being cagey. As far as I can tell the message is what it is. Not exactly helpful, but not completely unhelpful.

I keep searching. There are other, earlier emails from Bradley, most of them banal messages about setting up meetings to discuss a project he wanted to team up with me on. Nothing more about the headset. No mention of anything called Deep Dive at all. And, so far as I can tell, there's nothing in my account from anyone named Jerry.

Not to be deterred, I Google the company's website. On the *About Us* page I pull up a picture of one Jerry O'Laughlin. He definitely looks like an asshole, with his beady little eyes, slicked-back hair, and bespoke suit that probably cost more than my three off-the-rack suits combined. Of course, there's no email or phone number under his bio. In fact, no one on the staff page has any contact information listed. Outside of a phone number for media inquiries, the only way to get in touch with anyone from Boundless seems to be a contact form.

I almost close the browser and message Meg to see if she's still got anyone's info, but she already thinks I'm off my rocker so I enter my name and email address in the appropriate field on the Boundless contact form, then type out a message:

Hi. This message is for Jerry O'Laughlin.

Jerry, my name is Peter Banuk. I'm not sure if you remember me, but I'm the creative director at Omega Studios. I was friends with Bradley Moss. We were working together on a virtual reality project before Bradley died. I think it was called Deep Dive?

I pause, considering how best to phrase my question without coming across as crazy.

> *I was just wondering if you were still developing the headset.*
> *I know negotiations fell through after Bradley passed away,*
> *but my team and I have been working on a sci-fi game that*
> *I think could work well in a virtual reality setting. I'd also*
> *be happy to pitch you something else.*
>
> *Anyway. Whoever gets this message, if you could pass it*
> *along to Jerry O'Laughlin, I'd really appreciate it.*

I add my cell phone number, then click Send.

I sit back in my chair, staring at the message thanking me for contacting the company. I'll give it a few days, and if no one responds, talk to Meg again.

Feeling suddenly very proactive, I run another Google search for false memories and virtual reality. Ignoring the articles pertaining to the studies I'd mentioned to Dr Blake, I scan the search results for any online forums or message boards where both topics are discussed.

The first few hits prove to be busts. Most of the links take me to conspiracy theory websites that devote the majority of their bandwidth to raging about topics even Fox Mulder would've rolled his eyes at. How *The Matrix* was right and that it was time for the masses to wake up and join the Church of Neo. How the government has been using video games, in particular virtual reality headsets, to secretly implant subliminal messages into children's brains in order to train them to be assassins. And my personal favorite, how an Artificial Intelligence from the future is using virtual reality to time-travel into the past in order to influence events in the present timeline.

But then I go to Reddit. I've never been much of an online participant – I even eschew multi-player campaigns in favor of single-player games, much to the derision of my contemporaries – but every once in a while, when I need to clear my head, I'll read some subreddit or another to take my mind off whatever's frustrating me.

I type "false memories + virtual reality" into the search box and hit enter. A single subreddit pops up.

Body jangling with nervous excitement, I lean forward and start reading.

Sadly, my enthusiasm instantly ebbs. Most of the initial comments would be right at home on the conspiracy theory websites. How the government's spying on us through gaming consoles, how NPCs are actually sentient and killing them amounts to real-life murder, how this one guy took acid before donning a virtual reality headset and had the most amazing trip of his entire psychedelic life.

Half a page down, however, things start to get interesting.

Redditor shamudeservedbetter: *when i was a kid my parents signed me up for a research study involving virtual reality. Which, wow, great parenting, right? to this day I'm convinced i swam with whales even though they swear it never happened. I mean, how messed up is that shit?*

Under this, agentsmith69 says, *holy shit are you FUCKING kidding me? I was in that study, too! I still haven't forgiven my parents. Making me think I swam with some damn whales and then telling me it's bullshit? It's like fucking Santa Claus all over again.*

Two more Redditors chime in, stating with many exclamation marks how they were also part of the study. Ganondork says, *they went so far as to pay for a trip to Vava'u, Tonga, a Polynesian island group in the South Pacific, in order to swim with humpback whales.*

It was awesome, but I gotta tell ya, it's been three years since then, and that shit back when we were kids still feels as real as when I went to Tonga. And I KNOW I went to Tonga. So, like, what does that say about memories?

"That our brains aren't hardwired for this shit?" I mutter.

If you can't tell the difference between a "real" memory and a memory conjured through virtual means, then, like Dr Blake said, you could argue that it doesn't matter which one's real and which one's not, and that's some straight up bullshit.

None of this is helping me, though. Like I told Dr Blake, thinking you swam with whales when you didn't is one thing. I've got an entire life populating my brain.

But then I see Redditor brainbandit666's comment.

I wasn't part of this research study, but I used to be big into VR games until they started messing with my brain. Are there any support groups for living with false memories?

Beneath this question, everyone in the thread chimes in with a "no clue", "other than this thread, you mean?" or "hey, that's not a bad idea, if you start one lemme know."

I can tell none of them are taking the question seriously, but it sparks something in me. Call it desperation, call it a long-shot, call it succumbing to the new narrative driving my life. Whatever the case, my cursor is on the move.

Before I can second-guess myself, I break my own lurker rule and create a Reddit account of my own.

Newly minted as Redditor VirtualCousteau1114, I hop back over to the whale subreddit and start typing.

Are you experiencing one false memory or several? I write to brainbandit666. *I'm only asking because I recently used an experimental full dive headset and now I'm having memory issues, too.*

I don't have much hope that anyone will respond. The subreddit was started five months ago. People responded to brainbandit666's question four months ago. Since then there's been no activity. Reddit archives its posts after six months, which means in less than thirty days no one will be able to leave any new comments.

I'm not sure I can survive thirty days without answers. Not that I think brainbandit666's experience is the same as mine, but you never know. At this point I'm grasping at straws, but dammit, I want my life back.

I keep the page open while I do my best to see if there's any gaming news I've forgotten or misremembered, but now that I have no clear line of investigation my brain can't seem to focus on much of anything. It doesn't help that the house, save for the background hum of the air conditioner, is almost completely silent. I can't remember the last time I experienced this kind of quiet. It's unnerving, largely because it reminds me of what I've lost. What I think I've lost.

Overwhelmed by solitude, I close my laptop and make my way upstairs. When I reach the doorway to the office that isn't Evie's bedroom, I finally hear something.

Crying.

Alana is lying on the couch, eyes clenched, body twitching with sobs. Essays are strewn haphazardly across the desktop and the floor.

"Honey?"

She flinches, eyes popping open as she lifts her head and hurriedly rubs at the mascara carving black lines down her cheeks. "I'm sorry. I ju– ju–"

I lay down beside her, sliding one arm under her head and draping the other across her torso as she presses up against me, fresh tears falling like warm rain onto my forearm.

"I'm not going anywhere," I murmur into her head, the sharp, aberrant scent of recent hair dye tickling my nose. "You and me, forever and always. Right?"

She sniffs stutteringly, nods into my arm, and exhales so strongly it feels like she's deflated. I pull her closer, the intimate puzzle of our bodies millimeters away from a perfect fit, and hope for her sake as much as mine that we make it through this in one piece.

CHAPTER EIGHT

That night we go to dinner with two of Alana's teacher friends, a couple who, like this version of us, doesn't have kids.

Alana almost said no when they messaged, but neither of us felt like cooking, and after I successfully argued that I'd made it through the day with no further hint of a breakdown, she reluctantly agreed to the invite.

I – of course – don't remember Alana's friends, but the situation is at least one I'm used to. Namely, when more than two teachers get together, they are incapable of not talking about school. Granted, gamers are just as bad. Not only do we talk about games we've played as much as we actually play them, we also spend time online watching live streams or recorded footage of other gamers playing games.

Luckily, Trenton is a gamer like I am. The moment he brings up *Scorchfell*, his husband, Jamal, rolls his eyes.

"Here we go," Jamal says. "He's been dying to talk about this game since he finished it last month."

There's fondness in Jamal's voice, though, and he grins as Trenton swats his arm.

All around us, the sushi restaurant hums with a dozen quiet conversations. It's the sort of place we could never take Cassie and Evie. Not because they're ill-behaved, but no matter how often I attempt to get them to try any food that's even distantly related to fish, they both make these awful gagging noises and run screaming from the room. Neither of them believes me when I explain that plenty of sushi is rice and veggies, two foods they both like.

"Ignore Jamal," Trenton says. "He pretends like he thinks gaming is for teenagers, but you should've heard him in the background when I was playing *The Last of Us*." Trenton puts one hand on his chest, widens his eyes, and affects a high-pitched voice. "Watch out for that Clicker! Oh my God use the flamethrower, USE THE DAMN FLAMETHROWER! That's right, Joel, you show that sonofabitch who's boss!"

Alana laughs, and even though I do everything in my power to stop it, a small part of my cold, fractured heart begins to warm to the notion that this place, this us, isn't so bad after all.

No. The girls need you. You need them.

Trenton leans over and kisses Jamal on the cheek. "Don't pretend like there weren't tears in your eyes by the end of the game."

"It's an amazing story for sure," I say. "I only wish mine were as good."

"Please." Trenton takes a sip of red wine. "*Scorchfell* was stunning."

Crap. He probably thinks I was fishing for a compliment. I really wasn't, not consciously. Game devs, like any creative person, are praise hounds for sure and love getting compliments about their work, but for as much as I crave success, I'm also the first to self-deprecate.

Oh look, now I'm spiraling about this.

I smile and take a big nervous sip of wine.

Jamal leans over and whispers loudly to Alana, "Trent's already started a second playthrough. I'm like, but you know how it ends."

Alana whispers back, "I feel your pain. Peter's played this one cowboy game at least three times. Whenever I walk into the room his character's always skinning a deer."

They grin, clinking glasses in solidarity. Trenton raises his wineglass toward me. "Backseat gamers, am I right?"

"I'll drink to that." We clink glasses and spend the time until the food arrives comparing favorite games while Alana and Jamal talk about the latest idiotic rule to come down from the school board.

"If you don't mind my asking," Trenton says, picking up a strip of yellowtail sashimi with practiced ease, "what inspired the girls in *Scorchfell*?"

I nearly choke on an eighth of my California roll. In the corner of my eye I see Alana tense, and it takes everything in me not to glance over at her. Even so, I can feel her watching me as I swallow down the piece of sushi and say, "I mean, lots of things, I guess."

"It's just, you guys don't have kids, but I would never know that based on Cassie and Evie. Their relationship felt so real. Did you get pointers from the actresses who played the girls?"

Hearing my daughters' names uttered by a relative stranger re-fractures my heart. To everyone else at this table, the girls aren't real. I can't bring myself to talk about them as though they're only fictional video game characters, to keep the pervasive sense of loss I'm drowning in from co-opting my voice.

Trenton's staring at me, though, waiting politely for an answer. Thankfully, Alana saves me. She reaches out and places her hand on top of mine, squeezing it gently. "Those two girls were just the sweetest. Everyone at Omega doted on them when they came in for motion capture."

"That must've been so damn cool to watch," Trenton says.

And there's my in, a way to derail the conversation without completely wrecking the train.

"You should come by some time," I say nonchalantly, dipping a round of sushi into my bowl of heavily wasabied soy sauce.

Trenton damn near drops his chopsticks. "For real?"

Jamal laughs. "Peter, you just made this fool's day."

"Of course." Alana withdraws her hand, content that I'm not about to have a nervous breakdown in the middle of the restaurant. "Peter's schedule is pretty full, but maybe in a few weeks?"

I shrug. "Sounds good to me."

"That would be amazing," Trenton says.

The waiter comes by, asks if we want another bottle of wine. A chorus of exuberant yeses sends him jaunting over to the bar, the bounce in his step indicative of the tip he's going to get.

As much as relaxing into the moment feels like I'm betraying Cassie and Evie – and, to a certain extent, Alana – I give myself permission to enjoy the company. The past twenty-four hours have royally sucked. What I need right now is to do exactly what Dr Blake prescribed: relax, clear my mind, regroup when I can think better.

The rest of the meal passes pleasantly. Alana and Jamal manage to turn the conversation from gaming back to teacher talk. Trenton regales us with a story about the time one of his students left to go to the bathroom and returned with a box of steaming hot fried chicken from the fast food restaurant right around the corner from the school.

"And to think I actually believed the little shit when he told me he had it in his locker the whole time." Trenton shakes his head. "I'm not gonna lie, I was a little impressed he'd made it there and back so fast."

"You should sign him up for track," Alana says.

Trenton grins. "I did."

All four of us die laughing.

When it comes time to pay the bill, I'm surprised to find that I'm sad the meal's over. Trenton and Jamal hug Alana goodbye, wave to me, and climb into their silver Audi. As they drive off, the orange glow from a streetlamp catches the hood, and for a second I'm back in the labyrinth, stepping through the red metal doorway and into that sea of silver light.

Alana takes my hand, interlacing her smooth, slender fingers through mine, her wedding band pressing against my skin. "You OK?"

"Just tired. Are you good to drive?" I ask as we walk over to her Beetle.

She squeezes my fingers, releases her grip, and digs in her purse for the car keys. "I'm pretty sure you and Trenton took care of most of that second bottle."

"Did we?" I slide into the passenger seat and realize that I am, in fact, slightly drunk. "Whoops."

"I'm sorry we spent so much time bitching about school." Alana eases the car out of the parking lot, then opens up the engine as we hit the main road. "Did you at least have a good time talking shop with Trenton?"

Spur of the moment, I lift her hand and kiss her palm. "This was exactly what I needed."

I almost mean it.

The smile Alana levels at me lights up the night more than any streetlamp blazing outside the car. "Good."

I recline my head against the headrest, listening to the low murmuring roar of an alt-rock radio station while Alana talks about some of the kids in her classes and how they'll spend more time avoiding doing work than it would've taken to just do the work in the first place. I think about Cassie stressing about getting her weekly homework assignments done the day they're assigned, about how Evie will claim she's made her lunch but in reality has stuffed an apple and a bag of pretzels into her bag because making lunch is boring.

The inside of my chest feels like someone's grabbed hold of my ribcage and is slowly cracking every bone inch by painful inch.

Alana looks over, smiles, and lays a hand on my knee. I place mine on top of hers and watch the streetlamps come and go in a tear-blurred slipstream of pumpkin-colored light.

* * *

It's almost midnight and I'm wide awake.

The wine should've knocked me out, but here I am, exhausted, still a little tipsy, and way too alert to try to chase sleep like I chased that car.

I've already checked the Reddit thread, and my email is full of nothing but advertisements and newsletters I don't remember subscribing to and spam that isn't even trying to hide the fact that it's spam.

Staring at my phone isn't doing me any favors in the sleep department, but perusing random websites is better than lying here kicking myself for randomly thinking about how I still haven't taught Evie how to ride a bike.

I cave and Google myself.

Reading print articles about me is weird enough. Watching muted interviews that I don't remember giving where I talk about *Scorchfell*'s success and the future of Omega Studios is totally surreal and more than a little disconcerting – the semi-articulate words coming out of my mouth might as well have been spoken by someone else for all that I recall fumbling my way through them. Same with the positive reviews of *Scorchfell* – they feel like they've been written about a game someone else developed. Reading them is a strange, bittersweet experience.

Next to me, Alana murmurs something about grading pasta and rolls over so her back's to me. I lower my phone, reach out a hand, and brush a strand of hair off her face. I still can't believe how long it is.

She smiles at my touch and snuggles deeper into her pillow. I pull the blankets up over her bare shoulder, then return to staring at my phone. There's only so much self-Googling I can handle, though.

I sigh, well aware that I need to try and sleep. Fatigue isn't going to do me any favors. But as I go to thumb off my phone, an email notification appears at the top of the screen.

It's from Reddit, alerting me that someone has replied to my comment.

I thought I was awake before, but now I'm buzzing like I've tossed back three successive double shots of espresso.

When I open the email, I expect to see a reply from brainbandit666.

Instead, the comment is from someone who's dubbed themselves trustn01.

As much as I love the *X-Files* reference, it's not the most promising start to a conversation about false memories. Neither, for that matter, is the first line of the comment itself.

Bullshit. Full dive tech doesn't exist.

I feel my hackles rise. This is why I avoid talking to people online. There's always some troll who waxes high and mighty about a subject they actually know nothing about.

Still, I click on the link embedded in the email. It takes me directly to the subreddit, and there's my comment.

Are you experiencing one false memory or several? I'd written to brainbandit666. *I'm only asking because I recently used an experimental full dive headset and now I'm having memory issues, too.*

Beneath it is trustn01's full reply. *Bullshit. Full dive tech doesn't exist. Go find some conspiracy subreddit and jerk off there, asshole.*

I know I shouldn't respond, shouldn't give this troll the satisfaction of engaging in a flame war. But I'm tired, edgy, and beyond done with people telling me what does or doesn't exist, especially when there's zero reason for them to give me shit.

Just an FYI, your upload failed, I reply.

Trustn01's response arrives two seconds later. *What the fuck are you talking about?*

Your upload. You know, all the PDFs and screenshots you meant to include as evidence to support your highly refined argument.

Do yourself a favor, trustn01 says, *delete your account before you dig yourself a hole you can't crawl out of.*

Embracing this bold, snarky version of myself, I respond with a gif of an animated shovel.

For real, trustn01 says. *One false memory isn't worth the shitstorm you're about to walk into.*

Jesus, and I thought I was acting extra. *Try an entire lifetime, buddy. But whatever. I just wanted to talk to other people who might've experienced what I experienced. You're clearly only here for the lolz. Go troll someone else.*

JFC, you're serious, aren't you?

I'm logging off.

Wait.

I almost sign out, but then trustn01 sends me a private message. Curiosity gets the better of me and I open it. All I see is a link inviting me to ChatSafe, an encrypted messaging app I've heard of but never used.

"What the hell?" I mutter. This just went from a stupid flame war to something much, much stranger. I should walk away.

Alana rolls toward me, murmurs, "You OK?"

Shit. I didn't mean to wake her, especially not for this.

"Just getting up to pee," I whisper, kissing her forehead. "Go back to sleep."

"Love you."

"Love you, too." I slip out of bed, pad across the floor, and creep downstairs.

The living room is a study in shadows, each patch of darkness fringed with the diffuse silver light of the moon shining in through the windows.

I drop onto the couch, the fabric cool enough to send a shiver up and down my body, and open my phone.

This is how people get duped by con artists, I tell myself even as I download the app for ChatSafe and set up a burner account using the same VirtualCousteau1114 alias I created on Reddit.

Seriously, you're going to regret this, my brain insists as I return to the link trustn01 posted on Reddit, click it, and tap the Accept button when a page appears displaying an invitation to a private chatroom.

So far as I can tell, trustn01 and I are the only two people

in the room. I give it a minute, and when my secretive
new acquaintance continues to remain silent I initiate the
conversation.

<VirtualCousteau1114> *Why am I here?*

<trustn01> *This is the best I could do on short notice. You never
know who's watching.*

<VirtualCousteau1114> *Wow, paranoid much? Seriously,
what do you want?*

<trustn01> *What did you mean, an entire lifetime?*

<VirtualCousteau1114> *Exactly what I said. Why am I here?*

<trustn01> *I might know something about full dive VR.*

<VirtualCousteau1114> *You literally called me an asshole for
suggesting it exists.*

<trustn01> *That's called subterfuge.*

Oh for the love of…

<VirtualCousteau1114> *Yeah, you're a regular James Bond.
But fine, I'll bite. What do you know about full dive VR?*

<trustn01> *More than you, apparently.*

<VirtualCousteau1114> *Cut the cryptic shit. You're the one
who invited me here. If you're just going to dick me around,
I'm leaving.*

<trustn01> *Fair enough. OK. Let's say for the sake of argument
that I have some experience with the kind of virtual reality
tech you're talking about. What I want to know is, how the
hell do you?*

And there it is. The question I'm not prepared to answer.
In all likelihood this guy's pulling some weird scam, a fucked
up catfishing scheme to get me to unintentionally divulge
clues that will help him guess the passwords to all my online
accounts.

Problem is, even though I'm well aware that being stuck in
this outlandish, psychological quagmire is making me act more
erratically than normal, there's a chance, however remote,
that he's not messing around with me. That he does know
something about full dive tech. If I log off, I'll always wonder

if this was my one opportunity to figure out what the hell is happening to me.

You're already hooked. Might as well let him reel you in.

I start typing.

<VirtualCousteau1114> *For the sake of argument, let's say that two days ago I went to my friend's office building. This friend is a tech whiz. He and I had partnered up on a project, it's not important what. What's important is that my friend's half of the partnership involved creating a full dive virtual reality headset that got around the issues users typically experience while creating an immersive experience unmatched by any similar device. With me so far?*

<trustn01> *I'm still here, aren't I?*

<VirtualCousteau1114> *You're a cranky son of a bitch. You know that, right?*

<trustn01> *So I've been told. Keep talking, shitbird.*

I hate to say it, but I'm kind of starting to like this person.

<VirtualCousteau1114> *Anyway. Saturday morning my friend messages and says he's finished the headset and wants me to come try it. So I do.*

<trustn01> *And? Did it work?*

<VirtualCousteau1114> *It did. Until it didn't.*

<trustn01> *Now who's being cryptic?*

<VirtualCousteau1114> *I put on the headset and it was like nothing I'd ever experienced.*

Even now, I can feel the hot desert wind wicking sweat from my skin, can still taste the dust on the air.

<trustn01> *Full sensory immersion?*

<VirtualCousteau1114> *And then some.*

<trustn01> *So what happened?*

<VirtualCousteau1114> *Honestly, I have no idea. One minute I was in this amazing simulation, and then all of a sudden things went haywire. I thought my brain was about to explode. The next thing I knew I was slumped over in my truck with a huge migraine and no memory of how I got*

there. And then…

I can't bring myself to finish the sentence.

Trustn01 does it for me.

<trustn01> *Something changed, didn't it?*

Another shiver passes through me, and not only from the chill in the air. I grab the afghan, pull it over my legs, and draw my knees up to my chest.

<VirtualCousteau1114> *You've used this kind of headset, haven't you?*

<trustn01> *Just keep talking.*

<VirtualCousteau1114> *I tried to call my friend, but his number wasn't working. All the contacts on my phone, all my apps, everything had been wiped. I drove home, thinking my wife was probably wondering where the hell I was considering it was two o'clock in the morning. I'd missed my youngest daughter's birthday, so I knew my wife would be pissed. But all I was worried about was getting home and kissing my kids goodnight. Except, when I got home, my kids weren't there.*

<trustn01> *What, your wife had taken them to her mother's or something?*

<VirtualCousteau1114> *Not there meaning they'd up and fucking vanished. All their toys, their clothes, the drawings on the fridge, all of it was just gone. So there I was, scared shitless and thinking I'd lost my damn mind, walked into the wrong house, gotten stuck inside the virtual simulation. Anything to explain the impossible. I ran into my bedroom and woke my wife. Know what she told me when I asked where the girls were?*

<trustn01> *That they didn't exist.*

My entire body starts shaking like someone's set off a nuclear bomb inside my stomach. It's all I can do to keep hold of my phone.

<VirtualCousteau1114> *How the hell did you know that?*

<trustn01> *Like I said, I've had some experience with the*

interface.

<VirtualCousteau1114> *So it's real? I'm not crazy?*

<trustn01> *Believe me, brother, I wish you were. Crazy is way fucking simpler than the shit you've stepped in. But yeah, much as I wish it weren't, Deep Dive is as real as you and me.*

Deep Dive.

It's real.

I didn't suffer some sort of mental breakdown.

Unless this guy's lying.

But he knows about Deep Dive.

He guessed right about the girls.

Which means.

Which means.

The nuclear bomb in my stomach sets off a mushroom cloud of emotions so dense I have to set my phone in my lap and lean my head back on the couch. Tears well in the corners of my eyes, tracing wet lines down my stubbly cheeks while I sit there, heart pounding.

Cassie and Evie are real. I didn't make them up.

<VirtualCousteau1114> *Where are my kids?*

<trustn01> *That's… complicated.*

<VirtualCousteau1114> *You're kidding, right?*

<trustn01> *Look, I get that this is a lot to process. I'm going to propose something, but first I need to know how far you're willing to go.*

<VirtualCousteau1114> *To the ends of the fucking earth.*

<trustn01> *Good answer. All right. There's a diner in the city on the corner of Anderson and 13th Avenue. Village Eats. Shitty food. You know it?*

<VirtualCousteau1114> *I can find it.*

<trustn01> *Good. Meet me there in one hour.*

<VirtualCousteau1114> *Wait, what?*

A notification pops up stating that trustn01 has left the chatroom. I stare incredulously, willing trustn01 to reappear, but a minute passes with no sign of the bastard.

"Now what?" I mutter.

It would be utter madness to meet a total stranger at some random diner in the middle of the night.

My eyes stray to the time at the top of my phone. It's after one o'clock in the morning. Alana will be up in five hours.

A quick search shows that the diner is twenty-five minutes from my house.

I can be there and back before she's awake.

Just in case, I leave her a note on the kitchen table saying I couldn't sleep and went for a drive to clear my head, then sneak upstairs, pull on a T-shirt and a pair of jeans, and creep back downstairs and out the front door.

This is quite possibly the dumbest idea in the history of dumb ideas, but evidently I've fully embraced my role as the intransigent main character in some bonkers conspiracy flick.

Throwing my truck into neutral, I let it roll out of the drive and into the street before starting it up. The engine grumbles to life like a slumbering monster disturbed from its hibernation. It still smells like Windex and vomit. I shift into drive, depress the pedal, and accelerate down the road, praying to every deity I can think of that I'm not making a huge mistake.

CHAPTER NINE

The diner is in a seedy section of downtown, right near the edge of the city where it goes from urban to rural. In the distance, late-night trucks roar down the highway. The moon is bright and full in the sky, a silver spotlight illuminating my path.

A neon sign flickers in the diner's window advertising twenty-four-hour breakfast and the best coffee in the city. Through the front door I can see an old white woman in a pink waitressing getup straight out of *Grease* leaning on the counter, playing with her phone. There are four other cars in the parking lot, none of which look like the white hatchback that may or may not be following me.

As I get out of my truck, wondering all the while if trustn01 owns a white hatchback, a cop car races past the diner, red and blue lights flashing silently.

That bodes well.

A bell chimes above the front door as I push it open. My nose is immediately assaulted by the smell of fried potatoes and overheated coffee. The waitress glances up from her phone, gives me a once-over, and, apparently deciding I represent no imminent threat, says, "Sit wherever you like. Menus are on the tables."

"Thanks."

She grunts, goes back to whatever app has her in its thrall.

I scan the diner, searching for any sign of someone who fits the mental image I have of trustn01. The only other people in the place are two men sitting in a far back booth. The one facing me is on his phone. The one with his back to me has his head on the table.

The counter forms a curved L, so I take a seat on a stool along the short leg where I can see the front door. The ceiling lights are painfully white, the glare reflecting on the window making it nearly impossible to see outside.

The waitress tucks her phone in her apron pocket and saunters over, a beige cup in one hand and pot of coffee in the other. She doesn't say a word, simply lifts both in the air. A name tag over her left breast pocket reads *Dolores*.

I nod. "Coffee would be great."

Grunting again, Dolores pours me a steaming cup. "You ordering food? Not trying to rush you, it's just I've got to let Clive know if he needs to fire up the stove."

I wasn't hungry when I left the house, but now that I'm sitting here my stomach starts to grumble. "Eggs, bacon, side of grits?"

"All out of grits. Bread, too. Clive makes a mean buttermilk flapjack, though."

"Sure, let's go with that."

"Lovely. Scrambled or over easy?"

"Scrambled."

I sip the coffee, all the while watching the front door. The coffee tastes awful, but at least it's warm, and will help counteract the last bit of red wine lingering around my bloodstream.

By the time Dolores returns with my food, the two guys in the booth have paid their bill and driven off.

"Can I ask you a question?" I say.

"Shoot." She takes a rag and starts wiping down the counter.

"Has anyone come in here asking about a, ah, person they met online?"

Dolores pauses, furrows her brow, and says, "You here on a blind date or something?"

"Not exactly. I'm just supposed to meet someone and I'm not entirely sure what they look like."

Dolores snorts. "Back in my day we called those blind dates, but whatever. Other than you and those two what just left, no one's been in here since before midnight."

"Oh. OK."

"You need any more coffee?"

"Actually, could I get a glass of orange juice?"

"I'll see what we've got in the fridge."

The bacon is charred, the eggs are runny, and the pancakes are dry and nowhere close to Cassie's standards of fluffiness, but I devour every bite as though it's the first meal I've eaten in days.

Another twenty minutes pass, and I'm still the only other customer.

Kicking myself for believing I was finally on to something, I signal to Dolores that I'm ready for the check. Luckily there's still plenty of time for me to get home and sneak back into bed without Alana ever realizing I was gone.

"Looks like your friend's a no-show," Dolores said, sliding the bill stub toward me.

"Apparently." I pull cash from my wallet and lay it on top of the check. "Keep the change."

For the first time since I arrived, Dolores pops a grin.

"Hey, thanks," she says. "Sorry about your not-a-blind-date."

"Me too. Night."

I climb into my truck and sit there for a minute, staring into the diner.

I can't believe I fell for this shit.

Whatever. There's still the message I sent to Jerry O'Laughlin, and if I don't hear back from him, I can always suck it up and ask Meg if she's got any points of contact at Boundless.

That decided, I reach for the gearshift when a deep, grizzled voice growls from behind me, "You ever wonder what a bullet from a Glock 19 semi-automatic can do to a man's liver?"

Time slows, stutters, comes to a screeching halt.

My heart trips over itself, caught between one beat and the next.

My hands are petrified in place, one wrapped around the steering wheel, the other holding the keys half an inch from the ignition.

"If you're thinking of running, don't," the voice continues. "The Glock has a clip capacity of fifteen 9mm rounds. At this range I can't miss. Even if I did and you somehow get your door open, I've still got fourteen more chances to put your insides on the outside before you manage to make it more than ten feet from the truck. So unless you want me to turn your dashboard into some bullshit modern art exhibit on the dangers of city life, you'll do exactly as I fucking say."

Inside the diner, Dolores is watching something on her phone while she walks the length of the counter, wiping down the Formica top without even looking at it.

"Start the truck, and don't bother honking to attract her attention. She won't hear you." Are they in it together? Dolores and the man in my back seat? Was she lying the whole time, keeping me occupied thinking my "date" hadn't shown up so that I'd sit long enough for him to crawl unseen into my truck?

Of all the obvious traps to fall for.

"Get moving, shitbird."

Shitbird.

Fear thrums like acid through my veins. Less than an hour ago, trustn01 called me a shitbird. I finally locate my voice hiding deep inside my throat. It takes no little amount of effort, but I manage to drag it out in the open.

"You're from the chatroom."

"And you," trustn01 says, "talk way too fucking much for an asshole being held at gunpoint. I said start the goddamn truck."

I nod, hyperaware that I need to play the part of the compliant captive if I want to get out of this alive. My heart finally gets its shit together and starts trying to punch its way through my ribcage, pushing blood back into my brain.

Trustn01 shifts behind me, and taps what I'm assuming is the barrel of his gun against the metal prongs connecting my headrest to the seat.

"What about 'do exactly as I fucking say' did you not understand?"

It takes two tries for my trembling hand to insert the key in the ignition.

The truck rumbles to life even as mine flashes before my eyes.

"Good. Back out of the parking lot. Slowly."

"I have money," I croak. "In my wallet. Or the truck. Take the truck. I won't even report it stolen."

"I don't want your fucking money or your gas-guzzling truck. Back out of the parking lot. Now."

Not willing to take the chance that he's lying about having a gun, I ease the gearshift into reverse, toe the gas pedal, and steer the truck backwards until we reach the street.

"Drive."

My eyes flick up to the rearview mirror. All I can make out is a shadowy, baseball-capped head silhouetted by the diffuse glow of ambient light outside the truck.

"I have a family," I say.

"No shit." He leans forward, his breath against my ear warm and redolent of stale coffee and cigarettes. "Just an FYI, you even think about pulling any sort of Formula 1 bullshit I'll put a hole in your stomach."

I accelerate slowly, doing my best to keep the truck in the middle of the lane. Up ahead, a yellow stoplight winks on and off.

"Take a right at the intersection," he says.

I do as he says, rounding the corner with all the hesitant stiffness of a senior citizen whose license should've been taken away years ago.

The road stretches out before us, orange and white construction cones on either shoulder. The moon is an uncaring silver eye hovering in the top right corner of my windshield.

"Stay on this street until I say otherwise. Also, hand me your cell phone."

Lowering my right hand, I slide the phone out of the center console and hold it up over my shoulder. My short-fused assailant yanks it out of my hand. A second later, the sound of shattered glass fills the cab. The backseat window on my side of the truck whirs open, letting in a draft of cool night air.

"Try tracking that, you pricks," the guy mutters as he closes the window.

My eyes shoot to the side view mirror just in time to see a tiny black shape bouncing end over end across the road before disappearing into the darkness.

Dammit. That was my one lifeline.

"Why are you doing this?" I ask.

"Because you just had to go blast all that shit all over the internet for everyone to see. So now I have to clean up your mess before it spills out into the open and ruins everything. Take a left at the stoplight."

The adrenaline racing through my body is beginning to abate, making plenty of room for my old pal nausea.

"I don't understand," I say, steering the truck onto the next street.

"That's really fucking obvious, otherwise you wouldn't have gone on Reddit and started blabbing about that fucking headset." He coughs, makes a hurking noise. "I mean, honestly, it's like you want them to track you down."

"No one's trying to track me down."

Tell that to the white hatchback.

"If they weren't before, they definitely are now." Trustn01 coughs again. "Be happy I got to you first. See that exit sign for the highway? Take it."

I spy a large green sign up ahead on the right with two arrows pointing in opposite directions.

"Which way?"

"What?"

"I can go north or south. Which way?"

The man grumbles to himself for a moment, then: "North."

Instead of making me feel better, his temporary uncertainty only heightens my anxiety. And when I'm anxious, I say stupid, ballsy things I have no intention of actually following through on, like:

"You know, if I roll this truck, there's a very good chance we'll both wind up dead."

"Then don't roll the fucking truck, dumbass." He lets out a rattling, mucous-thick bark that makes it sound like one of his lungs is about to implode.

Part of me wants to roll the truck anyway, because fuck this B-movie goon. My seatbelt's on. The steering wheel has an airbag. The truck is big and sturdy.

But I can't, for three very good reasons.

Alana, Cassie, and Evie.

I don't want to die. I want to live. I want to find my daughters.

So I do what the bastard in the backseat tells me and take the northbound exit.

Aside from long-haul truckers, it's late enough at night that the highway is only sporadically dotted with cars. For the next half an hour or so, my abductor stays silent, leaving me plenty of time to dwell on my numerous regrets. I keep wondering if I should try to engage him in conversation, start rambling about my family in order to make him realize I'm a person just like him, try to ferret out what it is about my involvement with Deep Dive that's made him willing to kidnap me at gunpoint. Because the one thing I'm certain about is that this has everything to do with that damn headset. Why, I have no idea, but this guy obviously knows more than he's letting on. I have to hope that he'll keep me alive long enough for me to coax information out of him.

Unless he coaxes information out of you first.

And by coax, my brain means torture.

I do my best to compartmentalize my emotions.

Turns out I'm not very good at compartmentalizing my emotions.

Regardless, the fact remains that trustn01 obviously needs me for something, otherwise he would've shot me back in the parking lot and called it a day.

A few minutes later, he finally breaks his silence. "Take the next exit."

Once again, I play the dutiful prisoner, and a mile down the road veer to the right. The exit ramp forms a sharp S curve that spills out onto a four-lane secondary road. We pass a gas station, a couple of fast food joints, a barbed wire fence surrounding some sort of warehouse complex.

After half a mile the buildings disappear, taking the streetlamps with them. The road goes from four lanes to two. Darkness closes in, broken only by the truck's headlights. Its beams reflect off deposits in the asphalt, illuminating the tall trunks of the pine trees lining either side of the road. The suspension judders as we bounce over potholes and fissures where unseen roots have formed miniature mountain ranges in the road, which gives up its straightforward path in favor of a winding route that takes us deeper and deeper into the heart of a dense pinewood forest.

Without warning, trustn01 leans forward and taps my shoulder with the barrel of his gun.

"Slow down."

Until this moment, I'd almost convinced myself that he was full of crap, that he didn't really have a gun. That maybe, just maybe, I actually stood a chance of getting out of this mess.

That sentiment is long gone.

Doing my best to ignore the renewed sense of panic seizing control of my limbs, I ease my foot off the gas, dropping the speedometer until we reach fifteen miles per hour.

"Slower."

I drop it below ten miles per hour. The truck crawls down the road.

"Good enough."

I can smell his breath again, the coffee and cigarettes. "Look," I say quietly, calmly. "I appreciate that you're pissed at me for posting something online that I shouldn't have. But in my defense, I was out of options. Let me go and I'll delete my comments and wipe the search history from my laptop. Hell, I'll even delete my account, reset my modem, and change my IP address."

"It's too late for all that," trustn01 murmurs. "Stop there."

He thrusts his gun arm past me, using the barrel to indicate an opening in the trees fifty feet ahead.

I react without thinking. My foot slams on the brake even as I jerk my hands off the steering wheel and grab hold of his gun hand.

"What the–"

He tries to wrench free of my grasp, but I've got a pretty tight hold. Fueled by terrified desperation, I twist his arm this way and that, doing everything I can to make him drop the weapon.

"You stupid fucking idiot!" he shouts. "What the fuck are you trying to do, get yourself killed?"

The gun goes off.

Amplified by the small space of the cab, the retort concusses my right ear with all the Zeus-like fury of a hundred-thousand thunderbolts. The bullet screams past my knee close enough that I can feel the heat of its passage even as it punches a hole through the center console.

It's so loud, so excruciatingly painful, I lose my grip on the gun and clap my hands against my ears. The inside of my head clangs like an orchestra composed solely of small children with cymbals has set up shop at the base of my skull, each and every one of them smashing their instruments in tandem.

I can't think straight, can't see straight, can't hear straight.

Two seconds later, the truck rolls off the road and crunches into a tree.

We're going slowly enough that the airbag doesn't deploy, but the impact still throws me forward.

My forehead smacks the top of the steering wheel, adding a whirling galaxy of stars to the high-pitched whump and whine hammering the inside of my right ear.

Groaning, I press my hands to the top of the dashboard, trying my best to stop the world from spinning off its axis and taking me with it as it hurtles off into deep space.

As if from a great distance I hear trustn01 shouting, "You stupid son of a bitch!"

I don't have time for him right now. I grit my teeth, dig my fingernails hard into my palms. My vision starts to clear. What I really want is for the ringing in my ear to stop, for my hearing to return to normal, but I know that's not going to happen for a while, if ever.

I've watched a ton of gun-centric movies, played plenty of first-person shooter games, done actual research into what it means to fire a gun. A gun goes off this close to your ear, that ear is fucked.

Trustn01 shakes me by the shoulder. "Are you hit? Are you bleeding? Fucking answer me, Banuk! Are. You. Hit?"

The sound of my last name is almost as shocking as the retort of the gun.

I never told trustn01 my name.

How the hell does he know my name?

Very, very slowly so as not to spook him into accidentally discharging another round and actually shooting me this time, I lift my head off the steering wheel, gently crane my neck around, and look at the man in the back seat.

I can't place him at first. But then he takes off his tattered baseball cap and glares at me.

"Damn it all to hell," he says. "Why'd you have to go and fuck things up like that?"

Trustn01 is Christopher Doran, the receptionist at Boundless.

CHAPTER TEN

The last time I saw Doran he was wearing an expensive suit and waving me into Bradley's office.

Now, a worn tight-fitting T-shirt and cut-off camo pants have replaced the suit. His eyes are hooded, intense, his face covered in dark scruff, his hair chin-length and matted. Gone is the overbearing stench of too much cologne. In its place is the ashy scent of cigarettes and coffee.

He looks like a man on the brink, which is not what you want a man with a gun in his hands to look like.

"You're Doran," I say. "You work at Boundless."

My words are muffled, like when you're sick with a sinus infection and every time you speak your voice sounds like it's coming from a speaker inside your head.

"*Worked* at Boundless. I left after Mr Moss died."

"To do what, become a professional mercenary?"

"It's not like that."

"You threatened to shoot me in the liver!"

Doran sighs, scratches his scalp with the butt of his gun. "Yeah, OK, maybe I was a little overzealous. But I wasn't sure I could trust you. There's no telling who they've gotten to."

I have no idea who *they* are, but right now, I don't care.

"Where are my kids, Doran?"

He lowers the gun, staring at it like he's seeing it for the first time. "Like I said, that's… complicated."

"Try me."

He shakes his head. "We're too exposed here. We need to get off the road."

What I need to do is get out of this truck and away from Doran. Maybe he has answers, maybe he doesn't, but right now I'm not safe.

Ever so discreetly, I reach my left hand back toward the door.

"Don't," Doran says.

I almost do, because at this point I have nothing to lose and being lost in the woods seems better than remaining a hostage, but then something warm and wet drizzles off my cheek and onto my forearm.

I reach up and touch my deafened ear.

My fingertips come away coated in blood.

Shit.

My skin goes cold and clammy. My pulse ratchets up several notches. I clench my jaw, willing to world to stop spinning.

"I think you broke my ear."

"Fuck you I broke your ear. You're the dumbass who went all John McClane." Doran points his gun at the passenger seat next to me. "Scoot over."

"Fuck you scoot over!"

I can't believe I'm trading insults with someone who was holding me at gunpoint less than sixty seconds ago, but I guess this is my life now.

"Jesus Christ," Doran snaps, "if I wanted you dead you'd be dead. Will you please just scoot the fuck over? We need to get out of sight."

I want to argue, but my equilibrium goes sideways again. I don't so much scoot into the passenger seat as give in to the direction my wobbly body is already heading.

There's a split second when Doran climbs out and the truck fills with the scent of pine sap that I reconsider jumping ship, but then he's in the driver's seat and it's too late.

He cranks the ignition. The engine sputters, growls, emits a series of metal clanks, and goes still.

"Balls." He turns the key again. Again, he gets the same result. "Guess we're walking." He doesn't bother to cajole me with the gun, he simply gets out and stands by the hood, waiting for me to join him. When I don't, he kicks the bumper. "Let's go."

I stay put. "How do I know I can trust you?"

"You're still alive."

"I don't think trust means the same to you as it does to me."

"Look, I realize we got off on the wrong foot." Doran makes a show of holding the gun up in the air before stuffing it behind his lower back. "But right now, I'm the only thing standing between you and a whole world of hurt."

I point at my ear. "You're doing a bang-up fucking job."

"That's on you, dickbrain. But fine, whatever. Follow me, don't follow me. I honestly don't give a shit at this point. You're clearly useless."

And off he goes, storming away from the truck like a petulant child and taking with him whatever answers he may or may not have about Deep Dive and, more importantly, Cassie and Evie.

I hold out for all of two seconds. "Wait!"

Doran stops. Pivots. Crosses his arms. And taps his foot. "If you're coming, then hurry up. I don't have all fucking night."

Grumbling to myself, I slide out of the truck and am immediately thrown so off balance by my pistol-punched ear that my first step sends me reeling into the wheel well. My hip glances painfully off the truck. Wincing, I throw out my arm, hooking it over the side-view mirror like a drunk struggling to stay upright.

I hang there for a few moments, struggling to regain my balance. This isn't helped by the caustic cloud of gas vapors perfuming the piney air. I shift my feet, hear an odd splashing sound, and look down.

Based on the dark puddle pooling on the ground beneath the engine, I don't have to guess where the bullet went when I tried to wrest the gun from Doran.

Nice job, Peter.

The cloying scent of spent fuel only adds to the residual nausea clinging to my insides like some possessive demon desperate to avoid exorcism.

"Hurry up!" Doran barks, and resumes his march into darkness.

Moaning and lurching like a *Bloodborne* brick troll, I stumble after him. "Where are we going?"

"I've got a place about a mile from here. Totally off the grid. We should be safe there." The moonlight filtering through the pines betrays his apprehension.

"What about my truck?"

"I've got spare parts at the cabin. Gas, too. Soon as it's light we'll repair the fuel line, top off the tank."

There's a turnoff fifty yards down the way. Doran leads me down a dirt track barely wide enough to fit my truck, dodging around a rusted barrier arm blocking the path.

It's been a long time since I've walked in the woods, let alone in the middle of the night with a person most sane people would characterize as a madman.

To my left, the night noise of nocturnal critters fills the air, chirps and hoots and undergrowth rustling with the passage of unseen bodies.

To my right it's nothing but white noise.

I trip to a halt.

White noise.

"Dammit, will you keep the fuck up?" Doran says.

"I need to call my wife." In all likelihood Alana's still asleep, but she'll be up soon. Granted, I don't remember her number, but Doran doesn't need to know that.

"Yeah, that's not going to happen. Or did you forget I kidnapped you?"

Oh, I haven't forgotten.

"She's going to wonder where I am."

"That's sweet. You obviously have a tight marriage. Congrats on beating the odds. Now get moving."

I stand my ground. "I'm serious, Doran. She already thinks I've lost my mind because of all this kid stuff. If she wakes up and I'm not there, she's going to think something happened. Guaranteed she'll call the cops." I shrug. "But hey, if you're cool adding an all-points bulletin to your list of problems, then who am I to argue?"

Doran mumbles to himself. "First, we talk. Depending on how that goes, I'll think about letting you message your wife. Deal?"

I search his moonlit face for any sign of dishonesty. "Deal."

Down the path we go, Doran tromping silently alongside me, me with so many questions crowding my head I don't even know where to begin. My steps are more tentative than his – my body seems to want to lean toward my throbbing ear, threatening to send me into an endless circle like a dog chasing its own tail.

"You know," I say, "you could've just been like, 'Hey, wanna grab a coffee?' instead of sneaking into my truck and threatening to shoot me."

Doran grunts. "Like I said, I had to make sure I could trust you."

"And?"

"Jury's still out." He angles his head, giving me a squinty-eyed once-over. "You really used Deep Dive?"

"The headset?"

"No, the swimming pool at the Y. Yes, the damn headset."

I frown. "What, you think I made it all up?"

"That's the thing." He slaps the back of his neck. "There are only about a dozen people in the world who know about Deep

Dive. Until you commented on that subreddit, your name was not on that list. Which begs the question, which one of those assholes at Boundless gave you access to it?"

"Bradley."

The name hits like a mic drop. This time it's Doran who stops in his tracks. A hush falls over the forest. "Bullshit."

I shrug. "I've been getting that a lot lately. It's still true."

"That doesn't make any sense. You said you used the headset Saturday morning, but Mr Moss has been dead for over a year."

"Welcome to my world." A mosquito lands on my arm, which I promptly smack into pulp.

Slow and lethal, Doran gets up in my face, one hand behind his back. "Shepard put you up to this, didn't she? Trying to drive me out into the open?"

"I don't know anyone named..." My brain reverses to a few days ago, when I first walked into Bradley's office. He was on the phone talking to someone about contracts. "Wait, do you mean General Shepard?"

Doran scoffs. "General? Please. That wet-work whack job only wishes she were in charge of an army." His eyes narrow. "I thought you said you didn't know her."

"I overheard Bradley mention her during a phone call, that's all."

Doran moves in until our noses are mere inches apart. "I don't believe you."

If this were any other situation, I'd probably back down. Avoiding confrontation, especially the physical kind, has always been my default. But this is different. This matters. So I remain rooted in place, damned if I'm going to let this asshole intimidate me.

"I don't really give a shit what you believe," I say. "Besides, you're the one who wanted to meet in real life. How do I know *you're* not setting *me* up?" Suddenly, the car I keep seeing makes a whole lot more sense. "Admit it, you've been tailing me since yesterday."

Doran's brows crinkle like toxic caterpillars about to go to war with each other. "Bitch, I only saw your question on Reddit a few hours ago."

"Then who's been driving the white hatchback?"

In one fluid motion, Doran whips out the Glock, chambers a round, and holds the pistol up to his sightline as he scans the forest. "Are you telling me someone's been following you and your dumb ass just thought to mention it?"

I resist the urge to punch him in the head. "Excuse me for not thinking straight or volunteering information. My brain's been a little preoccupied what with, oh, I don't know, being held at fucking gunpoint."

Doran grunts, finishes his sweep of the woods, and lowers the Glock. "This is not what I fucking need," he mutters. Turning, he studies me in the moonlight, his eyes black like distant patches of starless sky. The tops of the pines rustle and sway, blown by a breeze that doesn't reach the ground. "For what it's worth," he finally says, "I'm not. Setting you up. But someone clearly is."

We stand there staring at each other, two men caught up in a standoff neither of them fully understands. Somewhere close by, a whippoorwill trills out, the ghostly call that gives the bird its name sending chills racing up and down my spine.

"So what now?" I say. "Compare notes and pretend like we trust each other?"

"You got a better idea?"

"Not really."

He slaps his neck again. "Ugh, these fucking bugs. Look, I'll tell you everything I know, but I'm getting tired of standing around in the middle of the woods."

With that, he resumes his trek down the path. I rush to catch up before my only chance at answers disappears into the trees.

The cabin is a ramshackle place, built decades if not centuries ago and so overgrown with ivy, moss, and rot that it's developed its own natural camouflage. Tall pines loom all around it, providing an additional layer of privacy. If Doran hadn't taken me directly to it, I never would've been able to find it.

Fingers crossed no one else does.

There's a click, and the front door groans inward on hinges long overrun by rust. The smell of ancient dust and black mold wafts out of the cabin, sucker-punching my nose.

Coughing violently, I follow Doran into the main room. He gestures at a fireplace on the far wall. "Throw some logs in there. I'll be right back."

There's a stack of old, yellowing newspapers next to a rusty metal bucket full of logs. The pages damn near crumple to dust when I start to pry them apart, but I manage to ball up enough to shove under the grate in the fireplace.

It's been a long time since I've lit a fire, but much like riding a bike, the muscle memory developed from years of childhood camping trips comes back to me. I arrange small pieces of kindling into a multi-tiered square, then steeple larger pieces of wood into a pyramid around the square.

Doran returns, tosses me a matchbook, then produces a faded bottle of lighter fluid and douses my carefully constructed structure.

I back away, light a match, and toss it into the fireplace.

With a hollow *whoompf*, a ball of soot and flame explodes up the flue. There's a startled shriek, followed by the sound of wings flapping as whatever bird or bat had made its home in the chimney beats a frantic escape.

Wood crackles cheerily in the fireplace, casting flickering shadows around the room. Taxidermied deer heads peer down at us from the wall, their beady eyes reflecting the flames. Two couches competing for which will decompose first form a V around a chipped coffee table with legs made of antlers. A recliner that was old when I was young sits nearby. To the left of the front door, what passes for the kitchen space sports a cast iron stove and a set of wall-mounted shelves full of pots, pans, and dishes coated in years of spiderwebs.

"This is a lovely place you've got here," I say. "Super inviting."

"Just be glad no one else knows about it." Doran strides over to an armoire that in another setting might be considered an antique, opens one side, and removes two glasses and a bottle of amber liquid. "Hope you like bourbon."

I don't, but after the night I've had – hell, after the past three days I've had – I'll drink anything that takes the edge off.

Filling each glass to the brim, Doran hands one to me, then plops down onto the couch. A cloud of dust engulfs him, obscuring his face for a moment.

I lower myself carefully into the recliner, and when it doesn't immediately fall apart, allow myself to relax into its tattered, bony embrace.

Raising his glass to me, Doran says, "To Mr Moss."

He tosses down half the glass, utters a contented sigh, and rests his head against the back of the sofa.

I incline my glass toward him, then lift it to my lips, swallowing a much more moderate amount. The alcohol burns as it courses down my throat. The fire snaps and pops, warming my legs. I take another drink, relishing the burn this time, and touch my ear. It seems to have stopped bleeding, which is good, but it's starting to feel like a phantom limb, which is more than a little worrisome.

Doran and I start to speak at the same time.

"You–"

"What–"

He tips his glass at me. "Geeks first."

There are so many questions floating around my head I hardly know where to start, so I go with something simple. "What did Deep Dive do to me?"

Doran lifts off his cap and rakes his hands through his hair. "Fuck if I know."

The firelight goes red, and I'm half out of my seat before I realize I've moved. "You son of a bitch. You told me you knew what it was!"

Doran rolls his eyes. "Cool your jets, tough guy. I never said I knew what it did to you. I said I had experience with it."

I swear to God, gun or no, I'm about two seconds away from cold-cocking this guy.

Fists clenched I say, "So help me, Doran, if you don't start talking straight, I'm walking."

"Says the man who claims Mr Moss called you on Sunday to beta test the headset, at which point it wiped your memories and replaced them with new ones?"

I work my jaw, tugging at my right earlobe in a fruitless attempt to ease the pressure. "Look, this conversation is clearly going nowhere. For the sake of moving on, can we agree to disagree on the timeline of events?"

Doran acts like he wants to keep arguing, then shrugs. "Whatever. Fine by me."

"Good." I tug at a strand of thread that's come loose from the recliner's arm. "What's your deal, anyway?"

"I don't follow."

"I get you worked for Mr Moss, but that doesn't explain why you're acting all cloak and dagger about this headset, let alone why you decided to kidnap me instead of, you know, have a conversation."

Doran studies the amber liquid sloshing around in his glass. "They've got my brother."

Now I'm the one not following. "Who's got him?"

"O'Laughlin and Shepard."

"O'Laughlin like Bradley's senior vice-president?" The guy I'd emailed earlier, a fact I decide to hold in reserve for the time being. "And what exactly do you mean by 'got'?"

Doran squints at me suspiciously. "I've gotta say, you've either got the best poker face in the entire world or you really have lost your marbles."

"If only it wasn't the latter."

"Yeah, well, that remains to be seen. Anyway. I'll play along for now." Doran tosses back the rest of his bourbon, refills his glass, and cradles it in both his hands. "When Mr Moss died, Boundless' stock took a major hit. Even before that the board of directors had been whining about all the time and money he'd thrown at developing the headset as a commercial gaming product. So when O'Laughlin took over as interim CEO, the first thing he did was nix the negotiations with Omega Studios. Your company."

He says this last bit all accusatorially.

"I'm aware," I say.

"Oh, that you remember?"

I'm not about to drag Meg into this. "Look, I appreciate the history lesson, and it jibes with what I've heard, but what does this have to do with your brother?"

"Don't rush me, dude. I'm getting there." Doran turns the glass in his hand, watching firelight refract in the bourbon. "We'd done plenty of contract work for the military, so O'Laughlin took the headset to one of his contacts at the Pentagon. They already use VR for a lot of training simulations, but O'Laughlin convinced them that this was some next-gen, full immersion shit. The project got greenlit pretty quickly."

"So was your brother part of the R&D team or something?"

Doran laughs humorlessly. "Please. James couldn't R&D his way out of a lunchbox. No, my brother's a grunt, through and through."

"He's in the Army?"

"Ranger. Served five tours in Afghanistan. Planned on getting out after one last assignment." Doran stares at me over the brim of his almost empty glass, firelight dancing in the booze like liquid flames. "Wanna guess what that assignment was?"

"Deep Dive."

"Ding ding ding. We have ourselves a winner, folks. Once the prototype headset was ready, they needed some guinea pigs to test it. James's unit had redeployed back to the States, and when I mentioned Deep Dive to him he was all about it.

So I talked to O'Laughlin, James got his CO to take it up the chain of command, and the next thing I knew my brother and his team were on board. I got a promotion out of it, to assistant project manager of all fucking things, so I was feeling pretty damn good about myself."

The Pentagon's history with technology aside, none of this sounds particularly sketchy. In fact, it sounds like a pretty sweet deal if you're a fan of the whole military-industrial complex thing. What it doesn't sound like is an answer to my predicament, let alone a reason for Doran to turn armed kidnapper.

"Something went wrong with the headset, didn't it?" I ask.

"Not initially. We had a fully immersive headset and a battlefield training simulation that James said was as realistic as any of the firefights he'd been in. The fact that there was no risk of dying meant he and his team were loving it. But then things got... weird."

"Weird how?"

"Weird like false memory weird."

I sit up so fast I almost drop my glass. Beneath me, the recliner creaks in protest. "Way to bury the lede, asshole. Why the hell didn't you mention that in your fancy chatroom?"

Doran smirks. "Thought that might get your attention. It was small stuff at first. One dude on James's team came out of his dive talking about taking leave to go to his sister's wedding, only this was the first James and the others had ever heard of him having a sister. Another guy started reminiscing about a team member who'd died in Afghanistan, a team member who no one else remembered and who didn't show up on any previous rosters."

The more examples Doran lobs at me, the more my body quakes with fear. If what he's saying is true, then...

"They're not real," I whisper.

Doran pauses. "What are you yammering on about?"

"My girls. If those soldiers all started experiencing false memories because of Deep Dive, then that means..."

A chasm opens up where my heart used to be, releasing an icy torrent of hopelessness that floods my entire body with an unbearable sense of loss.

Alana was right. We don't have children. All those late nights when Evie used to crawl into bed with us, all the times Cassie held my hand in a death grip while we watched scary movies – none of that happened. Every single memory I have of my daughters is absolutely, completely, unequivocally false.

This whole time I've been chasing a lie.

Utterly defeated, I slump in my chair and stare dead-eyed at the dying fire, the crackle of flames a hellish soundtrack to the tragedy of my life.

CHAPTER ELEVEN

Doran leans forward, snapping his fingers an inch away from my face. "Did I say story time was over?"

Snarling, I bat his hand away. "Fuck off, Doran. I'm done listening to you."

I was so convinced the girls were real. I still want them to be, more than anything else in this divergent world, but I'm not so far gone that I can't see myself for what I've become: a manic treasure hunter pursuing an endless series of fallacious clues.

"Stop acting like a little bitch." Doran's face is full of derision. "You think I'd go to all this trouble just to give you the sads? This shit is way more left fucking field than false memories."

"I don't care." Not anymore. Occam's razor has cut me so many times I've become woozy from blood loss. If I don't staunch the bleeding, if I don't accept that the simplest, most logical explanation is the right one, I might never recover from whatever Deep Dive did to my brain.

Doran's face is a study in fire-lit shadows, black shapes writhing across stubbly cheeks like tiny demons. "Then I guess you don't want to hear about how they kept accumulating false memories. How O'Laughlin insisted everything was fine and continued sending James and his team on dives until one day they entered the simulation and never came out."

A sap pocket pops, releasing a hiss of steam as one of the logs

131

crumbles into pieces and sends sparks and embers shooting up the flue.

As much as I'm feigning disinterest, I can't help but be intrigued. "What do you mean, they never came out?"

"Their virtual avatars are nowhere to be seen, and their bodies are as unresponsive as coma patients. They are, for lack of a better phrase, lost at fucking sea."

Anger carves tight furrows into his forehead. He reaches for the bottle of bourbon, upends it, and fills his glass to the rim.

I take the bottle and refill my glass with a much less lethal amount. "I don't understand."

"Neither did we, at first. But then one of the techs discovered some blips in the simulation logs."

"What kind of blips?"

"Every member of James's team, everyone who'd experienced false memories, disappeared not only from the simulation, but from real life."

I pause in the act of taking a drink, bourbon lapping at my lips like an incoming tide. "Define disappeared."

"As in vanished. For only a few nanoseconds, but during those nanoseconds, James and the others literally disappeared from every sensor we had hooked up to Deep Dive. I'm talking in virtual reality and reality reality."

I swallow a gulp of booze. "Now I know you're just screwing with me."

"Give me one good reason why I'd make all this shit up." He gets up and tosses another log on the fire. "Go on, I'll wait."

I scowl at him, but the truth is, I can't think of a thing.

"That's right, you've got nothing. So do me a favor," he says, settling back on the couch. "Suspend your disbelief and listen to what I'm telling you."

I tilt my head so the left side's angled toward him. "I'm all ear."

Doran actually laughs. "Gallows humor. I like it. There might be hope for you yet, Banuk. Anyway. I was as skeptical as you are when I read the report. People don't just disappear, right? Then I watched the footage from the simulation and the security cam in the Deep Dive chamber side by side."

He leans forward, his eyes full of firelight. "Both videos were slowed down as far as the processors could take them, but even in slow-mo it was one of those blink and you miss it moments. Eventually I saw it. My brother disappeared. I saw his team disappear. The moment their avatars walked through that door in the simulation, their bodies–" he snaps his fingers again "–winked out of existence. Just for a microsecond. But it was long enough to do something to their minds, because not a single damn one of them has woken up since."

The only sound is the sizzle of flames attacking fresh fuel. I can tell Doran is waiting for my response, for me to express an appropriate amount of shock and awe over what he's just told me. It's not that I'm not gobsmacked, but the thing that's stuck in my brain like a burr isn't the fact of his brother's vanishing act.

It's what Doran said about his brother walking through a door.

The moment their avatars walked through that door in the simulation, their bodies winked out of existence.

The memory of that red metal door in the labyrinth and the sea of silver light behind it is forever seared into my mind.

Doran crosses one leg over the other, rotating his glass of bourbon like a sommelier examining its coloration. "What's the matter, cat got your tongue?"

"The door."

Doran pauses, the glass halfway to his mouth. "What about it?"

"I walked through one. In the simulation. Right before I came to in my truck."

Doran slowly sets his glass on the coffee table and scoots forward. "And you didn't think that might be pertinent information to share with the class?"

"How was I supposed to know it was important?"

He steeples his fingers, the gesture eerily reminiscent of Dr Blake. "Anything else you've neglected to tell me?"

"Doran, I've already told you everything I–"

"Bullshit!" He slaps his hand down on the coffee table, the sound as loud as a gunshot. "I'm done playing around. I don't know if you used Deep Dive after-hours and that's what messed up your brain like it did James's or if you really are just fucking with me, but it really doesn't matter. What matters is that this is your fault, and now you're going to help me fix it."

"My fault? How is this my fault?" I glance at the nearly empty bottle of bourbon. "Why don't we–"

Slow as death, Doran stands, unfurling until he's looming over me like a demon made of firelight and shadow. "I'm done with the innocent act, dickweed. Mr Moss might have designed Deep Dive, but that battlefield simulation is one hundred percent on you."

"Now you're just talking out of your ass." I stay seated, forcing a veneer of calmness, but inside my brain is begging me to run. "I've never worked on a first-person shooter, let alone a…"

My voice trails off as my mind flashes back to the conversation I had with Meg after I left Dr Blake's office.

Your "secret project"? The one you've been designing on the sly for, like, the last year? What, you think I didn't notice how weird and distant you've been acting lately?

No, no way. There is no way what Doran is suggesting is true.

"It's coming back to you, isn't it?" he says. "How many times have we passed each other in the hall? Me, running interference between O'Laughlin and the project manager, you always rabbiting around troubleshooting software glitches like some nervous nelly?"

I rub my wrist nervously. "I– I don't–"

Doran circles the coffee table, picks up an iron poker, and, bending down, jabs it into the fire. Sparks swirl up the chimney like fallen stars rising back into space. "The military's good at a lot of things, but designing high-quality virtual simulations ain't one of them. O'Laughlin realized we needed someone from the private sector, someone who actually knew game development. *Scorchfell* wasn't half bad, and we'd been in talks with Omega Studios once already, so I suggested we go back to you. Several non-disclosure agreements later, you came on board as Boundless' newest creative consultant."

Now I'm the one calling bullshit. "You're lying."

"Like I said before, what possible reason do I have to make this shit up?"

This is too much. I close my eyes, rubbing my temples as though I can erase everything Doran has just said.

"You're telling me," I say through my hands, "that I'm the one who designed the battlefield simulation."

"Unless you've got an identical twin you never told anyone about, then yes, that's exactly what I'm saying."

"No joke, at this point I wouldn't even discount that."

My brain says Doran is full of it, but then my brain also says that I have daughters when my own wife swears we don't, that *Scorchfell* flopped when it didn't, that Bradley is alive when he isn't.

I don't know what to believe anymore.

Doran hangs up the poker but remains squatting by the fireplace, his expression less aggressive. "I'm not trying to be an asshole, no matter what you think. I honestly don't care if you're full of it or if you really don't remember shit. The fact of the matter is, my brother's a vegetable and you're not, which means that you walked away from Deep Dive relatively intact. Somewhere in that discombobulated brain of yours is the answer to fixing James and the rest of his team."

There's an internal logic to everything he's saying that makes it hard to argue.

"So that's why you kidnapped me?" I say. "To help save your brother?"

"When I saw you in the diner and realized who I'd been chatting with, yeah. Before that I thought you were some defector I could grill for intel. See, ever since James and his team went comatose, O'Laughlin's shut me out. I'm pretty sure he's out of his depth and trying to stage a cover up supported by the military, and I'm not having any of that shit. My brother deserves better."

"So, what, we're going to break into Boundless?" I say, not quite able to believe I'm actually considering becoming party to whatever Doran has in mind.

Doran taps the side of his head, then points at me. "Smart man. The way I see it is, you built it, you can fix it."

"Please tell me you have a plan."

"Formulating one as we speak. For now, though, we need to make sure we stay off O'Laughlin's radar."

My stomach, already soured by the events of the past couple of hours, curdles even more. "Um."

Doran rises from his crouch, his glare hotter than the fire. "Um what?"

"I might have already emailed O'Laughlin about Deep Dive."

"Why the ever-loving *fuck*," Doran hisses, "would you do something stupid like that?"

"In my defense," I say, "I didn't know it *was* stupid at the time. I was looking for answers and thought he might have some."

"Shit."

"I'd offer to check my email to see if he's responded, but *someone* decided to throw my phone out of a moving car."

Grumbling to himself, Doran pulls his phone out of his pocket. "Here. It's got a satellite uplink, so no one can track it. Don't look at my search history."

I don't even want to know what Doran gets up to online. "Yeah, about that."

"Sweet baby Jesus, what now?"

"There's a chance I don't remember my passwords."

The glow from the fireplace enshrouds him like flames straight out of Muspelheim. "By chance you mean…"

"At all."

"Shit on a stick! Are you trying to fuck us from the start?"

"Like you remember all your passwords."

He shakes his phone. "It's called autosave!"

"Well, all *my* passwords are autosaved on the phone you chucked out the window and my laptop at home."

Home, where Alana's probably, hopefully, still asleep. She sometimes has issues with insomnia, but once she's out, she's out. I could play *Doom Eternal* at full volume ten feet from our bed and she'd keep right on snoozing. It's an impressive skill, one I'm eminently jealous of.

Today of course will be the day Alana wakes early and realizes I'm gone. The note I left will only tide her over so long, assuming she even sees it. The first thing she'll do is call out my name. When I don't answer she'll anxiously pull on her slippers because her feet are always cold and start searching for me. But the house will be empty. Silent. Her worry will kick into overdrive. She'll message me if she hasn't already. I won't respond. Any headway we've made since I barged into our room demanding to know what happened to Cassie and Evie will become completely moot as her brain posits a thousand terrifying scenarios that all end in something horrible befalling me.

She doesn't deserve that. Not after everything I've put her through. Which means I need to get home. Now.

I stand and hold out my hand. "Keys."

"Yeah, that's not happening."

"Look," I say, "you're going to have to trust me at some point. Unless you'd rather barge into Boundless totally blind, I need to check my email to see if O'Laughlin responded. Plus, didn't you say Shepard blocked all your access codes? Unless you plan on holding up someone else at gunpoint, we need my ID card."

Wherever the hell that is.

"You crashed the truck," Doran says.

"And you said you could fix it."

We have ourselves a good old-fashioned staring competition. Surprisingly, Doran blinks first.

"Fuck. Fine. But so help me, Buddha," he says, getting up in my face, "if you do something stupid like tell your wife what's happening, memory loss will be the least of your problems. Capiche?"

And now we're in an Italian crime drama.

I hold up three fingers. "Scout's honor."

"Please. Like either of us were ever in the Boy Scouts." He reaches into his front pocket, removes the keys, and drops them into my hand. "Wait here."

He vanishes into the back of the cabin. A loud crash followed by a louder curse echoes through the den.

"Need any help?" I call out.

"Fuck off!"

A minute later Doran emerges from the shadows carrying a gas can, a roll of duct tape, and a cobweb-covered length of hose. "Let's do this."

We set out into the cool early morning air, two men on a mission that most people would characterize as sheer madness bordering on outright lunacy.

Above the treetops, dawn is just beginning to bruise the sky. Shadows flit in and out of the trees like the ghosts of dark elves haunting Alfheim.

I trudge alongside Doran, shifting the red five-gallon gas can from hand to hand. We make better time to the truck than we did to the cabin. Thankfully my balance has mostly corrected itself, and I don't trip over my own feet as we hurry down the uneven dirt track.

I don't know whether it's good or bad that my right ear doesn't hurt as much as it did when we first got to the cabin. It's still tender to the touch, and the whining drone of mosquitoes has been replaced by the dull roar of the ocean, but it seems like – I hope that – my body's slowly adapting to losing half of one of its senses. I have no idea how I'm going to explain it to Alana. I suppose it's a hopeful sign that I'm thinking that far ahead. Or it's straight-up delusion. At this stage it's hard to differentiate between the two.

When we reach the truck, I jack up the left front wheel and Doran crawls underneath. The front bumper is dented all to hell, which is something else I'll have to figure out how to explain.

Working in tandem like a TV doctor and their surgical assistant, I hover at the fringes of the repair job, passing him tools while he removes the perforated section of gas line and duct tapes a new one into place.

When it's done I pour gas into the tank while Doran checks for leaks. Satisfied it's as good as it's going to get, he lowers the jack, tosses the toolbox into the back of the truck, and climbs into the passenger seat.

"Fire this bad boy up," he says, slapping the dash.

The key is halfway in when I hear a soft tinkle of glass, followed by a wet, sickening crunch.

I pause, staring in confusion at the latticework of cracks radiating out from a small hole that's suddenly appeared in the windshield, then look over at Doran.

"Did you–"

The question dies on my lips. Doran's head is lolling to the side as though his spine has quit supporting his neck. It's light enough now that I can see a black hole in the center of his forehead that wasn't there a few seconds ago. Blood pumps sickeningly out of the hole, painting a gristly, sinuous line down the side of his face.

"Doran?" I whisper, gaping in horror at my inexplicably but undeniably dead acquaintance before a surge of unbridled panic jump-starts me into motion.

The truck rumbles to life, but as my hand grabs hold of the

gearshift, a shadowy figure materializes outside the driver's side window, rips open the door, and points a gun directly at my face.

"Move," he says, "and I'll blow your fucking head off."

CHAPTER TWELVE

A second figure appears behind the first, leveling an assault rifle at me. Both are dressed in tactical body armor, their faces hooded by their helmets.

"Hands on the steering wheel," the first one orders.

I stare in numb disbelief at the massive handgun hovering a foot from my left eyeball. The gun stares back at me, its single, lidless, all-knowing eye boring into my very soul.

"I said hands on the fucking steering wheel!" the first soldier says.

"Do it now!" the second one barks, inching toward his partner.

Despite my lack of action, I really do want to comply. But my brain and body seem to have suffered a sudden divorce, because neither is speaking to the other at the moment.

"Fuck this noise. You got me?" the first soldier says.

The second one shifts sideways, adjusting the angle of his rifle. "Good to go."

The next thing I know, the first soldier grabs hold of my arm and hauls me out of the truck, dragging me several yards away before tossing me unceremoniously onto the ground.

The impact jolts me out of my static state. I lurch to my feet, fully intent on making a desperate dash for the questionable safety of the trees, but my assailant kicks my feet out from under me, dropping me to the ground so hard it knocks the breath out of my lungs and sends a shower of shooting stars cascading across my vision.

Breathless and half-insensate, I lay there as one of my attackers pins my legs while the other wrenches up my arms and binds my wrists, cinching the zip-tie with frightening, professional ease.

"Try that again," he growls, "and I'll break your fucking kneecaps."

Between the hard, biting plastic of the zip-tie and the uncomfortable weight of his partner pressing down on my legs, escape is now officially off the table.

This is it. Game over.

Branches and rocks dig into my body like the claws of hungry ghouls emerging from unmarked graves. I can taste dirt on my tongue, smell its dry, fungal earthiness inside my nose. My head's pounding, the ear that was deafened earlier pulsing in painful counterpoint to the rapid thump of my heartbeat. It's hard to suck in more than a partial breath.

All of that pales, however, to the image of Doran, slumped over in the truck's passenger seat, the headshot that ended him still weeping blood like a third, sightless eye.

I've played my fair share of violent games, mowed down thousands of NPCs, and I can honestly say with one hundred percent certainty that even the most lifelike shooter does nothing to prepare you for the reality of a freshly murdered corpse.

I don't even realize I'm about to puke. My mouth opens of its own accord and vomit bursts out, splattering the ground inches from the feet of the soldier crouching near my head.

"Aw, Jesus, what the fuck?" The man leaps up, kicking bile off his boots.

His partner, the one holding my legs in place, he laughs.

He *laughs.*

Doran is dead.

Doran is fucking *dead*, murdered, and this asshole *laughs*?

I thrash and twist, writhe and wriggle, consumed by the need to do some damage, to make them pay for what they did to Doran.

The man on my legs curses, trying to hold me in place. "Finn!" he shouts.

Finn drops down, pressing one hand into the space between my shoulder blades while the other shoves his gun into the base of my skull.

"I already have one good reason," he says, leaning down and giving me my first good glimpse of his bent nose, acne-scarred cheeks, and humorless eyes. "Please, Banuk, give me another."

The sound of my name is almost as shocking as Doran's lifeless body. This guy knows me. How the hell does this guy know me? I certainly don't recognize him.

"I think you've made your point, Finn," a third, decidedly feminine voice says. "Get him up."

Grumbling to himself, Finn waves at his partner, who climbs off my legs as Finn slides his hands beneath my armpits and lifts me roughly to my feet. My entire body aches so much from being manhandled it's all I can do to stay upright.

The newcomer is about Alana's height. Slim. White. Blonde hair cut into a razor-sharp bob. Upturned nose. Thin lips. Long neck. A tight white T-shirt and a gray vest overtop. Black jeans like a second skin. Steel-toed boots like Finn and the other guy. The spitting image of a modern-day, pulp fiction gangster. I'm honestly surprised there's not a cigarette dangling from her lips.

She leans against the side of my truck, apparently unbothered by her proximity to Doran's body, and crosses her arms. "If you'd told me last week that I'd be standing in the woods debating whether to bring you in or let Finn finish you off, I'd have told you you'd taken leave of all your senses." She sighs, shakes her head. "Honestly, Peter, what the hell were you thinking, conspiring with Doran?"

The familiarity with which these bastards say my name makes my skin crawl. It's almost as disconcerting as their apparent lack of concern for the dead body in the truck.

Finn smacks me upside the back of my head. "Ms Shepard asked you a question."

I jerk away, fury as intense as any I've ever known radiating out from me like I'm the epicenter of a bomb blast, tempered only by my bound hands and the fact that my brain's running at half-capacity so it takes a moment before I register what Finn called the woman.

Shepard.

This is the one Doran warned me about, the one who works with O'Laughlin. If they know me well enough to call me by my first name, then Doran was right. I must work at Boundless.

Fuck.

Somewhere in the forest a screech owl lets loose a series of high-pitched hoots. The thinnest of breezes blows through the trees, the dawn-cool wind doing nothing to calm my nerves. Overhead, pink and orange clouds frame the brightening sky like nuclear fallout. I keep hoping someone will drive by, see me, call the cops, but we're too deep in the sticks for passersby this early in the morning. Which, in terms of their safety, is probably for the best, but it thoroughly sucks for me.

"My patience isn't what it used to be, Peter," Shepard says.

I'd rather spit in her face than give her the satisfaction of capitulating, but I'm at so many disadvantages here it's not even funny, and honestly, I'd really rather not wind up like Doran.

"I guess I wasn't thinking," I mutter.

"There seems to be a lot of that going around." She pushes off from the car. "For what it's worth, I apologize for this morning's unpleasantness. This certainly isn't how I envisioned events playing out, but, well, needs must."

"Needs must? You killed Doran!"

"Doran knew what would happen if he went up against us."

Shepard's eyes are black in the dim light of dawn. "And now so do you."

There's no aggression in her tone, but the threat comes through loud and clear, made all the more frightening by the fact that she's talking about the murder of a coworker as though she's done nothing more than push paperwork through a shredder.

"Please understand," she continues, turning to peer inside the truck. "While Doran's death was pretty much inevitable, your own is something Mr O'Laughlin and I would very much like to avoid. At the moment, we simply want to have a conversation with you."

The underbrush rustles with movement. Finn's partner shifts his feet, raising his rifle as he takes a few steps toward the tree line. Finn doesn't react at all.

I flex my wrists, grimacing as the zip-tie cuts into my skin. "You have a pretty fucked up way of getting people to talk to you."

Shepard reaches into the truck, removes something from Doran's body, and then closes the door. "Despite what you think," she says, rotating back around with the Glock in hand, "I didn't enjoy ordering Doran's death." She stuffs the pistol into the waist of her jeans. "But rest assured, I'm fully prepared to do whatever's necessary in order to protect my interests."

"You're not going to get away with this," I say, because that's what you're supposed to say in a situation like this even when you know full well the other person will absolutely get away with it.

She sighs. "Peter, it's been a long morning. I haven't had breakfast yet. So please, cut the bullshit. Otherwise I'll be forced to let Finn have his way with you."

The expectant joy on Finn's face turns my marrow to ice.

"Fine. You want the truth? I have no fucking idea who you are."

Shepard smirks. "Oh, I'm well aware you're not who you say you are."

My entire body goes rigid, which apparently is confirmation enough to Shepard that she's right. I don't actually know if what she's saying is true – I've lost all capacity to say who I really am, because I legitimately don't know anymore – so it takes little effort on my part to act perplexed by her question.

"I have no idea what you're talking about."

"You claim to be Peter Banuk, correct?"

Claim to be?

"Yeah. So?"

She gives me an appraising glance. "I must say, the resemblance is remarkable. But then I guess it would be, wouldn't it?"

Resemblance? Resemblance to who?

"Seriously," I say, "do any of you not talk out of your asses?"

"I get that you're not quite ready to cooperate." Shepard shrugs, raps her knuckles on the truck. "Admittedly, some of that's on me. But I need you to understand that the longer you stall, the more likely it becomes that I'll be forced to talk to Alana. She seems like a very nice woman, and I'd really rather not drag her into this, but rest assured, if it comes to that, I will not hesitate to do so."

My periphery goes red like I'm on my last hit-point. "Don't you lay a fucking hand on her!"

"How sweet are you?" Shepard smiles, her cheeks dimpling. "Don't worry, involving your wife is a last resort."

I force my shoulders to relax, try to keep my voice level despite the panic spreading through my veins like poison. "Alana's got nothing to do with this."

"Oh, I highly doubt that. In fact," Shepard taps her lips, "I'd hazard a guess that your wife is well aware that everything is not as it seems. What do you think she'll do when she finds out the truth, hmm? I for one would love to be a fly on the wall for that conversation."

Shepard's whole enigmatic act is wearing thin. Problem is, I'm in no position to challenge her. For one, I'm half hogtied. For another, she clearly knows more than I do. All of which puts me at a distinct disadvantage, seeing as I still have no fucking clue why she shot Doran or what she wants with me. What I do know is that the only way I'm going to survive long enough to uncover the truth – and, more importantly, keep Alana safe – is if I pull off the biggest bluff of my life by convincing Shepard that I'm still holding a viable hand.

"Leave her alone and I'll cooperate," I say.

Shepard spreads her arms wide. "See? That wasn't so hard, now was it? I must say, Peter, I'm looking forward to hearing your side of this strange little story."

If only I had a legitimate story to share instead of a headful of empty pages.

A phone rings, its trill disturbing the relative quiet of the woods. Shepard lifts a finger as she answers it. "Yes?" She listens without moving for a moment, then nods. "Understood." She shoves the phone back in her pocket and turns to Finn's partner. "The cleaning crew is on its way. When they're finished with the cabin, I want you to follow them back to Boundless with Peter's truck." She pauses. "Actually, for now, see if you can move it farther back into the woods. No reason to risk some hapless local getting nosy."

"Yes, ma'am."

"Oh, and do something with this." She removes Doran's pistol from her waistband and passes it to him, then returns her attention to me. "So, are we ready?"

Not really, no. I nod.

"Wonderful. Our ride's just up that way. Finn, if you wouldn't mind chaperoning our guest?"

Finn shoves me forward. "March, asshole."

I stumble, catch my balance, and glare at him. He grins, exposing a mouth of bleached white teeth, and gets up in my face. His breath smells like spearmint. This close I can see the pucker in a scar bisecting his forehead. "What, you got something to say?"

"Finn!" Shepard snaps. "I said chaperone, not bully."

Finn's partner snickers. Finn shoots him a nasty look, then taps the tip of my nose. "You and me, we're gonna have some fun when this is all over and done with." He snaps his jaws at me, leers, and tries to shove me again.

I'm ready for it, though. Side-stepping the blow, I stride down the road a few paces ahead of him, the set of my shoulders belying the fear souring my stomach. I make it about twenty feet before the sound of my truck stuttering to life causes me to glance guiltily over my shoulder.

From this distance it would be easy to assume Doran is simply sleeping off a bender while Finn's partner prepares to drive him home.

But Doran is never going home, and if I'm not careful, neither am I.

I'll make this right, I promise him. *I don't know how, but I will find your brother and make this right.*

Shepard's ride, a black SUV with heavily tinted windows, is parked about fifty yards up the road. Finn opens the rear passenger door and watches impassively as I duck my awkward way inside, then rounds the car and climbs in beside me. I scoot as far away as I can and try to get comfortable, but there's no way I can sit properly with my hands bound behind me. I settle on pressing my butt into the seatback and hunching my shoulders slightly forward. It doesn't diminish the discomfort, but it distributes it more equally.

Shepard slithers into the driver's seat and angles the rearview mirror until she can see me in it. "Everyone ready?"

Finn raps the window with his knuckles. "Good to go."

"Lovely." Shepard puts the car in gear, pulls a U-turn, and heads back down the road.

My truck's already gone, hidden deep in the woods where no one will see it. The only sign it and Doran were ever there is the dent in the tree we crashed into, its mangled bark a poor substitute for the gravestone he'll never get.

CHAPTER THIRTEEN

Back in the city, life's going on as normal as can be. Cars zip up and down the roads. Early-bird pedestrians stride along the sidewalks. Pigeons perch on rooftops. Clouds course through the warming, summer-blue sky. It's a picture-perfect montage of ordinariness that further emphasizes just how fucked up my life's become.

At one street corner, I look to the side and catch a glimpse of a park we sometimes take the girls to on the weekends when I'm actually home and the weather's nice. No one's there right now save for joggers and dog walkers, but it's not hard to imagine sitting on one of the benches while Cassie and Evie run around the playground.

I'm exhausted, scared, and not entirely convinced this is going to end well for me, but as the light changes and we pull away from the park I utter a silent prayer that I earn the chance to watch my girls play there again.

Next to me, Finn fiddles with his gun, flicking the safety off and on, making a show of sighting down the barrel and popping the cartridge in and out. When he catches me watching he flashes a wolfish smirk, places the gun in his lap, and clasps his hands behind his head as if daring me to make a move.

Seeing as the zip-ties are preventing me from flipping him off, I do the next best thing and, channeling Evie at her snarkiest, stick my tongue out at him.

Finn reacts with a sort of twitchy, confused double-take, which gives me way more satisfaction than it should, all things considered.

"Fucking weirdo," he mutters. "No wonder your simulation went belly up."

Shepard clears her throat. "No shop talk in the car, boys."

I want to goad Finn into divulging more – something tells me it wouldn't take much to get him riled up – but that would clue them in to just how clueless I am. Plus I don't want to get pistol-whipped. So I do my best to hold my tongue, the very picture of a compliant prisoner with information to trade.

"You look like hell, by the way," Shepard says, regarding me in the rearview. "When's the last time you slept?"

What the hell do you care? I shrug. "It's been a while."

"I bet. Well, I'm sure you'll have some time to rest once we reach Boundless. After all, lack of proper sleep can impair cognitive functionality, and we certainly can't have that."

"I've heard a bullet to the head can have a similar effect," I mutter, staring out the window at an abandoned parking lot choked with weeds and populated by rusting shipping crates.

"Yes, well." Shepard purses her lips and goes back to minding the traffic.

Finn mimes playing a tiny violin. "Doran broke the rules. He's lucky he went out like he did."

"Oh, bite me. The thought didn't occur to you to, I don't know, fucking *talk* to him first?"

"Believe me," Shepard says, "we tried. Unfortunately, the moment he went AWOL, Doran became a clear and present danger to the program. He had to be dealt with."

"Don't give me that Tom Clancy bullshit. You had a choice."

"So what's your excuse?" Shepard says.

"For what?"

"You made a choice to post on Reddit, Peter. Had you not done that, you might've been able to fly under the radar for a little while longer. Doran for sure would still be alive."

"Don't you dare lay that shit on me!"

"Sit back!" Finn barks, his gun abruptly inches from my temple. "Now!"

I blink rapidly, unaware I'd shot forward. Cheeks flushed, I unclench my jaw, relax my arms, and do my best to regain what little comfort the zip-ties afford me.

"For you," Shepard continues, unruffled by the tension in the backseat, "that choice made complete sense at the time, as did mine. Honestly, you're lucky it was only Doran. Our higher-ups don't take kindly to seeing matters of national security posted online for all the world to see."

"What the hell do false memories and a virtual reality headset have to do with national security?"

It seems that now we've started, Shepard is more than happy to chat. "Deep Dive is the most significant technological achievement in all of human history. It's also the most dangerous. Your presence here is proof enough of that. In a way, I suppose we should thank you for opening our eyes to the truth. If you hadn't shown up, it might've taken months, maybe years, before we realized its true power."

If I hadn't shown up? Based on everything Doran told me, Shepard and I are coworkers. The way she's acting right now it's like we're meeting for the first time. And yet she also recognizes me and knows everything about my life.

None of this makes any sense. There's definitely way more going on here than false memories and the disappearing act Doran claims his brother pulled, but I'll be damned if I can figure out what could possibly merit murder.

Sadly, the signal has to remain lost in the noise for the time being, because half a minute later we reach our destination.

Boundless HQ.

The place where everything started.

The place where, unless something changes, everything's about to come to a dismal end.

My stomach knots so much even Alexander the Great couldn't slice his way through it.

Instead of going through the visitor's gate, Shepard drives around behind the building to the private entrance. The guard who emerges from the shack next to the security arm is dressed in blue and gray camouflage and carries a massive, wicked-looking machine gun that makes Finn's pistol seem like a child's toy.

Shepard rolls down her window and hands the guard her ID card. I manage to catch a glimpse of the front before the guard takes it and disappears into his shack. On the left side of the card is Shepard's face. In the middle is the word *Security*. And in the top right corner, a small oval containing the acronym DARPA.

Oh shit.

I've done my fair share of research, personal and professional, so I know exactly what DARPA stands for.

The Defense Advanced Research Projects Agency, an offshoot of the United States Department of Defense that studies, manages, and creates emergent technology for the military.

Like most scientific entities, DARPA isn't good or bad. But as is the case with agencies that exist on the fringes of, or outright dabble in, futuristic technology, there's a lot of room for abuse. Just look at how $E = mc^2$ contributed to the atomic bomb. Based on what Shepard did to Doran and how dangerous she's made Deep Dive out to be, something tells me that this particular division of DARPA has definitely gone the route of super villainy.

I am so screwed.

As discreetly as I can, I lean forward and squint at the side-view mirror, gauging the distance back to the road. In all likelihood, Finn would mow me down before I made it ten steps, but I'm beginning to wonder if that's better than whatever's waiting for me inside Boundless.

My leg twitches, and I start to twist my hips so that my back's facing the door, giving my hands easy access to the handle.

"I double dog dare you," Finn says.

I freeze, try to act nonchalant like I'm just stretching.

"Tell you what," Finn continues, "I'll give you a head start. Say a twenty-count? Don't worry, I'll probably just wing you. Sound good?"

"Finn," Shephard snaps.

"Aw, I'm just having a little fun with my buddy here."

The guard reemerges from his shack and returns the card to Shepard. "You're all good, ma'am."

Behind the security arm, red emergency lights flash above a heavy metal garage door. With a series of clunks, the door rises until it's just high enough for the SUV's roof to clear it.

"Have a nice day," Shepard says to the guard, and then into the belly of the beast we go.

Wheels squeak as we spiral down several levels. I knew Boundless was big, knew there were rumors about clandestine services renting space, but I had no idea it extended this far underground.

When we reach the bottom, six floors down, Shepard pulls into a parking spot designated for head of security. I wait for Finn to let me out, then follow Shepard as we trudge across the parking garage toward a yellow- and black-striped door.

Right before we reach it, I glance to the right and do a double-take.

There, parked a few spaces over from a jet black Mercedes, is a white hatchback with tinted windows.

I wasn't being paranoid after all. Yay.

Shepard holds her ID up to a card reader embedded in the wall. The screen pulses red once, twice, then goes green, displaying a grainy image of her face. The scanner emits a pleasant beep, and the lock on the yellow-jacket door clicks open.

On the other side of the door is a whitewashed concrete corridor that smells cloyingly of old socks and motor oil.

"Fun fact," Shepard says as we trudge down the passageway. "Boundless was built on top of a Cold War-era bunker that was originally designed to act as a temporary seat of government should DC get turned into a mushroom cloud."

How appropriate.

I can practically hear the claw clicks and guttural growls of mutated monsters stalking the last survivors of the human race. In another time and place, this would be the perfect location to set a post-apocalyptic first-person shooter. Now, it only serves to remind me how unlikely it is that I'll ever see Alana again, let alone Cassie and Evie.

Shepard stops as we reach a set of double doors. "Now, this can go one of two ways. Cooperate, and I'll do my best to see that you get home. Put up any sort of resistance and I'll have Finn start breaking fingers. Understood?"

Finn starts to pop his knuckles one by one.

I swallow, nod.

"All right." She twirls a finger. "Turn around."

Half-convinced she's been playing me this whole time, that Finn's about to put a bullet in the back of my head, I slowly face the wall.

Finn jerks at my arms, causing waves of pain to radiate out from my shoulders. I wince, grit my teeth, and fight the urge to donkey kick him.

"Here's how this is going to work," Finn growls, his breath hot and humid on my ear, his rough, beefy hand tight around my forearm. "You're going to keep your eyes down and your mouth shut. Someone says hi, you ignore them. Someone passes you a birthday card to sign, you sign it and move on. You do anything to make anyone think you're here under duress, you even act like you're about to rabbit, I will march you into the nearest supply closet and waterboard you with a mop bucket. Do I make myself clear?"

I nod again.

"Good. Then hold the fuck still."

There's a faint *snick*, and then the zip-tie falls away.

I hate how grateful I am, how amazing it feels to be able to do something simple like stretch my aching arms in front of me and rub circulation back into my raw, enflamed wrists. When I turn around and look at Finn, the self-satisfied smirk on his face tells me he's well aware of my conflicted relief.

Shepard swipes her ID through another card reader, unlocking the doors. They open onto a spacious common area. Potted plants stand alongside desks and cubicles occupied by dozens of people, most of whom barely glance up as we pass by. Several vending machines stand against one wall. A kitchenette is stationed in a corner complete with a fridge, a stove, and the kind of hand-pulled espresso machine that would make a perfect *I'm sorry I put you through this* gift to Alana.

Those who do acknowledge our presence raise their hands in greeting. Like a queen promenading past her subjects, Shepard accords each of them the briefest of nods. Contrary to Finn's threats, none of them pay any attention to me. I certainly don't recognize anyone.

In truth, this is the opposite of what I expected. It's so... normal. Nothing here indicates someone as sociopathic as Shepard or Finn could ever be an employee.

We exit the common room, head down one last corridor, and follow Shepard into a small office, where a young man sits doing paperwork behind a bland metal desk.

"Is he in?" Shepard says as the kid looks up.

He presses a button on the intercom next to his computer.

"What?" a gruff voice snaps.

"Mr O'Laughlin? It's Edward. Shepard just–"

"She's here?"

"Yes, sir. Should I–"

"Shepard," O'Laughlin's disembodied voice shouts, "get your ass in here!"

"I see he's in a good mood," she says to Edward.

"He's on his third espresso of the morning if that tells you anything. Go ahead and–"

The door behind us opens.

"Edward," says the vaguely familiar, very pregnant woman who walks into the room while reading something on the tablet in her hand, "is Mr O'Laughlin available? I need to run some numbers by him." She looks up, sees our merry trio. "Oh. I'm sorry, I didn't realize…"

Her voice trails off as she notices me. Ambient light glints off a silver stud piercing her left nostril. Shoulder-length braids bob around light brown cheeks speckled with dark freckles.

And that's when it hits me. Who she is.

The last time I saw her she had a silver ring in her right nostril instead of a stud in the left and was definitely not pregnant, but there's no doubt about it.

It's Reggie, the computer technician who was with Bradley when I used the Deep Dive headset.

CHAPTER FOURTEEN

"Um, never mind," Reggie says. "I can come back."

She spins around, but O'Laughlin's voice stops her. "Dr Manasa? Is that you?"

"Sorry, Mr O'Laughlin," Reggie calls out, still inching out the door. "I didn't mean to interrupt. I can show you the latest figures when you're done."

"That's fine," O'Laughlin says. "Wait, hold on. This likely pertains to you, too. You might as well come in."

Shepard seems to be a master at schooling her expression, so it's impossible to tell whether she's happy about the addition to our party. Finn simply glowers and hooks his thumbs into his waistline, the pinkie finger on his right hand grazing his holstered gun. Reggie, on the other hand, is toggling from one foot to the next as if she can't decide whether to listen to O'Laughlin or make a break for it.

"I really don't mind coming back later," she says.

"Regina, get your ass in here!"

She sighs. "Yes, sir."

She hangs back as we file into O'Laughlin's office, Shepard in front of me, Finn behind, then comes in after us.

"Do you need anything else, Mr O'Laughlin?" Edward asks.

Without looking up from the file he's reading, O'Laughlin, a portly, balding white man about my age, flaps a mitt of a hand dismissively. "See if you can scrounge up another espresso. And hold all my calls."

"Yes, sir." Edward closes the door, sealing us in.

O'Laughlin licks the tip of his finger, flips to the last page of the file, then lays it down and leans back in his chair, hands propped on his prodigious gut. He gives me a derisive once-over, then looks at the rest of the crowd gathered in his office.

"I thought you said you were bringing in Doran," he says.

"Unfortunately," Shepard responds, "Mr Doran experienced an unexpected change of heart and won't be joining us."

Finn coughs into his fist, hiding his smile. Reggie makes an almost imperceptible strangled sound. I glance at her, but she remains focused on Shepard.

"Shit. OK." O'Laughlin runs a hand over his balding pate and shrugs. "What about Banuk's wife?"

"We have eyes on her but see no reason to involve her yet."

The amount of dread that floods my body could drown a roomful of lab rats.

O'Laughlin nods and turns his attention to me. "Your hair's different. His hair's different, right? Longer? And maybe the nose, too?"

"There are some dissimilarities, yes," Shepard says. "In general, though, the resemblance is a near perfect match."

Alarms explode in my head, but beyond a general sense of self-preservation, I don't know what they're warning me about, just like I don't know what Shepard means by a near perfect match.

I swear to God, if I'm a clone, I am going to fucking lose it.

"If you say so." O'Laughlin clears his throat, adjusts the folder he was reading so that it's lined up at perfect right angles to the corner of his desk, and says, "All right, here's the deal. Unless you'd like to spend the rest of your days at the bottom of a very deep hole, I would think very carefully about how you answer my questions. Understood?"

"Yes, sir," I say, because men like O'Laughlin thrive off being referred to as sir.

"Fantastic." He points at Reggie. "Go."

She blinks rapidly, confused at being summoned only to be dismissed, and turns toward the door.

"Dammit, Reggie, I meant go like tell me what you came to tell me!"

"Oh. Right." Reggie walks past me, tucking her arm close to her side, and places her tablet on O'Laughlin's desk. "You can see where we've attempted to restimulate the motor cortex by administering light electrical pulses into the solution. Unfortunately, other than a few muscle spasms, we've been unable to bring them out of their comas."

I don't understand most of what she's saying, but there's no doubt in my mind she's talking about Doran's brother James and James's team.

"What about the simulation?" O'Laughlin asks.

"No one's been able to gain access to it since he–" her eyes flit briefly to me "–since Mr Banuk, ah..."

Her voice trails off. As one, every head in the room swivels toward me.

Shit, what did I do now?

"This fucking day just keeps getting better and better," O'Laughlin mutters. "All right, keep me apprised of any new developments."

"Yes, sir." Reggie picks up her tablet, turns to go, then stops. "Mr O'Laughlin?"

"What is it?"

"It's just, I thought, since he's here now, it might be a good idea to scan his brain for abnormalities. It might help us understand what caused the others to go catatonic."

This version of Reggie is more nervous than the one I met in Bradley's Deep Dive room, which I suppose makes perfect sense considering all the other personality shifts I've witnessed. That doesn't make it any less disconcerting, though.

O'Laughlin mulls this over. "What do you think, Shepard? Can we trust him not to do anything stupid?"

Shepard shrugs. "Peter claims he's on board."

Out of sight of O'Laughlin, Finn bares his teeth in a wolfish grin, makes a gun with his hand, and mimes shooting himself in the head.

"Fine. I'll arrange some time for you later this morning," O'Laughlin says to Reggie.

She dips her head. "Thank you, sir." She backs up, bumps into the closed door. "I'll be in my office."

She pivots awkwardly and disappears. Grumbling to himself, O'Laughlin reaches down and jerks the waistline of his pants up over the bottom of his stomach. One of the buttons on his shirt pops free, releasing part of the undershirt held hostage beneath it.

"Now," he says, returning his attention to me. "You've got about ten fucking seconds to tell us what the shit damn hell you and Doran were planning, otherwise things are gonna get real ugly real quick."

At this point I have no reason to lie. "Doran was worried about his brother. I told him I'd help him. That's it."

O'Laughlin leans forward, his belly enfolding the edge of the desk like a supernatural blob devouring everything in its path, and rests his forearms on top of the file folder. "Do I look like a moron?"

Yes. "No, sir. Not at all."

O'Laughlin slams his hands down so forcefully the entire desk trembles. "Do not dick me around, asshole! It's no coincidence you showed up right after James and his boys had their brains turned into vegetable puree. You're here for a reason. What's your endgame, Banuk? Steal our tech? Replace us all one by one? Recon for an invasion? Why. Are. You. Here?" He punctuates each word with another hand-slam.

In the corner of my eye I see Finn's entire body stiffen. I don't know what to make of it – hell, I don't know what to make of any of this. Nothing O'Laughlin's raging about makes a lick of sense. Steal tech? Replace who? An invasion?

I feel like I'm in an episode of *The Twilight Zone* written by David Fincher.

"I'm not trying to dick you around," I say. "I want answers as much as you do."

"That's rich," O'Laughlin scoffs. "Well, whatever your fucking angle is, we'll figure it out, even if we have to take your brain apart neuron by fucking neuron."

That does not sound pleasant at all.

"Look," I say, scrambling for a reason to keep my place in the room. "Dr Manasa said there's something wrong with the Deep Dive simulation, right?" I'm still not convinced Doran was right about my role in developing it, but playing along is still one of the only cards I can throw. "Let me take a look at it. Maybe I can fix it."

"Oh, you'd fucking love that, wouldn't you?" O'Laughlin sighs theatrically. "You know what? I'm bored. Shepard, take our guest to his *quarters*. Maybe some time alone will loosen up his tongue. If not, we'll just have to bring in the wife." He presses the button on his intercom. "Edward, where's my goddamn espresso?"

Like a dying star, all my pent-up emotions go nova the moment O'Laughlin mentions Alana. Filled with a burning, incandescent rage, I throw myself sideways, for once catching Finn off guard. He grunts, fights to maintain his balance, and lurches into a filing cabinet. Shepard curses, tries to grab me, but I duck beneath her arms and lunge toward O'Laughlin, fully intent on wringing his neck for threatening Alana, for threatening to lock me up, for what he and his cronies did to Doran.

My fingertips have just grazed his neck when something hard slams into the back of my head, plunging me into darkness.

* * *

The first mistake I make is opening my eyes.

My retinas react to the sudden introduction of outside light by sending a silent scream down my optic nerve and directly into my brain, triggering a migraine-like headache on par with a thermonuclear explosion.

Even closed, the insides of my eyelids are a battlefield of swirling black motes and blinding white pulses set to the tempo of my jackhammering pulse.

Eventually, the battle tapers off and a ceasefire is reached. My pulse slows and the pounding in my head abates, leaving behind a residual desire to throw up.

This time, when I open my eyes, I do so millimeter by careful millimeter, tempering the tender eggs of my retinas with the boiling milk of ambient light.

When I'm mostly certain my eyeballs are no longer at risk of curdling, I blink the lids all the way open. Like a lag in gameplay, the room around me judders into focus, frame by skipping frame.

The first thing I notice is that I'm lying on a cot and my hands are bound. The second thing is that I'm no longer in O'Laughlin's office. This room is much smaller, maybe taking up half as much square footage. The walls around me are bare concrete blocks painted a jaundiced yellow broken only by the gunmetal gray of a door with no discernable means of opening it from this side. Above me, too high to reach, is a twisting network of PVC and metal pipes.

Groaning, I press the heels of my hands into my throbbing eyebrows, take a few deep, steadying breaths, and then shimmy up into a seated position.

The room starts to spin again.

I rest my head against the concrete wall, but this only ignites another solar flare of pain. Dipping my head toward my chest, I ever so gingerly press the base of my skull.

There's a knot just above and behind my still deafened right ear that's painfully tender to the touch.

Despite my miserable, unhinged performance in O'Laughlin's office, I don't have a death wish. I really did plan on cooperating with him. Logically it's in my best interest, but the thought that I might never leave this building, that they might actually hurt Alana, blew all my gaskets.

It occurs to me that for all the threats against me and Alana, no one's said anything about Cassie and Evie. If I were in O'Laughlin's position, I'd be using the girls as leverage as often as I could. The fact that he hasn't suggests he and Shepard aren't quite as all-knowing as they'd like me to believe.

It's not much of a stamina boost, but it's enough to relieve a tiny bit of the tension in my shoulders.

Feeling like I've gained a bit of a second wind, I lower my feet and attempt to stand. The room immediately teeters sideways. I steady myself against the wall until the dizziness passes. One step at a time, I cross the room until I reach the door.

"Hey!" I shout, banging my bound fists on the cold metal surface. "Let me out, you bastards! Let me out!"

No one answers.

I pound harder on the door, ignoring how each blow amplifies my headache. "Let me out, let me out, let me out, let me *out*!"

With one final, fruitless wallop, I lower my smarting hands and press my forehead to the door.

"Feel better?" Shepard says.

I whip around, scanning the room, but unless she's managed to turn invisible, there's no one here but me.

"Up here, Peter."

I crane my head, searching the ceiling. And that's when I see it, buried in the corner above the cot. A tiny, ball-shaped security camera painted puke yellow to blend in with the walls.

A single red light blinks on and off, signaling it's active.

I stride to the middle of the room, lift my hands, and shoot two shaky middle fingers at the camera.

"Wow, that's mature." Shepard's voice crackles with static.

I stare daggers at the camera lens. "Fuck you, Shepard. Fuck you, fuck O'Laughlin, fuck Finn, fuck everyone here."

"Correct me if I'm wrong, but I did explain what would happen if you didn't behave, right?" Her words breathe through the camera's speaker like a ghostly wheeze. "Those conditions haven't changed. Yes, Mr O'Laughlin is feeling a bit out of sorts with you. However, he's also a businessman, and therefore recognizes the value of keeping you alive. That said, he has his limits. I'd suggest not pushing them more than you already have."

Like a petulant child, I continue glaring at the camera.

"So be it," Shepard says.

"Wait!"

"Oh, so you do have something to say."

"I'll tell him what he wants to know."

"You'll forgive me if I don't believe you after your little performance in his office."

"Please, Shepard."

Silence, then: "Kneel."

I blink. "What?"

"Kneel. If you're serious, kneel."

"You're joking."

"Peter, in the short time we've known each other, have I ever given any indication that I'm the sort of person prone to stand-up?"

This is true. Shepard's about as excitable as the knot on the back of my head.

Feeling like I've fallen into some anachronistic LARP mockumentary, I awkwardly drop to one knee.

"Now repeat after me. I, Peter Banuk, under penalty of death, do solemnly swear to follow each and every command given to me by Mr O'Laughlin and his associates, including but not limited to yours truly."

This is beyond humiliating. "I swear," I say through gritted teeth.

"The whole thing, if you please."

I repeat her oath word for word, hating myself with every uttered syllable.

"There now. That wasn't so hard, was it?"

I resist the urge to tell her what I really think. "What now?"

"Now you rest. Dr Manasa will be along shortly to administer an MRI. After that... well, we shall see what we shall see, won't we? In the meantime, try to get some rest."

"What if I have to pee?"

Shepard doesn't answer.

"Shepard?"

The silence stretches into minutes, then an hour. I have no real way of knowing how much time has passed, but at what feels like the two-hour mark, there's a faint beep. The door swings open on noiseless hinges, and in steps Shepard. There's no sign of Finn, a fact for which I'm eternally grateful.

She crosses her arms, regarding me like a parent checking on a child sent to time-out. "Ready?"

I nod, half-expecting her to make me kneel again.

"Come along, then."

She steps back into the hallway. I join her. We're in the middle of a long corridor, its walls the same puke yellow as my cell.

"That way," she says, gesturing to the right.

I start walking, fighting the urge to glance over my shoulder to see how close she is. "Why does O'Laughlin want to run an MRI on me?"

"Oh, speaking of, you're not claustrophobic, are you?"

"Not that I'm aware of," I say.

"Good. That will make Dr Manasa's job easier."

"You didn't answer my question."

"Oh, you noticed that, huh? Turn left."

We head down another corridor. At the end of it, a tall red safety shower like you'd find inside a chemistry classroom stands sentinel next to a door.

That bodes well.

Before we open the door, Shepard pulls out a folding buck knife, flips open the blade, and looks me in the eye. "If you even think about doing anything stupid, I will stab you in your carotid artery. Got it?"

I gulp, nod.

She slices through the zip-tie, freeing my hands once again, then stows the knife. "All right. Let's go."

On the other side of the door is a waiting room that would be at home in any doctor's office. Four chairs surround a low table strewn with old copies of *Scientific American* and *PC Gamer*.

To the left is another door. Next to it, a long glass window overlooks a darkened room full of tiny blinking lights. Shepard knocks on the door. There's a startled yelp, and the door opens, revealing Reggie.

"Are you all right, Dr Manasa?" Shepard says.

"What? Oh, yes." Reggie lays a hand on her stomach. "Sorry. He just started kicking." She takes a step toward Shepard, smiling shyly. "Do you want to feel?"

Shepard's expression makes it seem like Reggie just asked her to touch a live wire while standing in a puddle of water. "Ah. Thank you, but no."

"Oh."

"Is the machine ready?"

"The machine? Oh, the MRI scanner. Yes, it's ready."

Shepard stands there expectantly. When Reggie continues to stare at her she says, "Do you want me to bring in Mr Banuk so you can insert the IV?"

"Oh. Yes, please!" Reggie disappears into the control room.

"That woman," Shepard mutters, shaking her head as she ushers me through the control room and into the MRI chamber.

"She's just scattered," I say, warily eyeing the table extending from the person-sized hole inside the donut of the scanner. "It happened to…"

My voice trails off, unwilling to voice the memories jostling my mind, to give Shepard more ammunition to threaten me with.

She arches an eyebrow. "Yes?"

"Never mind."

Shepard regards me for half a beat too long, then points to a privacy curtain across the room. "You can change behind that."

I duck behind the curtain and start to undress. What I almost said to Shepard was that I remember how scattered Alana was when she was pregnant. More so with Cassie than with Evie, probably because Cassie was our first. It wasn't all the time. Mostly it was whenever Alana decided to cook. She never had strange food cravings like dill pickles and vanilla ice cream or salt and vinegar potato chips crumbled on top of scrambled eggs. When she cooked, though, she would often forget to add key ingredients. I lost track of the number of times she made chocolate chip cookies and left out the chocolate chips or the eggs or, in one classic case, substituted half a cup of salt for sugar. It frustrated the hell out of her at the time, but now Alana jokes about having pregnancy brain anytime she forgets something.

Shepard, so far as I know, still has no idea I have kids. I'd like to keep it that way. Reggie, however, is a different story, and right now I need to exploit any and every option available.

As I take off my shirt and kick off my pants, I try to map out the corridors we walked down to get from my cell to the MRI chamber. Problem is, even if I got past Shepard, I was out cold when they tossed me in the cell. I have no idea where the exit is in relation to that room. Not to mention, if I were to run now, I'd be running forever, always looking over my shoulder, always wondering if I'd ever see my girls again.

And so, ensconced in one of the most humiliating articles of clothing ever invented, I step out from behind the privacy curtain in a turquoise hospital gown and prepare to have my brain scanned.

CHAPTER FIFTEEN

Inside the control room, Shepard sees me and nudges Reggie. Reggie looks up like she's surprised that I'm standing there in my turquoise frock.

She frowns, then waddles out to meet me, one hand pressed to her lower back.

"Go ahead and lie down." She grabs a small wheeled tray loaded with medical supplies and rolls it over to the table extending from the MRI.

I stretch out on the cold slab, tugging the gown down over thighs pimply with goosebumps.

"Comfortable?" Reggie says, spritzing the back of my hand with antiseptic spray before wiping it off with gauze.

The pillow under my head is rough as four hundred grit sandpaper and smells like off-brand detergent, so not really. I glance into the control room where Shepard's watching us and say without moving my lips, "You mean aside from the whole being held against my will thing?"

Face fixed with the same displeased expression she donned when she first saw me, Reggie picks up a thick purple rubber band, cinches it around my forearm, and taps the back of my hand, raising a vein. Nodding to herself, she picks up an IV needle. "This will only sting for a second."

There's a pinch as the needle slides into my vein. With

practiced ease, she tapes it down, then reaches for a syringe and a bottle of clear fluid.

"What's that?" I say, suddenly fearful she's about to dope me with some sort of truth serum, or worse.

"Gadolinium." Reggie inserts the syringe into the top of the bottle and extracts a small amount of the liquid. "It's a contrasting agent, which is a fancy medical term for the dye that helps make the image clearer on an MRI scan."

"It's not gonna turn my pee blue or anything, will it?"

She starts to smile, catches herself, and purses her lips. "You don't have a history of kidney problems, do you?"

"None that I'm aware of."

"Good." Lifting the IV off my hand, she inserts the syringe needle and depresses the plunger. When the syringe is empty, she lowers my hand. "You should be good to go in a few minutes. There's a speaker inside the scanner, so once you're inside we'll still be able to talk if you experience any problems."

"OK."

She wheels the tray of medical supplies out of reach, then returns to the control room, pulling the door shut behind her.

I stare at the ceiling. So far, my plan to engender sympathy and get her talking is not going well. If I had to guess, I'd say we have some sort of acrimonious work history, which would just figure.

I roll my head over to see the control booth, where Shepard is looming over Reggie, who's now sitting in front of a bank of computers. Behind me, the MRI clicks and hums. I try not to fidget, but it's hard to lie still when you're wearing nothing but boxer briefs under a thin smock that some invisible breeze keeps trying to lift up while employees who work for a sketchy government agency prepare to look inside your brain.

"All right." Reggie's voice buzzes over the intercom above the plate-glass window separating us. She's speaking into a long-stemmed microphone. "In a minute I'm going to slide you into the scanner. It's going to feel claustrophobic, but I need you to keep as still as possible, otherwise the MRI won't be able to scan you properly."

I give her a thumbs up.

"Like I said, we'll be able to talk while you're inside, so if you start to feel sick or have any questions, feel free to speak up. Otherwise–"

Her voice breaks off in a crackle of static as Edward, O'Laughlin's assistant, abruptly enters the control room. I can't hear what he says, but whatever it is annoys Shepard. She shakes her head, points at me. Edward looks over, blinks, turns back to Shepard, and lifts his hands in apology.

Scowling, Shepard leans in front of Reggie and toggles on the microphone. "It appears that my presence has been requested elsewhere. You remember our deal, right?"

"Oh, I remember."

"Lovely." She throws the full weight of her gaze on Reggie. "Dr Manasa, does the door to the chamber lock?"

"Yes, but–"

Shepard snaps her fingers. "Edward, secure the door."

Edward practically leaps into motion. The lock clicks closed.

"All right, Peter, I shouldn't be gone too long. Behave yourself." Shepard waggles her fingers at me, then she and Edward exit the control room.

Reggie pulls the microphone toward her. "Guess it's just you and me now. Ready?"

I nod, nervous for a plethora of reasons.

"Here we go."

The examination table trembles beneath me, and then I'm gliding backward into the belly of the scanner like a human pizza.

I normally don't have issues with tight spaces, but Reggie's right: this thing is the definition of claustrophobic. My chest constricts. My heartrate ratchets up several notches. I clench my fists, trying to stave off the rising panic by taking deep breaths.

"How you doing?" Reggie asks, her disembodied voice piercing the solitude like a benevolent god debating whether or not to deliver her people from the darkness. My good ear chases the sound, desperate for an anchor to keep my mind from sailing off into angst-filled seas.

"Oh, you know, just trying not to freak out."

It's hard to tell, but I think I hear Reggie chuckle. "If it helps, I nearly lost it the first time I went into one of those. They had to pull me out halfway through the scan."

It does help, a little. "So how long will this take?" I ask.

"Twenty minutes, half an hour tops."

Shit. Not much time. There's no telling when Shepard will be back. "What exactly are you looking for?"

All around me, the machine emits a rapid, repetitious, low-decibel noise that sounds like a muffled jackhammer breaking through plasterboard.

"Brain abnormalities."

Jesus, making this connection is like pulling my kids' teeth, which is why I leave that job to Alana, because ugh. "Such as?"

"Swelling, excessive activity in the neocortex and thalamus, things like that."

Until now I've never considered the possibility that using Deep Dive might've harmed me beyond my memory issues. All of a sudden I'm convinced I'm about to have a stroke.

Licking my lips, I say, "So, um, how's it looking?"

"Have you ever had any sort of intracranial neurosurgery?"

"Um, not that I'm aware of. Why?"

"No reason."

Translation: she's seen something and isn't going to tell me what.

I swallow the lump in my throat, self-diagnosing myself with brain cancer, early onset dementia, any number of a hundred different varieties of deadly diseases that will explain my memory problems. All the while the rounded walls of the MRI squeeze in more tightly.

There has to be some way to get through to Reggie, some way to flip the script, but I'll be damned if I can see it.

The noise inside the MRI picks up its pace, the dull thumping growing more feverish and high-pitched like the machine's developed its own pulse. I feel like a baby inside a uterus listening to its mother's frantic heartbeat.

Oh my God, I'm so stupid.

If there's one thing I know, it's that soon-to-be parents love to talk about their babies.

"How far along are you?" I ask.

"Sorry?"

"You're pregnant, right?"

Oh God, please let her be pregnant.

"Almost thirty-seven weeks."

Phew. "Congratulations."

"Thank you."

"Do you know what you're having?"

"A boy."

"Got a name picked out?"

"Elijah. It was my grandfather's name."

"You nervous?"

"Terrified." That seems like all she's willing to volunteer, but then she surprises me. "It's been tough, juggling work and doctor's appointments, but I'm managing. Kellye, my wife, she's been super helpful."

"That's definitely a plus."

I take a deep breath, praying I've read Reggie right and that she's not like Shepard and O'Laughlin, because if I throw my ace of *Hey I Have Kids Too And I Really Hope That Means You'll Help Me Get Out Of This Fucking Mess So I Can See Them Again* and it backfires, then I am totally screwed.

"I remember when my wife was nearing her due date." I keep my voice low. "I was so manic. Kept trying to hold her arm while we walked places, chopping vegetables so she didn't cut off one of her fingers, that sort of thing. She'd get so annoyed with me. I wasn't as neurotic the second time around, though."

There's a long pause, the air filled with the rapid digital trill of the MRI scanning my brain. I tense, unaware of how much she's aware of my memory issues, so I have no idea how she's going to take my baby bombshell.

"You have kids?" she says slowly.

"Two girls."

"Shit."

I frown, thrown off balance by her response. I could be wrong, but it almost seems like she believes me. "Reggie?"

"Shut the fuck up, I'm thinking."

Now I'm worried I've pushed it too far too fast, but I'm running out of time, and need as many allies as I can get.

In for a penny, in for a pound, right?

"Cassie is ten," I say. "Evie just turned seven. Last Saturday, actually. I was supposed to make her favorite meal. Fried chicken fingers and macaroni and cheese. The goopy kind, not the casserole stuff I grew up eating. But then I went into work because I just had to try out that damn headset."

As I talk, it's so unbelievably easy to see how stupid I've been, wasting my time at work trying to make my family proud of me when all they really wanted was for me to be around. To spend time with them. To actually *be* a family, not just in name but in actuality.

Reggie's still quiet. I keep talking.

"I'm sure this sounds crazy to you," I say. "No one else believes me. My own wife thinks I've lost my mind. I mean, I get it. I tell her I have this whole life in my head that she doesn't remember and just expect her to roll with it? But I couldn't let it go, you know? Even after seeing the cover of *Scorchfell* and the therapist with his *you've got dissociative amnesia because your job's stressful and your friend worked himself to death*, I still refused to believe that they were figments of my imagination."

The MRI clicks and beeps.

"Reggie?"

"Jesus, you really don't remember, do you?" she says.

My body goes cold. "Remember? Remember what? Reggie, do you know something about my girls?"

She doesn't respond. My brain freefalls down a rabbit hole of possibilities so dark and cataclysmic that even Alice wouldn't have come out the other end mentally intact.

"Please, Reggie. I just want to see my girls again. If you know something, anything…" I swallow hard. "Shepard lied, Reggie. She had Doran killed. He didn't even know what hit him. One second he was talking to me, the next he was dead, a hole in his fucking head."

The MRI lets out a series of swift knocks, then goes quiet.

"Why the *fuck* are you telling me this now?" Reggie says, her voice suddenly harder.

"Because I'm afraid that I'm going to wind up like Doran." I close my eyes. "I don't know what Shepard and O'Laughlin want from me. All I know is something happened when I used Deep Dive, and then everything went to shit. I just want to go home. I want to go home and hug my daughters and kiss my wife and never, ever, ever let them go."

More silence, then:

"Goddam motherfucking shit ass fuck!" There's a loud thump. "You bastard. I told you before–"

Through the microphone comes the sound of a door opening, followed by Shepard's voice.

"How's our patient, Dr Manasa? Do I need to have a word with him?"

My entire body tenses as I wait for Reggie to sell me out.

The speaker coughs static, then goes dead.

Crap.

If I read Reggie wrong, if I didn't get through to her, I've got about ten seconds before Shepard marches into this room, buck knife in hand.

I count to ten.

Nothing happens.

My palms bleed sweat, fingers clenching and unclenching.

I count to twenty.

Still nothing.

My heart is a battering ram against my ribs, drowning out the hum of the MRI.

When I reach thirty, I start to wriggle. I have to get out. No way am I dying in a tube.

At forty, the table vibrates beneath me, then slowly begins to slide out of the MRI.

When my head clears the edge of the scanner, I sit bolt upright, fully convinced Shepard's about to stab me in the throat.

But Shepard's not coming at me. She's not even in the MRI chamber. Instead, she's standing inside the control room next to Reggie, who's staring at me through the plate-glass window like I'm the last person she wants to see.

Shepard says something to her. Reggie doesn't respond, just keeps watching me. Shepard taps her on the shoulder, repeats whatever she said. Reggie blinks as though she's coming out of a daze, nods, and activates the microphone.

"How are you feeling?" she says, like we haven't just had what amounts to a treasonous conversation.

"Fine."

"No headache, nausea, itchiness?"

"None of the above."

"Good. Sometimes the gadolinium can have side effects, but they're usually mild. If you experience any of them, or notice a rash developing on your skin, please let me know."

Look at us, pretending like we're in a normal doctor-patient relationship while Lady Dimitrescu watches over us.

"I will."

"Thank you. Give me a minute and I'll come remove your IV."

The microphone goes quiet again. Shepard leans over Reggie's shoulder, asks a question which Reggie answers with a shrug and what I lip-read as *Maybe*. Half a minute later, Reggie pushes back from the computer, slides awkwardly past Shepard, and enters the MRI chamber.

I don't say anything. All I do is watch her purposely not making eye contact with me while she goes about the process of removing the IV from the back of my hand.

A droplet of blood wells up from the puncture wound.

I blink away the memory of Doran's head wound, bury it beneath images of Cassie and Evie putting on one of their plays while Alana and I sit and try not to laugh at how serious they're acting.

Reggie drops the IV needle on the wheeled table, temporarily blocking my view of Shepard.

"What did you mean when you said you told me before?" I whisper. "Told me what, Reggie?"

"Not now," she hisses, not looking up as she tapes down a piece of gauze over the spot of blood.

"When?"

"Later. Just shut the fuck up, OK?"

"Is he good to go, Dr Manasa?" Shepard says from the doorway, interrupting our tenuous conspiracy.

"Almost." Reggie removes a penlight from her pocket and examines my eyes. "Any dizziness?"

I shake my head.

"OK. I'll check in on you later to make sure the gadolinium has worn off."

I have no idea if this is a legitimate medical move or if she's coming around to helping me. Either way, I don't get my hopes up.

After I change back into my clothes, Shepard escorts me to my cell and wordlessly shuts the door behind her, leaving me alone in the room, my only company the security camera and a mind full of a thousand different ways that all of this is about to go completely to shit.

CHAPTER SIXTEEN

Time in my cell passes slower than *Scorchfell*'s loading screens, one of the many reasons it landed on several Worst of the Year lists when it released. I don't remember the loading screens being a problem during beta testing, but then a lot of things fell through the cracks toward the end.

My family, for instance.

The family I'm desperate to get back to.

Instead, I'm stuck in this fucking cell, tracing the labyrinth of pipes bolted to the ceiling and doing my best to ignore the security camera above my bed.

It can't have been more than a few hours since Shepard brought me back from the MRI chamber. It feels like days, though. Weeks. Years.

It's the not knowing that's getting to me.

Not knowing what Reggie saw on the MRI that made her ask if I've had intracranial neurosurgery.

Not knowing what she meant by *Jesus, you don't remember, do you?*

Not knowing if she's going to help me or turn me in.

Not knowing what Shepard and O'Laughlin have planned for me.

Not knowing if I'll ever have another chance to kiss Cassie and Evie goodnight.

Not knowing if I'll ever wake up in the middle of the night to find Alana curled up against me, little spoon to my big.

Frustrated beyond belief, I elbow the wall, instantly wincing as pain flares up and down my arm.

There's a lot of self-pity crammed into this tiny cell, let me tell you.

Rubbing my arm, I sit up, swing my legs over the side of the bed, and will the door to open.

It doesn't.

I stand up on the bed and jump for the pipes, but they're a body-length out of reach. I sit back down and lean over the side to examine the bottom of the bed, but it's a solid concrete slab.

If this were a video game, there'd be something in the room to help me escape, or the difficulty of besting my enemies would be scaled to my current level. Hell, if this were a video game I could commit one of the cardinal sins and simply go to the Load menu, click the Save file from right before I donned Deep Dive, and start over.

But this isn't a game. This is real life.

You can't reload real life.

Regardless, all of my musing is moot without Deep Dive. It's definitely the key to everything, but it might as well be at the bottom of the Mariana Trench for all that I can reach it.

I squint at the door.

Open, open, open.

It opens.

I do a double-take.

In lumbers O'Laughlin, the rat bastard.

There's no preamble, no hello, no hey, how's imprisonment going. Just him pointing a bratwurst of a finger at me and saying, "Get up."

O'Laughlin's got a good hundred pounds on me. Even so, I tense my legs, preparing to propel myself across the room and into his prodigious girth.

Shepard leans around him and arches her patented supervillain eyebrow. "Please don't, Peter. It would only end badly."

O'Laughlin crosses his arms over his pork-barrel chest. "I said get *up*."

Brushing a nonexistent piece of lint off my thigh, I push off the bed. "Where's your lapdog?" I ask Shepard.

"Oh, he's around here somewhere." She holds her hands up to the light, studying her lacquered fingernails. "That's the beauty of someone like Finn. He pops up when you least expect it."

With O'Laughlin in the lead like some comic book juggernaut and Shepard trailing behind me like an ever-present shadow, we march down one hallway after another. I do my best to memorize our path, counting the lefts and the rights we make, the number of times O'Laughlin has to hold his ID card up to a wall-mounted reader before the door blocking our way buzzes open and allows us into the next corridor.

I keep hoping we'll pass Reggie if only so she'll be reminded that I still exist, but no such luck.

Soon enough we reach a corridor that ends in an old-school metal grate. O'Laughlin grabs hold with both hands and lifts it up, the grate rattling like bones as it clatters up into the ceiling. Behind this is a service elevator, its beige metal door chipped and tarnished with brown and orange rust.

Entry to the freight elevator requires not only O'Laughlin's ID card but a passcode at least seven digits long and a biometric scan of his handprint.

His identity confirmed, the door groans open, and in we go.

O'Laughlin pushes the fourth button down. The door begins to close, but catches on something halfway and stops. Gears grind as the mechanism continues to push the blocked door along its tracks, shaking the entire elevator.

"I thought they fixed this fucking thing," O'Laughlin growls, mashing the button on the bottom left to no avail.

"They're still waiting on the work order to be approved." Shepard steps forward and kicks the stuck door once, twice, three times, the elevator shuddering precariously with each blow. On the third kick, the door lets out a banshee shriek and finally slides closed. "Try it now."

Grumbling about tight-wad accountants, O'Laughlin hits the fourth button again. With a series of clunks, the elevator finally begins to descend.

Shepard grins at me. "Percussive maintenance. Works every time."

O'Laughlin at least has the common decency to stare at the door while we drop into the depths of the bunker. Shepard, being the sociopath that she is, puts her back to the wall and stares at me. I do my best to return her unblinking gaze, because fuck her and her stupid mind games. By the time we reach the fourth sub-basement, I'm more than happy to break eye contact.

The door groans, but O'Laughlin's learned his lesson. He slams his foot into the base of the door, forcing it open.

The corridor beyond the elevator is as dissimilar to the one we left four floors above as night is to day.

Gone are the bright, boring beige hallways. In their place is a catacomb of exposed steel pipes and bare metal beams that run along the walls like the circulatory system of some subterranean robotic beast. Red light bulbs encased in black wire sconces paint the walls a pale shade of blood. Unseen drips echo in the background. The air is warm and humid and smells of spent motor oil and something more sinister, a sharp antiseptic scent that brings to mind hospital morgues and funeral parlors.

So this is the Cold War bunker Shepard said Boundless was built on top of.

It's the kind of place ripe for the next *Silent Hill* installment, a place where horror games go to give birth. The kind of place where you bury your darkest secrets, your blackest experiments, your most hideous creations.

It's the kind of place people like Shepard take people like me to die.

Down we go into the bowels of Boundless, skirting piles of discarded pallets and broken crates, our footsteps reverberating off the cavernous walls until my good ear starts to detect the hum and thrum of hidden machinery. We round our way to the left, and there, at the end of the next corridor, stands Finn.

He's reclining against a flywheel protruding from a large metal door mottled with water stains and rust. When he sees us, he pushes lazily off the flywheel, stretching his arms wide to the side as though we've just woken him from a nap.

"You still here, Banuk?" He yawns.

"Bite me, Finn."

He grins, his teeth as white as ghost light, and rests his hands on the machine gun now draped across his chest.

"How are they?" Shepard asks him.

Finn's expression slips, the curved line of his grin straightening out until his lips form a frown that almost humanizes him. "How the fuck do you think they are, Shepard? It's like a goddamn coma ward in there."

"They knew what they were getting themselves into," O'Laughlin says, brushing past Finn and grabbing hold of the flywheel. "If need be we'll just find new test subjects."

"What the fuck did you say?" Finn's fingers tighten around the machine gun's pistol-grip. In the red light of the corridor he looks more devil than human.

"Stand down, Finn," Shepard warns in a low hiss.

Grunting with effort, apparently unaware of the venom oozing from Finn, O'Laughlin spins the flywheel. Finn glares ICBMs at the back of O'Laughlin's head, and I swear to God, for a second, his finger strays toward the trigger. Shepard grabs his arm, shakes her head.

Interesting.

"The fuck you looking at?" Finn growls, stepping toward me with murder in his eyes.

I affect a mien of innocence, raising my hands palms out in the universal sign for *Please calm down, you gun-happy lunatic.* "Nothing. Nothing at all."

"Damn right nothing."

The flywheel rotates, screeching with every quarter turn. Metal bolts retract with a series of hollow thuds. Arms straining, veins bulging on the sides of his neck like worms writhing beneath his skin, O'Laughlin pulls the door open, releasing a blast of cold air into the corridor.

"Leash your dog or leave him outside, Shepard," O'Laughlin says. Without waiting for any of us he steps over the threshold of the doorway and disappears into the room beyond.

Finn's eyes bulge. Shepard plants a hand on his chest to hold him in place.

"O'Laughlin's not wrong," she says quietly. "They knew what they were agreeing to." Her eyes flick briefly to me. "Well, most of them, anyway. You know full well there's no way we could have predicted any of this."

Finn stabs a hand at the doorway. "I got no problem with what happened to Doran. He wasn't a soldier. But that's my team in there, Shepard. Folks I've worked with for years. They're goddamned Rangers, for Christ's sake! They deserve fucking better, and you know it."

I shift my feet, staring past them into the darkness where O'Laughlin has vanished. From my vantage point, all I can make out is an eerie pinkish glow.

Shepard and Finn suddenly remember I'm there. As one, their expressions harden, and they round on me.

"Stop gawking and get in there," Shepard snaps.

The red gleam in their eyes stills the tongue I'd very much like to keep. Giving them both as much of a wide berth as I can manage in the confines of the tunnel, I follow O'Laughlin into the room.

I'm not sure what I'm expecting to see – at this point, after everything that's happened, it seems like there isn't much left that can shock me.

I am so, so wrong.

The space on the other side of the flywheel door is much more cavernous than anything I've seen so far. Directly in front of me on the far side of the room is a massive screen that would be right at home in a multiplex. But it's what lies to the right that causes my jaw to drop.

"What the hell is that?" I whisper.

"A giant clusterfuck," Finn mutters, shouldering me out of the way as he sweeps into the room.

"Ignore him," Shepard says. "So, what are we feeling? Impressed? Frightened? Mystified?" She elbows me all friendly-like. "Perhaps a little bit of all three?"

I nod, unable to put a voice to the emotions churning through me. It's like something out of a mad scientist's lair. Glowing pods surround a massive central cylinder that stretches from the floor to the ceiling. Of the six pods I can see, five are empty. The one that isn't is filled with a pink, gelatinous fluid that glimmers with an unearthly light. And floating in the fluid...

My hand strays to my left wrist, rubbing the line left by the zip-tie. "Is... is that a person?"

Instead of answering, Shepard gives me a none too gentle shove toward the pod. I balk, my brain screaming at me to run, to get as far away from this nightmarish scenario as I can because nothing good ever, ever, ever comes of people in pods.

But my feet have developed minds and motion of their own. Drawn forward as if by some irresistible spell cast by the figure suspended in pink, I cross the intervening space in a sort of hyper-focused daze. As I near the pod, the rest of the room darkens, shunted to the farthest reaches of eyesight.

There is only the pod, and the figure within.

Save for underwear, the man inside is naked. His face is turned away from me, but the hose leading away from it and the strap encircling his head suggests he's wearing some sort of breathing apparatus.

And yet, despite the fact that I can't see the man's face, there's something intimately familiar about his figure, something about the design of the pod and the color of the fluid that conjures the smoky residue of a long-suppressed memory struggling to form itself into a tangible image.

I sense more than see Shepard stopping to stand alongside me. She's on my left, my good side.

"Who is that?" I say.

"Don't you know?"

I gulp, recalling what led me to this moment. "Is it Doran's brother? James?"

Shepard laughs. "If only it were that simple. Look closer," she says, an evil witch encouraging her victim to peer into a magic mirror.

Mesmerized, I'm unable to resist. I step closer, closer, closer, until the whole world is taken up by the man inside the pod.

His left leg twitches, kicking out to the side. I jerk in response, the muscles in my left calf spasming.

The internal screaming returns, low and intense like the snarl of a cornered animal.

Walk away. Walk the fuck away right fucking now.

But I can't. I'm entranced. Spellbound. A motorist gaping at the wreckage of someone else's life.

The body twitches again, but this time, the face slowly rotates toward me.

I stumble backward, gasping for air like I'm the one inside the pod.

"Do you understand now?" Shepard says.

I don't want to, but I do.

God help me, I do.

This?

This isn't the wreckage of someone else's life.

This is the wreckage of mine.

Because the man inside the pod.

He's me.

CHAPTER SEVENTEEN

I tell myself I'm wrong. The man in the tank can't be me. *I'm* me, and I'm standing right here, staring at a doppelgänger, a remarkable simulacrum, a clone who only looks like Peter Banuk but can't possibly *be* Peter Banuk because *I'm* Peter Banuk.

"Knock, knock," Shepard says, rapping her knuckles on the outside of the pod. The man inside – the *me* inside – doesn't react. He simply floats there, eyes closed, limbs twitching at random, totally unaware of our scrutiny.

I thought the girls' faces on the cover of *Scorchfell* was the most shocking thing I'd ever seen.

I was wrong. So very, very wrong.

Shepard studies the man in the pod, then turns to regard me. "Now that I see you both together, the resemblance is even more remarkable than I realized. I bet you're used to this, though, huh?"

What? How the hell could I be used to it? Disorientated doesn't even come close to explaining how I'm feeling. I'm not sure there's a word in any language that could adequately describe the chain reaction of emotions detonating one after the other. It's like my world has been struck by a meteorite, obliterating everything I once held to be true and leaving behind a smoking crater where my mind used to be.

I knuckle my eyes, praying that when I look again the man's face will have changed.

It hasn't.

"This isn't real." My voice is hollow, stripped of inflection.

Shepard tilts her head. "Isn't it?"

"You're screwing with me."

"Yes, because basic torture wasn't good enough for you, our special unexpected tourist, so we built this entire structure over the course of a few days for the sole purpose of toying with your fragile little mind."

Shepard leans nonchalantly against the pod and stuffs her hands in her pockets, the silhouette of her upper body backlit by the iridescent pink gel. "Think it through, Peter. It's pretty simple, actually, once you establish a few parameters. But don't take too long. Mr O'Laughlin has a lot of questions, and in my experience I've found it's best not to keep him waiting any longer than is necessary."

"Starting with where the hell you're from and what the hell you're doing here," O'Laughlin snaps over his shoulder. He's sitting in front of a computer beneath the massive movie screen, tapping away at the keyboard. Above him, the screen begins to emit a pale light like evening snowfall.

Where I'm from? I'm from here.

Aren't I?

As much as it pains me to do so, I focus on Shepard, hoping she can provide some sort of anchor to keep me from drifting out to sea. "I don't understand."

She studies my face, searching for signs of dishonesty. Her eyes widen. "My goodness, you really don't, do you? How interesting. Although I suppose that explains why you've been acting so erratic lately." She uncrosses her arms and pushes off the pod. "Let me see if I can jog that befuddled brain of yours. Last week, Peter Banuk–" she points at the man in the pod "–was tasked with patching the Deep Dive simulation, which had recently malfunctioned in some unknown way, resulting in several of our personnel being trapped inside their suspension pods."

"You're talking about Doran's brother James and his team."

"So you do remember something."

"Only because Doran told me."

Shepard frowns, then beckons me to follow her around the pod containing the man she claims is Peter Banuk. A man who can't be Peter Banuk, because *I'm* Peter Banuk.

Aren't I?

Moving as if in a daze, I shuffle after her.

Finn, who's been standing to the side glowering this whole time, trails after us like a demonic familiar.

There are six more suspension pods on the other side of the cylinder. Five of them are full. Like the other me, three men and two women float in pink goo, each of them sporting unflattering underwear, each one of them wearing a face mask, each one of them completely comatose.

"Any of this ring a bell?" Shepard says.

I shake my head. "No." I desperately wish it did, though.

The man floating nearest to me is slender but ripped, a body built for violence. There's something of Doran in his face. My guess is, this is James.

"Admiring your handiwork?" Finn growls from behind me.

"I had nothing to do with this, Finn. It was the other…"

I can't bring myself to finish the sentence.

The other me.

"Bullshit," Finn says. "I've seen the video feed. You might not have designed the simulation, but you sure as fuck did something to it."

"And he's going to help us fix it," Shepard says. "Aren't you, Peter?"

"I hate to tell you this, but I know zilch about the battlefield simulation, let alone Deep Dive."

There. I've said it. Admitted I'm not the man everyone thinks I am. It's a bit anticlimactic considering the other me in the submersion pod, but at least it's out in the open now.

Apparently, no one cares.

"Oh, I'm well aware you didn't design the simulation,"

Shepard says. "But Finn isn't wrong. You did something to the software, which means you're quite skilled with computers. However, as much as I'm very interested in learning how much of your life matches the Peter I know, story time will have to wait." Turning around, she raises her voice and calls out, "Jerry, are we ready?"

Across the room, O'Laughlin is a shadowy hulk backlit by the glow of the massive wall screen. "Get Banuk over here!"

"A simple yes would've sufficed." Shepard crooks her finger like a forest witch leading me to her gingerbread house. "Come on."

I try not to look at the other Peter's pod as we pass by, but that's like asking Narcissus to stop staring at his own reflection.

Who the hell are you?

For that matter, who the hell am I?

When we reach O'Laughlin, he slams his pinkie down on the enter key. The monitor blanks out. Above us, the wall screen flickers with a green phantasmagoric snow of static, and then the grainy footage of what looks like the feed from a security camera appears.

I back up far enough so that I can see the screen, fully expecting Shepard to chastise me for moving without permission. When I look at her, she points two fingers at her eyes, then turns them toward the screen.

Watch, she's saying.

All of a sudden, I'd rather not. But just like with the other-Peter in the tank, I can't look away.

The footage is of this room, the angle suggesting a camera located above the flywheel door. Pods of pink goo glow with iridescent light. Similar to how it is now, there are five empty pods nearest the wall screen, but the sixth one which should contain the other Peter is empty, too. Five of the other six pods contain the team of unconscious Rangers.

I glance at the bottom right corner of the screen, where a series of numbers is progressing in fast-forward. It's a time stamp, dated Sunday. The day I used Deep Dive. The day I lost my mind. The day I lost my family. The day everything in my life got turned inside out and upside down.

The footage runs in fast-forward, the room remaining unchanged as entire minutes are devoured in the space of each one of my thudding heartbeats.

And then there's movement. A shifting shadow, a change in light.

O'Laughlin taps a key, slowing the footage so that it moves in real-time.

"This is the good part. Pay attention to that pod," Shepard says, pointing at the empty one where the other Peter currently bobs.

Everything I've experienced since Sunday screams that what I'm about to see is the polar opposite of good. My flight response kicks in, but I ignore it.

The pink liquid in the pod begins to brighten. A tiny black spot, indiscernible if I weren't already looking for something, appears in the center of the tank. It pulses slowly, increasing in size while the liquid around it glows brighter and brighter.

"Whatever can that be?" Shepard says, nudging me as if she and I both know exactly what it is.

I can't even begin to fathom what's happening, but I don't have to wait long to find out.

By now the black spot is the size of a baseball, a fully three-dimensional sphere that glimmers with its own dark light. White bolts of electricity ripple and writhe within it like beams inside a plasma globe. The sphere pulses, expands again, basketball-sized now and spitting lightning that lashes the interior of the pod, churning the pink liquid like angry tentacles.

Shepard is practically gleeful. "Here we go!"

With one final pulse, the black sphere swells until it takes up nearly all the space inside the pod. There's a blinding flash, so bright I have to look away. When I can see again, the black sphere is gone.

In its place is a person.

Shepard places a hand on her cheek. "I wonder who that could be?"

The person bobs in the pink goop, not moving until without warning their limbs start thrashing like someone who's just realized they're drowning. They twist every which way, legs kicking, hands slapping at the glass walls. Their fingers reach up, grasp hold of some unseen aperture in the top of the pod, and drag themselves up and out.

Pink liquid sloshes over the rim of the opening, running in rosy rivulets down the side of the pod as the person follows suit. They hit the floor with a silent thud and lay there for a minute, chest heaving, face turned away from the security camera.

"Ouch." Shepard mock-winces. "That must have hurt."

After a few seconds, the person pushes up off the floor, sits with their head bowed, then lifts their head and looks around.

I knew it was coming, but the shock of seeing my own face is still enough to send my brain reeling. I have zero recollection of this place beyond the half-hour I've just spent here, but the person on screen is undoubtedly Peter Banuk.

The sixty four thousand dollar question is, I don't know if the Peter Banuk on the screen is me or the other me currently floating in the pod from which the man on the screen just emerged.

That question alone sends my brain for another dizzying loop on the mental rollercoaster of neurons jetting around inside my mind.

Shepard clears her throat. "Care to change your story now?"

I'd like to get off the ride now, thanks. "You don't know that's me," I say. "It could be the other Peter."

Despite my inability to comprehend exactly how in the name of *God* there's another Peter, I somehow manage to suggest just such a possibility with total sincerity.

"Don't be a nimrod," O'Laughlin says. "Of course it's you."

I open my mouth to argue, but Shepard presses a shushing finger to her lips.

"Keep watching," she says. "It's about to get really good."

On the screen, Peter grabs the side of the tank and pulls himself to his feet. He wobbles for a moment, then starts to make his way around the room, examining the pods first and then over to the very computer near which Shepard, O'Laughlin, and I currently stand.

He doesn't sit at first, simply stares at the computer, then the pods, then the computer again. If this is me, and the jury's still way, way out on that, I'm debating some course of action, fretting over what to do first, stalling out from too many choices. Typical behavior, in other words.

Somewhere deep in my brain, memories twitch like dormant tulip bulbs sensing the early onset of spring. They creep upward through the scorched earth of my mind, but as soon as I attempt to focus on them, they wither away, retreating back into the cool, dank darkness.

"Oh, here we go!" Shepard says.

In the video, Peter's head snaps around. Hands raised, he starts talking, but the feed has no sound and I've always been a bad lip reader so I have no idea what he's saying.

A flicker at the bottom of the screen draws my attention. A shadow joins the show, moving quickly from the unseen doorway beneath the security camera like an approaching ghost until it coheres into a second Peter.

Visibly agitated, Peter 2 speed-walks toward Peter 1, then comes to a screeching halt when he reaches the other him who's invaded this scientific sanctum. Both of them are wearing jeans and a black T-shirt, Peter 1's still very wet, Peter 2's dry. I can't see Peter 2's face, but I can see Peter 1's. It's the same falsely reassuring, calm-but-not-calm expression I wear whenever I'm trying to keep a petty fight between Cassie and Evie from escalating into outright warfare while simultaneously trying not to lose my shit and yell at them both to stop fucking bickering.

On-screen, Peter 1 takes a step forward, away from the computer. Peter 2 backs up a step, his arms raised like he's warding off an approaching mugger.

Shepard puts both hands to her cheeks in mock terror. "Oh my goodness, whatever is happening?"

"This is CGI," I say. "Or a game demo."

"Oh, come on, Peter," Shepard chides. "You don't honestly think we'd expend the time and resources to develop a simulation of you simply to fuck with your head, do you?"

I want to tell her that's exactly what they've done, but deep down I know it's not. Deep down, I know what I'm seeing is real.

On-screen, Peter 1 is still attempting to calm Peter 2, but Peter 2 is most definitely not having any of that shit. An accusatory finger jabs out at Peter 1, who shakes his head, his calm veneer cracking to reveal the stress marks beneath it. Without taking his eyes off Peter 2, Peter 1 points backward at the computer, then gestures at the suspension pods, his lips moving rapidly as he does his silent best to explain his actions.

Peter 2 shakes his head, jazz-handing *Nope, nope, not buying your lies, you lying liar*, and starts to turn, my guess is to flee through the door and summon security.

He only makes it a few steps when Peter 1 launches into action.

I've never been what you'd call an aggressive person. I've spent my life avoiding altercations, physical mostly but also verbal, the latter of which has put me at a huge disadvantage when it comes to winning arguments with Alana. Which is something I never do. So it comes as quite a shock when I see Peter 1 tackle Peter 2, taking him to the ground like the football player I never wanted to be.

"Damn, I did *not* see that coming," Shepard says. "Did you, Peter?" She laughs. "What am I saying? Of course you did."

I don't bother arguing. I'm too confused and engrossed by this deleted scene from *Fight Club* taking place on screen to offer up a snarky comeback.

Peter 2 pulls some gravity-defying wrestling move, getting his arm around Peter 1's torso and twisting himself up and over so that he's got Peter 1 in half a full-body hold. Peter 1 responds by reaching his foot back, hooking his leg, and yanking it forward, pulling Peter 2 off his feet.

He crashes to the floor with Peter 2 beneath him. Peter 2's head snaps back, smacking the floor hard enough that it causes his arms to release Peter 1 like the tines of a claw trap dropping its stuffed animal prize back into the pile.

Peter 1 rolls onto his knees, scurries forward, and shakes Peter 2. Peter 2 doesn't respond. Peter 1 places his fingers to the side of Peter 2's neck, taking his pulse. Whatever he discovers clearly relieves him, but then his head snaps up as, in the bottom of the screen, a third shadow enters the room. He stands, starts talking, but then his face contorts in a rictus of pain.

The video feed warps, every pixel flexing like a solid surface temporarily gone soft like Neo sticking his finger into the mirror, then snaps back into place.

Peter 1 drops to his knees, slapping his hands to the sides of his head, and–

The feed goes blank. Nothing but static shows on the screen.

"What the hell?" I glance at Shepard. "Where's the rest of it?"

"That's all there is." Shepard regards me like a parent fully aware of what her child has done but giving him the chance to come clean instead of making it worse than it already is. "So what I'm thinking is, you should start explaining what happened between that moment–" she points at the snowy screen "–and this." She swipes her arm sideways, indicating the suspension pod where the other Peter floats. "We have our theories, but right now it's all conjecture."

"I told you, I don't remember anything," I say, but O'Laughlin isn't having any of it. He steps in front of me, Goliath sneering at a David who showed up without his slingshot.

"Cut the memory loss bullshit, Banuk. This is your last chance to come clean before we–" He looks at Shepard. "What's that phrase you use? Oh, right." His eyes bore into mine. "–torture you until your teeth bleed enamel."

"Jerry's paraphrasing a bit," Shepard says, "but you're only hurting yourself by clinging to this pretense of ignorance. It's obvious from the video that something unexpected occurred, but I don't for one second believe you're as innocent as you claim. So why don't you take a couple of deep breaths and then tell us exactly where you came from and what you did that caused the Deep Dive apparatus to go haywire."

"Don't you think I'd help you out if I could?" I do nothing to hide the desperation choking my voice. "I've spent the past four days trying to piece my life back together, for Christ's sake!"

Shepard sighs with something almost like pity. "I really was hoping we'd be able to avoid any further unpleasantness, but I guess we're going to have to break out the big guns." She nods at O'Laughlin. "Do it."

The big man shoves past me and reclaims the computer seat. Within seconds, another security feed appears on the wall screen, only this one isn't shot from inside the room.

It's coming from inside a police station.

And it's focused on Alana.

She looks haggard, like she hasn't slept in days. Bruised eyes, hair up in a long, messy ponytail, a faded Siouxsie and the Banshees T-shirt, torn jeans, flip-flops. It's an ensemble normally reserved for yardwork, never for major public appearances, and definitely not the kind of thing I'd imagine her wearing to a police station. Not that I've ever imagined her in a police station, but there's no disputing what I'm seeing.

At the moment she's sitting next to a desk, talking to a uniformed police officer who's writing in a steno pad, pausing every few seconds to interrupt her for clarification.

"This is live, by the way," Shepard says, a phone suddenly

at her ear. "Right now she's trying to file a missing person's report. The police officer is explaining that they have to wait at least forty-eight hours from the last time she saw you."

Knowing this isn't recorded, that it's happening as I watch it, plunges me into the barrel-bottom depths of utter wretchedness. Alana must be so upset with me right now. Scared, too, judging by her face. And why wouldn't she be? Her psychologically unstable husband has run off on some Quixote-like quest in pursuit of children who don't exist.

I'm so, so sorry, sweetheart. I didn't mean to drag you into this.

On-screen, whatever the cop is telling Alana does not go over well, because she leans forward abruptly and slams her hand on his desk.

Shepard cups the receiver on her phone. "She's just called him, and I quote, 'an officious little asshole' and is demanding to know how he'd feel if his spouse started exhibiting serious mental health issues and then abruptly disappeared."

The officer Alana's talking to carefully lays down his steno pad, clasps his hands on the desk, and starts speaking.

Shepard begins to relay his words, but I cut her off. "Stop."

"Don't you want to hear this?"

"Leave her alone. Please. I'll help you. Just, let Alana go."

Shepard stares at me impassively. "Then tell me why you're here, what you did to Peter and the Deep Dive apparatus, and what you're going to do to fix it for me."

In the video feed, tears dot the corners of Alana's eyes. The police officer hands her a packet of tissues, says something else to her. She dabs her eyes, blows her nose, and nods.

"I swear to God, Shepard, I don't know why there's another Peter floating in that fucking pod, let alone what that *Terminator* black sphere bullshit was!"

Shepard holds up a finger and cocks her head. "You're in position? Good. Yes, he's watching. Be a dear and wave to the camera for us, would you?"

In the background, two desks behind where Alana sits, a

man stands up, casually stretches his arms above his head, and waggles his fingers at the security camera.

It's Finn's partner, the one who drove off in my truck with Doran's body slumped in the passenger seat.

The room goes a murderous shade of crimson. Blood boiling, I launch myself at Shepard with no thought other than to take her phone and use it to break open her skull.

I make it all of halfway to her before a meaty hand belonging to O'Laughlin clamps down on my forearm, swings me around, and sends me hurtling groundward like I weigh nothing at all.

He looms over me. "Time's up, Banuk. We'll still make you sing, but first you're gonna watch your wife die."

On the wall screen, the police officer is escorting a defeated-looking Alana off-camera. As they disappear from view, Finn's partner grins into the camera, waves, and follows them.

"I'll tell you!" I yell. "I'll tell you everything you want to know! Just tell him to leave her the hell alone!"

The words are out and into the ether before I can even begin to consider the implications of the lie that's left my mouth. But this is Alana. I will do whatever it takes to keep her safe.

"Hold on a second, Donald," Shepard says, then lowers the phone and stares at me. "Go on."

At the left edge of the wall screen, the back of Donald's head is barely visible.

"You're right," I say. "I sabotaged Deep Dive."

"What'd I tell you," O'Laughlin sneers.

Maybe it was me, maybe it wasn't. At this point I don't know, and I don't really care. All I know is, Shepard and O'Laughlin think it was, and that's something I can use to my advantage.

Granted, it may wind up getting me killed, but if it buys me time and Alana's life, I'm more than willing to take that chance.

Shepard waves a hand. "You sabotaged Deep Dive and…"

Facing a literal deadline, I spin a fiction faster than I ever have in my entire life. Dr Blake would've been proud.

"I'm from the future. Not like the far future, the near future. Next year, one of your research assistants is going to use Deep Dive and experience a moment of time dilation. He won't understand what happened at first, but eventually it will come out that he actually traveled forward in time for several seconds before being pulled back. Over the course of the next eighteen months your scientists will develop a way to safely time travel. It's highly restricted, but four days ago in my time I snuck into the Deep Dive chamber. I wanted to experience it for myself, only something went wrong. I was flung backwards in time instead of forwards. In the security feed you showed me, I was trying to hotwire the software so I could get home, but then the Peter from this timeline showed up. I'm not entirely sure what happened, but I believe it caused a temporary paradox that shorted out your computers. What you don't see in the video is me running off because I didn't want to get caught."

I have no idea if any of this is even close to being theoretically sound. I know jack shit about time travel, but I've watched enough movies and read enough books to know that a paradox is usually wildly misunderstood.

"Time travel? Seriously? That's your story?" O'Laughlin laughs derisively. "Try again, Banuk."

"I'm telling you the truth."

"Whatever." O'Laughlin snaps his fingers at Shepard. "Tell Donald the hit's back on."

"Belay that order," Shepard says quietly.

The sound of her calm command reverberates around the room like the echo from a whip crack. O'Laughlin's cheeks flush purple with embarrassment at having his supposed authority blown to hell in front of the likes of me, but he doesn't argue.

"I'll admit, your story smacks of desperation," Shepard says. "However, I'm willing to accept, for the time being, that you're telling at least part of the truth. The fact remains that Deep Dive is broken and our people, including some version of you, are trapped in their suspension pods, leaving you the resident expert in how to unfuck this."

"I can fix it, Shepard. I swear."

Her eyes narrow. "Alana only gets one reprieve."

A lukewarm wave of relief washes over me. It's only a temporary stay of execution, but right now I'll take anything I can get.

Granted, I have no idea how I'm going to fix this infernal machine, but if I can stall long enough, I might be able to convince Reggie to get word to Alana that she needs to take a long vacation and not tell anyone where she's gone.

"All right." Shepard lifts her phone. "Change of plans, Donald." She pauses, looking irritated at whatever Donald's response is. "I don't really give a shit how excited you were, if you'd like to keep your job, you'll do what I say." Another pause. "Thank you."

Shaking her head, Shepard slips the phone into her back pocket, then says to me, "You have two hours. I'd suggest you get started if you want to keep Alana alive."

CHAPTER EIGHTEEN

Shepard stands guard behind me. O'Laughlin's long gone. Finn ran off to sharpen his knives or oil his guns or something, so it's just me and her, alone in this massive room filled with the quiet hum of machinery and the psychedelic Pepto-Bismol glow of the suspension pods.

Wiping my sweaty hands on my pants, I lean over the keyboard and run a few basic diagnostics. I mostly know my way around a PC. Problem is, I'm limited to localized fixes, because the computer is hardwired to Deep Dive and operates off an internal intranet that Shepard claims is impervious to outside intrusion.

"We're still not entirely sure what caused the malfunction that trapped the soldiers in the pods," she says. "They'd gone on extended dives before, usually two to three days tops. Never had a problem with life-support or anything. Then all of a sudden, everything went to shit."

Her tone is relaxed, conversational, like I'm a new employee with whom she's trying to build a positive rapport. I don't buy it for a second. She's an awful human being no matter how pleasantly she schools her voice. What I need to do is get her out of here.

"Doran told me his brother disappeared from the scanners," I say. "Any idea why?"

"Our technicians detected some strange quantum fluctuations when they went over the data," Shepard says, "but we haven't been able to determine their precise nature." She pauses, taps her chin. "I wonder if they have anything to do with the time dilation you mentioned."

She says it all casual-like, but I know better than to assume she's not suspicious as hell of my story. Especially because I'm still thinking on the fly, racking my brain for a solution that might not exist, all the while acting like I know what I'm doing.

"Time's a funny thing," I say.

"What's it like?" Shepard says. "The future?"

And this is why we don't concoct big, elaborate lies on the fly.

"Pretty much the same. Climate change is still a problem, though there's talk of adapting the Mars terraforming initiative for use on Earth. There was a global pandemic a couple years back, which was not fun. No zombies, though, so yeah. Um, self-driving cars are outselling gas guzzlers. Oh, and they finally invented actual hover boards that use magnetic levitators, so those are all the rage. Also really expensive to insure. Otherwise, you know, same old same old." I change the subject. "Have you tried turning Deep Dive off and then turning it back on?"

"I'm told that would sever whatever connection still exists between the minds and the bodies of everyone in the submersion pods, including the other you." Shepard shrugs. "But hey, if you're game…"

"What? No!"

"Just checking."

Jesus Christ.

"OK, just bear with me for a second. I need to think this through."

"You're the one with the deadline," she says. "See what I did there? *Dead*line?"

I'm fairly proud of myself for maintaining my composure just then. "Anyway. So you can't turn off Deep Dive because everyone will die, which is bad." I stress this mostly for Shepard's benefit.

"You also can't reload the training simulation your Peter designed since everyone is technically still online and taking it offline will also sever whatever connection's keeping them alive."

"You see our predicament."

"I'm assuming some of the program files are corrupted?"

"That's our assumption as well."

That gives me pause. "Um, then why haven't you tried to repair them?"

"We can't."

"Why not?"

She glares down at me. "Because *someone* made them unsearchable."

"Oh."

"You're the someone, by the way," Shepard says.

"Yeah, I got that."

Shepard flaps her hand at the computer. "So make them searchable, Future Man."

I stare at the computer screen. "It's not that simple."

"Why is that?"

"I have to figure out where I hid them."

"I fail to see what the problem is."

I tap my head. "Remember how I said I've been having memory issues?"

Shepard sighs. "I'm beginning to regret giving you a chance to fix this."

"Call Alana if you don't believe me. She's been dealing with my fucked up brain for days." Even mentioning my wife in front of Shepard feels like a betrayal, but I'm running out of options here.

"You'd like that, wouldn't you?"

What I'd like is for you to go to hell and leave me and my wife alone. "My point is, it's hard for me to think with you watching over my shoulder."

She narrows her eyes. "Are you suggesting I leave?"

"It's just, you know how some people can't pee if someone

else is standing in the stall next to them? I'm like that when it comes to computer stuff."

"Fine," she says, surprising me.

I heave a sigh of relief.

"But it will cost you an hour."

My relief experiences an extinction-level event. "What?"

"I'll go, but I'm reducing your deadline from two hours to one."

The knife's edge on which I'm balanced starts to slice into my feet. I want to protest, to tell Shepard there's no way I can pull this off in an hour, but I desperately need her gone, and if that means appealing to her sociopathic tendencies, then so be it.

"OK."

"You understand," Shepard says, "if you're not done when I get back, I'll call Donald and tell him Alana's back on the menu."

I gulp down the leaden lump in my throat. "I understand."

"All right, I'll play along." She sets a timer on her phone. "I hope you know what you're doing, Peter."

So do I.

I watch her leave, then swivel nervously back toward the computer and open the command prompt, praying all the while that my victory isn't as Pyrrhic as it feels.

I've always been hugely paranoid about getting hacked, so in our early garage days I had Bradley teach me how to make folders unsearchable. In theory I know exactly where to look for the missing program files, because no matter the operating system, I always hide everything in the same place.

Of course, this is all contingent on whether I'm Peter 1. Shepard certainly believes I am, and I'm like nighty nine percent certain I'm not Peter 2, the one currently stuck in the submersion tank. Save for the action hero theatrics and the fact that I have no memory of ever setting foot in this chamber before today, the security feed presents a compelling amount of visual evidence to support her belief.

I take a deep breath and type in the folder path.

Five seconds later, an encrypted zip file appears.

I smile to myself as I type in the password. When Cassie was five, Alana taught her how to speak Pig Latin. Cassie was obsessed with it, and spent weeks responding to us using only Pig Latin. Years later, when Evie was around the same age, Cassie taught it to her. The girls would run around the house rapid-firing Pig Latin at one another. It drove me crazy. But it also stuck with me, and I wound up using the language for one of the puzzles in *Scorchfell*.

I also use it for encryption keys.

january242001fiddler*sgreen – otherwise known as the month, day, year, and name of the restaurant where Alana and I had our first official date – translated into Pig Latin looks like *anuaryjay242001iddler*sfayeengray*

The zip drive opens.

I'm in, and also feeling quite smug that these DARPA supergeeks got outclassed by the likes of me.

Inside the zip drive is a single folder labeled *VirtualCorps*. That must be the name Peter 2 gave the VR simulation. Not the snazziest title, but then anything fun and creative probably got overruled by O'Laughlin and Shepard.

As I open the *VirtualCorps* folder, I feel the hair-raising tingle of déjà vu, like I've been here before and done this already.

I look up at the dormant wall screen above me.

What the hell were you really doing here, Peter?

There are dozens of folders nestled within the main *VirtualCorps* one. Each of these sub-folders are packed with a crap-ton of files, everything from data and storyboards and motion capture to images and audio and animation, all the little bits and bytes that make up the beating virtual heart of *VirtualCorps*.

There's no way I can study each and every file in less than an hour. Luckily, I don't need to study them. I can just run repair on the busted ones, then make them unsearchable again and hold them for ransom until I have proof that Alana's safe.

It's a shitty plan, but right now it's all I've got.

Out of creative curiosity, I click on an animation folder, double-click the first file, and stare in horrified disbelief at the box of gibberish that appears on the screen.

I double-click the next file, then the next, then the one after that. Toggling back into the main folder, I open the motion capture folder, and click on those files.

But no matter which one I open, they all show the same thing.

A large text box full of gibberish symbols.

Every single file has been corrupted.

I glance at the submersion pods in confusion. If all the files are corrupted, the simulation should have totally crashed. James and his team should be dead. But they're not.

Something else is going on here. I have no idea what, though, and something tells me an hour is nowhere near enough time to figure it out.

Still, I start trying to repair the corrupted files so I at least have some form of bargaining chip. But much to my eternal dismay, nothing works. Changing the file format or using a different program to open the top file does nothing. Neither does opening the command prompt screen and running system and disk scans.

Virus, malware, logic bomb. Pick your digital sabotage of choice, it really doesn't matter. Whatever Peter 1 did to corrupt the files, whether accidental or purposeful, was thorough.

The *VirtualCorps* training simulation is toast.

All of a sudden, my usefulness has been greatly diminished. If I can't fix this, Shepard has no reason to keep me alive. No reason to keep Alana alive.

Shit shit shit shit shit.

I have to get out of here. I have to get to Alana. Now, before the inevitable countdown commences.

But how?

I cast about the room. Peter 2, James, and the other soldiers float in their pods, oblivious to the outside world. Above the flywheel door, which Shepard made sure to let me know she'd be locking from the outside, the security camera lens reflects the glow from the pods like Sauron's baleful eye, ever watchful, ever ready to bring all of Mordor, or in this case DARPA, down on me.

I glance back at the computer. In theory I could download another VR game and attempt to sync it with Deep Dive. But one, I can't access the Internet from here. And two, swapping out simulations might very well kill everyone still connected to Deep Dive. As much as I want to get home, I wouldn't be able to live with myself if I knowingly sentenced Peter 2 and the Rangers to death.

Even so, if I don't find some way out of this mess, Alana and I are going to run out of lives. But so far as I can tell I'm trapped in this mad scientist's lair with no feasible means of escape. The computer has zero access to the outside world, and the only door is locked from the outside. If it was electronic, I might be able to hotwire it, but the flywheel is straight-up old-school brute strength tech.

It's a no-win situation, the tic-tac-toe scene in *War Games* when Joshua says to David, "The only winning move is not to play." Except I have to play, because if I don't, I'm a goner.

I glance at my unconscious doppelgänger. If I was a bastard, I'd figure out a way to use him, James, and the others as hostages. But I'm not a bastard, not completely, and if Finn got wind that I was threatening to harm the Rangers, a hundred Shepards wouldn't be able to prevent him from using his machine gun to turn me into Swiss cheese.

Defeated, I plop down into the computer chair, glaring at the corrupted files taunting me from the monitor. Well, there's only one option left.

Beg.

Fall on my knees once again and beg.

As I spin around in the chair like a man about to take his last walk down death row, a loud metallic clang sounds throughout the room, echoing like a gong and startling me into stillness.

A second clang follows the first, and with a ponderous creak, the flywheel door glides open.

Speak of the Shepard and the Shepard appears.

I tense, fully expecting her, Finn, or O'Laughlin.

As it turns out, it's none of them.

"What are you–" I start to say, but Reggie presses a finger to her lips, then raises her other hand and points something at the security camera.

There's a barely audible *click*.

The light on the security camera goes out.

Holy shit.

Is Reggie here to rescue me?

"Shepard and O'Laughlin are in a meeting, so we have about twenty minutes before they realize something's wrong with the feed," she says, marching toward me like a vengeful guardian angel. "I jammed the elevator door, which should buy us a little more time, but I'm pretty sure Shepard has a way down here that only she and O'Laughlin know about, so this has to be quick."

Pushing up out of my chair, I say, "I wasn't sure if I'd scared you off earlier, but seriously, thank you for–"

I don't have a chance to finish thanking her.

With her next stride, Reggie reaches me, draws back her arm, and cold-cocks me right in the face.

Pain blossoms in my left cheek, spreading along my jaw as I stumble, trip over the chair, and narrowly avoid cracking my head on the computer desk as I hit the ground with a bone-jarring thud.

"What the hell!" I shout, cupping my cheek. It comes out more like a muffled *Ut eh ell!*

"You asshole," she hisses, looming over me, fists clenched, jaw set, eyes ablaze with fury, her very pregnant belly protruding like a boulder about to tumble off Mount Manasa and crush me where I sit. "One time wasn't enough for you?"

To say that I'm perplexed by Reggie's angry question is like saying Cassie and Evie have a passing affection for pancakes.

"Ut r u alking a-out?" I burble. Wincing, I rub my cheek and say, "One time what?"

"Don't play dumbass with me," Reggie says, stepping forward like she's about to use my head as a soccer ball. "I stuck my neck out for you once already. I am not saving your ass a second time."

"A second time? Look, I'm sorry if you're pissed off at me for all that manipulative stuff I said back in the MRI room, but I don't think it merits getting sucker-punched."

"It merits a whole lot more than a sucker-punch." She shakes her head, grabs the chair, and lowers herself carefully into it.

I work my clicking jaw back and forth a few times, trying to decide if anything's broken. "I don't know if you noticed," I say, "but I'm a little out of my element here. It might help us both if you started at the beginning."

Reggie studies me, her left side painted with the pink glow of Peter 2's suspension pod. "The truck," she says.

"Truck? What truck? My truck? Are you talking about when Doran kidnapped me?"

"Jesus." Reggie shakes her head, folds her hands on top of her stomach. "How do you not remember any of this?"

I scoot back and recline my head against the desk. "Hey, if it helps, Shepard doesn't believe me, either. But I'm telling you the truth."

As I say this, though, my brain tingles with an unreachable itch of dormant memories begging to be scratched.

"Technically it's his truck," Reggie says, flapping her hand at Peter 2 floating in his tank. "But that's not the point."

The itch in my head becomes more pronounced. "Four days ago," I say slowly, "I woke up in my truck."

"And how do you think you got to your truck?"

To be honest, I haven't given it much thought.

"Four days ago," Reggie continues, "I found you standing over that other Peter, the one I know. You gave me some rigmarole bullshit about it not being your fault and how you needed to get him in one of the suspension pods before the twin paradox or some shit destroyed everything and everyone, but then you went and had another seizure or something, and then you lost your damn mind. Before I could stop you, your happy ass did something to the computer and then took off yelling about needing to get home, leaving me to clean up your damn mess. I was not about to take the fall for whatever you did to my Peter, so I got Eddie to help me put him in the tank. Now I owe him a favor, and I fucking hate owing people favors."

I gawp at her. "That's impossible."

"Bitch, do I seem like the kind of person who'd scramble a security camera and risk my job – a second time, mind you – for *impossible*?"

"Reggie, I've never been in this room before."

But that's not entirely true, is it? According to the security feed O'Laughlin played, I have. And the way I acted all startled at the end suggested a third person had entered the room.

Was it really Reggie?

"If you've never been in this room before," Reggie says, reaching into her pocket, "then where did I get this?"

She lobs something at me. A Mobius strip of brown leather flies through the air, flipping end over end until it lands on my lap as softly as a feather.

I stare at the bracelet.

The memories scratching at the door of my mind form into one giant battering ram.

The world slows, narrows to a pinprick.

I've never seen this bracelet in my life, but I instantly recognize it. Cassie gave it to me. Except she didn't, because this is the first time I've ever seen it. Except it's not. I've had this bracelet for two years. Cassie made it at school, during art class. She was so proud of the letters she managed to cut in the center of the leather strip, the C and the E and the M and the D.

Cassandra.

Evangeline.

Mommy.

Daddy.

She gave it to me for Valentine's Day. I know this like I know the sound of Alana's laugh, like I know how ticklish Evie is, like I know that at any one time Cassie has at least five books hidden strategically around her bed.

I know this because it's true, but it's a truth I cannot possibly know because I've never once laid eyes on this bracelet until this very moment.

"It's yours, right?" Reggie says.

I lift my gaze to her. "I… Where–"

"It was on the floor, over there," Reggie says, gesturing to her right. "Near that Peter's pod. I found it the day after you pulled your little materialization trick." She leans forward, eyes intense. "So do you believe me now?"

According to Alana and everyone else I know, Cassie and Evie don't exist, therefore this bracelet can't exist because Cassie gave it to me and I've never seen it before this moment despite the fact that I can still see her hopeful, bashful smile as she tied it around my wrist the day she brought it home from school.

Fingers trembling, I pick up the bracelet.

The moment my skin makes contact with it, my mind explodes.

It's like a mirror shattering into a thousand shards of glass, each reflecting a lifetime of memories I've never experienced but undoubtedly belong to me. Wave after wave, moment after moment, image after image simultaneously crashes in, clawing over one another and begging to be acknowledged, begging to be seen, begging, begging, begging to be remembered.

And finally, I do.

I remember.

CHAPTER NINETEEN

"Are you sure you want to do this again?" Bradley said.

I shrugged, tracing the letters on the bracelet Cassie had given me. I'd felt a little silly the first time I put it on, but she'd been so proud of herself that I couldn't say no. I'd worn it every day since. It had become a physical reminder of everything I loved, everything I stood to lose if I wasn't careful.

"It's not like we've got much choice," I said. "We're the ones who opened the door. When they show up on our side it's up to us to show them how to get home."

"Technically you opened the door. I'm just tech support." Bradley handed me the Deep Dive headset. "We could just stop, you know. Or, better yet, rope some other suckers into taking over. No one would blame us."

I sighed. "You know we can't tell anyone else. The more people we involve, the greater chance it'll leak. But I mean, if you want to cause a global panic and have every government in the world demanding access, then sure, let's take out a wanted ad."

"Whatever," Bradley said. "All I'm saying is that you look like shit. This is clearly taking a toll on you."

We'd had this conversation far too many times to count. I wasn't even mad that we were rehashing it yet again. Mostly I was just tired. I missed the girls. Missed Alana. Things were different now, better than they had been. We felt like a family unit for the first time in years, in large part because I'd finally figured out how to be more present. But lately I'd been spending more time with Bradley. I was aware of it, and was making a conscious effort to pull back, but that didn't mean I could shirk a responsibility like this.

"I'm not going to leave them trapped in there," I said.

"Look," Bradley said, "they made their choice same as we made our choice. They didn't have to open the door if they weren't ready."

"Oh please. Like we were ready?" I shook my head. "Admit it, we got lucky that first time."

"Luck had nothing to do with it." Bradley slid into his chair and wheeled up to the dedicated computer we'd hardwired to Deep Dive. "Anyway. Let's get this over with so you can get home to your family. Alana's starting to hate me again."

"She doesn't hate you," I said as I walked over to the immersion rig and sat down, the headset in my hands feeling heavier than usual.

"Keep telling yourself that, buddy." Bradley hit a key. On the screen, the program began to load.

Truth was, Alana still didn't particularly like Bradley – her nickname for him was Techno Douche – but she didn't hate him. If anything, she'd developed a grudging appreciation for him. A lot of that had to do with the fact that ever since I sold Omega Studios to Meg and partnered up with Bradley, I worked normal hours instead of the long-haul stints I used to pull, so I actually got to spend quality time with Alana and the girls. Some days I missed the creative atmosphere of developing video games, but what Bradley and I were doing was far more important and, in many ways, a hell of a lot more exciting.

He wasn't wrong, though. I needed a break. The more time I spent hopping in and out of realities, the more exhausted I felt. We'd talked more than once about trading places, but at this point I'd become the default expert in traversing the Nexus, whereas Bradley was the tech genius who knew Deep Dive's hardware inside and out and could troubleshoot problems faster than I could cause them.

"How's your head today?" Bradley asked, tapping away at the keyboard.

I touched the top of my skull, where my scalp occasionally tingled.

Bradley told me I was imagining things, that there was no way I could feel the stent-based electrode he'd inserted via my jugular vein into a blood vessel next to the motor cortex. It caused occasional migraines, but if something went wrong, it was the only thing that could get me home.

"It's fine." I pulled on the headset, muting the outside world, and stretched out on the gaming chair Bradley had redesigned specifically for use with prolonged dives. "Ready when you are."

Bradley's voice came at me as if from far away. "Just running some last diagnostics on the stent."

Among other things, the stent, by tapping directly into the electrical activity of my brain, made it easier to manipulate virtual environments. It also made it possible to select realities inside the Nexus, the quantum crossroads that existed in the seam between actual reality and the virtual reality created by the Deep Dive headset.

We'd stumbled upon the Nexus by accident the very first time I used Deep Dive, when I opened the red metal door in the Scorchfell simulation and came face to face with that infinite sea of silver light.

We were still working out the physics behind it, but our running theory was that it had to do with the way the unique blend of electroencephalogram and focused ultrasound technology that formed the basis of Deep Dive's hardware stimulated our brain while within a virtual environment. Our conception of reality is based on our perception of reality, what we can taste, touch, see, smell, and hear. The experience of Deep Dive was so completely immersive that virtual reality became as objectively real as actual reality. Once the brain bridged that dichotomy and accepted the possibility of two opposing yet fully genuine realities, it grew capable of perceiving and accepting more realities.

Enter the Nexus, the quantum crossroads that underpins all realities, the place where all realities exist simultaneously. Just like the concept of infinity, the human brain is incapable of truly perceiving the Nexus. Therefore, in order to make sense of it, our mind creates a proxy, a virtual doorway, that acts as a gateway to the Nexus. A door of perception, if you will.

Of course, when we first stumbled upon this mind-blowing discovery, we had no idea what the hell was going on. I damn near got trapped in the Nexus. If Bradley hadn't cut the feed to Deep Dive when he did, I would've drowned in that sea of silver light and never seen my family again. I'd still missed Evie's seventh birthday, but I'd done a pretty decent job of making up for it since.

Bradley and I had learned since then, taken baby step after baby step. Established parameters and precautions. The stent was the latest of those. On top of allowing me to focus when I was inside the Nexus and select a reality rather than simply fall into one at random, the stent also acted as a beacon, a GPS of sorts, so that anytime I entered another reality, I was always able to locate my home reality the next time I reentered the Nexus.

"OK," Bradley said. "Here we go. In five, four, three, two, one."

The inside of the headset disappeared. In its place was a vast, rocky desert surrounded by towering, craggy mountains. In the center of the desert was a labyrinth the size of a city. In the center of the labyrinth was the door to the Nexus.

No matter how many times I did this, I always arrived in the same place, atop a cliff overlooking the desert.

Sometimes I walked to the labyrinth, relishing the immersive feel of the world I'd created for Scorchfell, *the game that broke my heart but gave me back my life when I sold Omega Studios. Other times I simply thought my way directly into the labyrinth and spent a while exploring its infinite corridors.*

That was how I discovered the ghosts.

At first I avoided them, but eventually I realized what they really were: lost souls, the virtual manifestation of minds that belonged to people from alternate realities who, using their own versions of Deep Dive, had found the Nexus, entered my reality, and become trapped in the labyrinth.

In the blink of an eye, I vanished from the clifftop and reappeared outside the door to the Nexus.

The five ghosts I'd encountered on my last trip – gray amorphous blobs that bore vague human features only if looked at sideways –

immediately flocked to me, silently clamoring for attention. Mind attracted mind in this place. I didn't know if they were aware of what had happened to them, but it didn't matter. What mattered was that they followed me through the door, into the Nexus, and back to their own realities. Otherwise, they'd start to fade, leaving their distant bodies forever mindless.

"Here goes nothing," I said. I'd done this rescue op a dozen times already, but every time always felt like the first.

Opening the red metal door, I stepped into the Nexus, and the ghosts followed.

As always, the first few seconds were almost completely overwhelming. My heart went into overdrive, and I almost triggered the tether, which, like the fast-travel system in any video game, would near-instantly transport me back to my reality. But I fought the urge, let the initial panic pass like I knew it would, and took in my surroundings.

All around me was an unending sea of silver light populated by an infinity of black bubbles. Each bubble represented an individual reality.

I held still. This was the tricky part. It was up to the ghosts to draw their reality to them. Or maybe it was the reality that drew the ghosts. I wasn't entirely sure. The fact of the matter was, the Nexus was almost as mysterious now as it was when I first stumbled through the door.

As much as there was hard science behind Deep Dive, a lot of my time traversing realities was spent trusting my gut. I had to hope the ghosts would do the same. Sometimes they didn't. Sometimes, they simply dematerialized. Other times, they found their bubble, or their bubble found them, and they were able to ruby slipper their way home.

"Come on, folks," I whispered.

The ghosts swarmed about me, undulating in place. A bubble floated by. Or maybe we flew to it. In the vacuum of the Nexus, it was impossible to tell who was doing the moving.

A succession of bubbles passed by. The ghosts began to lose shape and color, their gray shot through with streaks of silver.

"Shit."

But then another bubble crossed our path, or we crossed its. The bubble expanded, or we shrank. Either way, the ghosts began to sink into it like organic spaceships entering the atmosphere of a planet.

"Finally."

I could go home now.

Or.

Don't do it, dude, *I told myself.* You're tired. You told the girls you'd take them to the amusement park tomorrow. Play Magellan another day.

Lately, I'd taken to following the ghosts to their reality to make sure they got home in one piece. It also afforded me a chance to get a quick lay of the land. I wasn't looking to play godly arbiter, but the last thing any of us needed was for some nefarious organization to decide it might be fun to invade someone else's reality. A lot of times, the people who'd developed Deep Dive in other realities seemed mostly unaware of what it could really do. If I caught wind of ill-intent, I took it upon myself to corrupt their system. I had no idea if my efforts had much of an effect, but so far we hadn't been overrun by soldiers from another world, so that was something.

Also, Bradley liked it when I checked out local tech. I'd upload schematics to the tether, which he then later downloaded and used to develop his own versions, giving him an even bigger slice of the tech market pie.

Into the bubble I went, falling after the ghosts like a meteorite.

In the blink of an eye I found myself standing in the middle of a warzone.

Bullets whizzed past, gouging holes in the red-brick walls of the house I'd appeared next to. A drone roared by overhead, divesting itself of its payload and speeding off while its missile homed in on its target, completely obliterating a nearby water tower.

The shockwave from the explosion slammed into me like a Skyrim *giant's club, smashing me into the wall of the house.*

It took me a second to realize I wasn't dying, bleeding, or in any actual pain.

Oh thank God, *I thought.*

This wasn't real. It was a simulation, a virtual world like my labyrinth. This sometimes happened. Reality, virtual reality, and the Nexus were stacked like Russian dolls, one inside the other. In order to access the Nexus, you had to pass from your reality and into virtual reality. The same held true for visiting other realities. Once you left the Nexus, you often but not always entered the simulation connected to Deep Dive in the alternate reality. But because of my stent, I sometimes went straight through to the real world if a simulation either wasn't active or was malfunctioning.

In this case, the virtual destruction raging all around me was unsettling enough that I wished I'd gone straight through. Deep Dive was clearly being used in conjunction with a battlefield simulation. Maybe it was a game, maybe it was a benign training program. Or maybe it was a precursor to invasion.

Yes, reality hopping had made me paranoid. But paranoia had kept me alive so far.

I accessed my stent and homed in on the local Deep Dive signal.

The simulation blurred. My belly button felt like it was attached to a cable connected to a spinning winch that had been bolted to my spinal column. My skin crawled with electricity. My body seemed to fold in on itself. There was a brief, disorientating lurch like I'd been thrust forward only to be jerked roughly backwards, and then I was spit out into the real world.

Right into a vat of pink, viscous liquid.

I was so used to emerging on dry land that, like a baby taking its first breath, I involuntarily inhaled.

Warm liquid the consistency of watery vomit filled my mouth and nose, choking me. Panic kicked in. Flailing my arms and legs, I started swimming only to immediately bump up against a solid surface.

Shit, I'm in a tank!

Lungs burning, I thrashed around in search of an exit. All around me, the pink goop glimmered with its own internal light.

There!

I bunched my legs, pushed off the bottom of the tank, and shot toward what I prayed was an opening.

Like a surfacing whale, my head parted the surface, splashing pink liquid every which way. I grabbed hold of the opening, legs treading water while I threw up the gallon of goop I'd swallowed. Oxygen flooded my lungs.

Breathing deeply, I pushed up and out of the opening, slid down the side of the tank, and landed on the floor with a wet resounding thud.

I sat there hunched over for several minutes, letting my body reorient itself to solid ground and breathable air. When I finally felt steady, I pulled myself to my feet and stared at the tank for a moment before backing up for a better vantage point.

Of the twelve pods surrounding the central cylinder where the life-support systems that controlled them were stored, five were currently occupied. Three men, two women. Not a huge stretch to assume the ghostly minds I led here belonged to these half-naked bodies.

Using full-body submersion as a means for extending the time spent in a virtual world was one thing – after all, virtual reality was solely the domain of the mind. But the quantum mechanics required to send your mind and your body from one reality to another tended to break down when your physical self was contained in a submersion pod, as evidenced by the fact that a large portion of the ghosts I'd encountered in the labyrinth and followed to their home came from a reality where such pods were used alongside Deep Dive.

I say tended. That wasn't always the case. Some realities had discovered the right kind of conductive liquid to allow minds and bodies to properly transition. I'd read in one of Bradley's science mags about a liquid substance called perfluorocarbon that was rich in oxygen and could theoretically be inhaled as though it were air. Maybe the team that created Deep Dive in this reality had manufactured a similar substance that also amplified the electrical signals in the brain.

I certainly fucking hoped so, because otherwise there was a very good chance I was stuck here.

Thankfully, the fact that the bodies had remained behind here suggested that's what they'd done. It also suggested something else. That the Deep Divers in this reality didn't want their bodies to go with them when they entered another reality. Maybe this all was still relatively new to them and they were conducting

*reconnaissance, gathering intel on the experience, before fully
committing to mind and body traversal, and that's what trapped
them in the labyrinth. Maybe they'd discovered some benefit of
mind-without-body traversal that Bradley and I hadn't considered
yet. Shit, maybe they'd figured out a way to slip into other virtual
networks outside of Deep Dive and effectively possess anyone
connected to those networks.*

*I was reaching, nerding out as Bradley liked to say, but the fact
remained that the options were as limitless as the number of realities
they could visit.*

*Whatever the case, the why was something to debate with Bradley
once I was safely home.*

*At the moment, I had much more pressing concerns. In order of
importance, getting home and helping the ghosts. Unfortunately, I'd
have to tackle them in reverse order. None of the bodies were stirring,
which meant something had gone wrong during the transition from
the Nexus to this reality.*

Dammit.

*In all my reality hopping, I'd made a point of doing my best not
to harm anyone I encountered. Yes, there were faceless corporations
and jingoistic shadow governments that more than deserved to
be hamstrung, and I did what I could in that department. But if I
corrupted the Deep Dive software before the minds returned to the
bodies in the pods, I'd effectively be killing them.*

*Maybe the mind would survive in the simulation – the ghosts in
the labyrinth were proof that consciousness could cope, to varying
degrees, without benefit of a body. The body, however, cannot live
without the mind. Without the mind, the body has no source code, no
central processing unit to control the functions necessary to turn what
is essentially a biological meat sack into a sentient being.*

*There was no way I could upload malware to corrupt this reality's
Deep Dive software when doing so meant not only destroying my way
home but relegating the people in the pods to, at best, a bodiless virtual
life, or, at worst, no life at all.*

Which meant I had to fix whatever was malfunctioning in Deep

Dive and then go back into the battlefield simulation and find the ghosts all over again.

"Hey!" a voice called out from behind me.

Startled, I whirled around, but even as I laid eyes on the person who'd entered the pod chamber, my brain had already matched the voice to a face.

My own.

"This is a restricted area," Peter said, marching toward me. "You're not supposed to be in here."

Dismay curdled my stomach. This was one experiment I'd never wanted to conduct. Yes, I'd observed other versions of myself from afar, but I never interacted with them. The risk of paradox was too great.

That, apparently, was about to change.

"I don't know what you think you're doing," Peter said, "but…" His voice trailed off. He took one more step, then stopped. Confusion played across his face, which had gone a foggy shade of pale.

"Look," I said, raising my hands. "I don't want to cause any trouble."

Peter backed up. "You… you're…"

"You." I nodded. "Yeah. Hey. Nice to meet you. Listen, I get that this is weird, so how about this? You accept that this is really happening, I'll see what I can do about those folks in the tanks, then I'll be on my way and you can either tell everyone about me or pretend like I was never here and take the credit for yourself. Either way, everything will go back to normal. Sound good? Great."

I could tell by his panicked expression that he was most definitely not OK. That wasn't surprising. I'd always been high-strung, and I'd never been very good at reassuring myself. Alana was always telling me to relax, to stop overreacting about the small stuff.

This was decidedly not small stuff.

"Who are you?" Peter demanded.

A tremor passed through my head, the first inklings of an approaching migraine. "Before I answer that," I said, "what do you know about the Nexus?"

"The what?"

Shit. This me had no idea what he was messing with.

"You've got Deep Dive, right?" I asked. "A brain computer interface?"

At this, his face went from freaked out to suspicious. "How do you know about Deep Dive?"

"I'm you, remember?"

That, apparently, was the wrong thing to say.

Peter advanced on me, hands clenching into fists. "You are not me!"

"Whoa." I retreated a step. "Chill, dude. As much as I'd love to stay here and chat, compare lives, talk about the road not traveled, help you work through any identity issues you might be experiencing at the moment, we really don't have time. If I could just get a look at your files, I'll–"

"Stop! Just stop!" He jabbed one finger at me, pressed the heel of his hands into his forehead. "I can't – I have to–"

Without warning, he pulled a one-eighty and started to book it toward the door.

Crap.

No way could I let him get out and call in the local Stormtroopers.

Cursing my luck, I raced after him. When I caught up, I grabbed his arm.

The moment our skin touched, a static charge more painful than any electric shock I'd ever received slammed through me. The blast was so powerful it almost sent Peter and me spinning in opposite directions, and would have if my hand hadn't remained clamped to his arm, unable to let go, held there by some invisible force.

We collapsed in a tangled heap of twitching limbs, two identical twins separated at birth trying to prevent themselves from being forcibly conjoined by an incredible trick of physics straight out of Doctor Who. *I think we fought, but I'm not entirely sure.*

At some point, though, I heard Peter's head hit the floor.

The hollow thud echoed in my ears like an un-tuned drum, and then he went limp.

The astonishing power that had sealed my fingers to his arm released its hold, and my hand fell away. Wheezing, the threatened migraine beginning to take hold, I scrabbled drunkenly onto all fours. On the ground, spasms raced through Peter's body. My vision blurred, and I almost collapsed on top of him. Somehow, I was able to reach out and lay a hand on his neck.

Despite the spasms, my fingertips detected a pulse.

He wasn't dead.

Thank God.

I had no idea if this version of me had a family – some did, some didn't – but I'd never forgive myself if I kept him from going home to them.

Sadly, my relief was short-lived.

"What the hell?" said a new voice from a few feet away.

I looked up with bleary eyes and saw someone I hadn't seen in over a year, not since she and Bradley had a falling out over whether to go public with Deep Dive and she'd left to get her own tech start-up rolling.

"Reggie." I gasped out her name.

She laid one hand on her pregnant belly, gawping from me to the knocked-the-fuck-out Peter lying on the ground.

My right arm went out from underneath me. I hit the ground on my shoulder, my chin glancing off Peter's forehead. At the moment of contact, a nuke detonated behind my eyebrows, the mushroom cloud obscuring my vision as the electromagnetic pulse cascaded around my skull in coruscating waves of searing pain.

"Help," I croaked, reaching out with a trembling hand.

To her credit, Reggie reacted much better than Peter did when he first laid eyes on me. Face abruptly steel-set, she strode over, grabbed my hand, and pulled me to my feet, steadying me when I started to lose my balance.

"What do you need me to do?" she asked.

I needed to get back in the submersion tank.

"Can you – Deep Dive – the computer–"

Try though I might, I couldn't make my words form properly.

"What?" Reggie said. "What about Deep Dive?"

I opened my mouth, but my tongue had swelled so much the only noise I could make was a groan.

Pushing away from Reggie, I stumbled toward the computer and fell into the chair. I called up the Deep Dive program, searching desperately for the simulation software.

"Hey, you can't do that!" Reggie shouted.

My vision doubled. The monitor glitched. I could feel my brain slipping away, my grip on reality weakening. The top of my skull pulsed with pain. I fought through it, but there were too many files and not enough time to figure out which ones were broken.

So I did the only thing I could think to do.

I dumped everything into a folder and encrypted it.

I'd done this before, in other realities, so it was like muscle memory, which is the only reason I was able to pull it off. If I'd had to think my way through it, I never would have been able to lock down the files. But it had to be done. Whatever was happening to me was bad. If someone came in and messed with the software before I recovered, I might be stuck here forever.

Reggie was still shouting at me, but I ignored her. The encryption finished loading. Just in case, I doubled down and made the folder unsearchable, too.

The moment I finished, the room went sideways.

I fell out of the chair and crashed to the ground again, my awareness disappearing with each passing second. I thought of Cassie and Evie and Alana and how I wasn't ever going to see them again. The weight of that unimaginable sense of loss bore me down into darkness, and–

CHAPTER TWENTY

I gasp, releasing the breath I'd held while my memory returned to me, and damn near almost pass out again as the pressure in my chest eases with a dizzying rush of air.

"I'm guessing you remember now," Reggie says.

I swallow, nod. It's like a whole other version of me has crowded into my brain, only I know that's not the case.

The Peter in the security feed?

That was definitely me.

The conversation I had with Bradley before throwing myself back into the Nexus for the umpteenth time?

That was real.

All of it was real.

All of it was me.

"An explanation would be really fucking great right about now," Reggie says.

"I've been using Deep Dive for two years," I say. "From my reality, I mean."

"Say what?"

I give her the quickest rundown in the history of rundowns, from our discovery of the Nexus and other realities to my rescue operation to help the ghosts get back to this reality.

"So you came here to return their minds to their bodies?" Reggie says when I finish. "But then you ran into another version of yourself, which had never happened before, and it short-circuited both your brains?"

"Basically, yeah."

Honestly, I'm not entirely sure how to explain it. A contradiction, spatial disorientation, temporary mental misalignment due to coming into contact with another version of myself who held an entirely different reality in his head? A meeting of two minds, both alike in the certainty of their reality, that resulted in a paradox, an irreconcilable inconsistency where two similar but ultimately oppositional realities attempted to coexist within the same spatial realm?

Whatever it was, it wrung out my brain like a wet rag, burying the memories of the last two years like an amnesiac act of self-preservation that reset my mind back to the morning when I first walked into Bradley's office, when neither he nor I had any inkling about alternate realities or other selves or ghosts in the labyrinth and I was just a struggling game developer who spent more time at work than home with his family, all out of a vain, self-serving need to salvage the vestiges of a once-promising career.

I tie Cassie's bracelet on my wrist. "You seem to be taking this surprisingly well."

"Oh, inside I'm screaming," Reggie says. "But seriously, there are two of you in this room. How the hell else am I supposed to take it?"

"Fair point." I gesture at the computer above my head. "I screwed up, though. Most of the time I look out for the other Peters, partly to avoid a paradox, partly because I'm curious what their lives are like, but I got distracted."

"So you stalk yourself?" Reggie says. "That's kind of creepy."

"Are you saying you wouldn't do the same?"

"Before I got pregnant? Maybe."

I give her my best *Really?*

"OK, fine. Yes, of course I would have. Who wouldn't? It's the ultimate Google yourself." She looks down at her stomach.

"Now that Elijah's on his way, though, the last thing I want to do is intentionally endanger myself and risk him growing up without me."

The verbal barb stings whether she intended it to or not.

I haven't allowed myself to think of it in those terms, but the fact of the matter is, that's *exactly* what I've been doing. Putting myself at risk without really thinking about what might happen to Alana and the girls if I didn't come home.

The realization of my selfishness hits almost as hard as the migraine that smashed into my brain when I grabbed Peter 2.

"I'm such a fool," I say.

Reggie scoffs. "You're just realizing that now?"

This whole time I've been telling myself that working with Bradley is better than if I'd stayed at Omega Studios.

Truth is, it isn't.

Yes, I'm home more often than I was. I get to spend more time with the girls, with Alana. But I'm doing something much worse than spending too much time at work.

I'm risking my own life.

And for what? An adventure? The chance to do something that no one else in my reality can do?

Yes, I'm helping people. I could argue that I'm doing this for altruistic reasons. After all, I nearly became one of the ghosts in the labyrinth, but I got lucky. Bradley saved me. So now I'm paying that twist of fate forward, saving minds as often as I can.

But if I'm honest, that's not the real reason.

When we first discovered the Nexus, I spent countless hours exploring other realities. I saw multiple permutations of me, some with families, some without. I was given a glimpse into endless iterations of what my life would have been like if I'd taken a right instead of a left, talked to this person instead of that, arrived early instead of showing up late. Every single decision other Peters made resulted in a new branch of reality. It was like watching different versions of *The Family Man* with yours truly replacing Nicolas Cage.

I made sure to keep my distance – there was enough scientific and fictional literature about paradoxes that I didn't want to take the risk of causing my brain to break or reality to implode in on itself – but it was too intoxicating to stop altogether, even after I started helping the ghosts in the labyrinth return to their homes. In some ways, that gave me an even better excuse to take a peek at what some of the other Peters were up to. Some of it was depressing. Some of it clued me in on how to better myself.

In the end, though, much like any addiction, what started out as seemingly benign became an irresistible malignancy.

What I'm doing now is no different than when I was still at Omega Studios, busting my ass to recover from *Scorchfell*'s failure. Instead of wasting my life chasing after some false measure of success, I'm chasing what-ifs down rabbit holes simply because I can.

But I got sloppy.

Took it one quantum leap too far.

And now here I am, stuck at rock-bottom in another reality with no way home.

"Why didn't you stop me?" I ask. "The other day, I mean. You knew I wasn't your real Peter."

"I don't like what this thing's becoming. Deep Dive used to be all research and observation, pure science, that kind of shit, you know? Lately, though, it's gotten a lot more, I don't know, militant, I guess. Before you ran off you swore you could fix this, so Eddie and I shoved the other Peter into one of the tanks and spun O'Laughlin and Shepard a story about how he'd decided to go into Deep Dive to try and find James himself."

That sounds familiar.

"Speaking of. I hate to impose again, but I kind of–"

"Uh uh. No fucking way. I am done shoveling this shit."

"–need your help getting home." My cheek still pulsing from

her right hook, I grab the top of the desk and pull myself to my feet. "This is the last time, I swear. Please, Reggie. I just want to hug my kids. Imagine if you got separated from Elijah."

Reggie glares up at me, her hands cupping her stomach. "That's low, dude."

"I just need your ID card."

Her hand strays to the plastic sleeve hanging from the lanyard around her neck, eyes narrowing. "Why?"

I gesture at the computer behind me, where the screen still shows the last of the corrupted files I opened. "Something fried the Deep Dive software. I'm guessing my tether acted like some sort of weird electromagnetic paradox pulse. Whatever happened, the software is shot, but the hardware's still functioning."

I stare at the submersion pods, not really relishing climbing back inside one again. "Even if I could fix the files, I don't have time. I need to upload a new VR program before Shepard gets back. Otherwise, those submersion tanks are useless to me."

"That doesn't explain why you need my card."

"So I can get into that Peter's office. He has a computer, right? There's got to be some sort of dev kit buried in his hard drive from back when he was developing the battlefield simulation."

Digital never dies, it simply gets relegated to some dusty folder containing all the other missteps a developer makes.

"I still don't see how that's going to help you," Reggie said.

"If I can get a dev kit, I can upload it to this computer. As long as the simulation is running off Deep Dive's hardware, I should be able to find the Nexus."

Operative word being *should*. This was all theory. I had no idea if it would actually work. Not to mention I've never really used a submersion tank.

"What about those guys?" She gestures at the tanks.

I sigh. "Peter should be fine once I'm gone. As for James and the others, all I can do is promise to look for them in the

Nexus." Assuming that's where they still were. "But I can't guarantee anything. They didn't come back the first time, so they may be gone for good."

Reggie stares at me for several long seconds, then: "Fuck. Fine. Here." She lifts the lanyard over her head and flings it at me. "Do you even know where Peter's office is?"

"I was kind of hoping you'd show me."

"Bitch, I've already put my job on the line for you. I'm going to keep my butt planted right here. If anyone comes in while you're gone, I'll tell them I came down to discuss your MRI results but you threatened to punch me in the stomach if I didn't give you my card. What was I, a weak frightened pregnant woman, supposed to do?"

She bats her eyelashes all innocently at me.

"You're a very scary person," I say. "You know that, right? In every reality."

Reggie smirks. "Thank you. Peter's office is on sublevel two. Left out of the elevator, second right, fourth door down on the left. Just hurry the fuck up before my water breaks."

"I thought you said you were only at thirty-seven weeks?"

"Motherfucker, go!"

I go. Out the flywheel door, down the corridor, all the way to the elevator which, true to her word, Reggie has wedged open with a fire extinguisher.

I drag it inside, and as soon as the doors trundle shut mash my thumb into the right button. With protesting gears, the elevator rumbles to life, and up I rise. At sublevel two, the service lift lets out an off-key *ping*. The doors start to groan open but get stuck halfway. I don't bother to force them any wider. Instead, I lay the fire extinguisher between them to prevent someone else from summoning the elevator, then head left.

This level is more finished than the level with the submersion tanks. No exposed pipes, no dripping water, just boring beige walls interspersed with boring gunmetal doors.

I take the second right and start counting doors. When I reach the fourth, I hold Reggie's ID card up to the wall-mounted scanner. It emits a little chime, then the red light turns green and the lock on the door clicks open.

The office bears all the hallmarks of a game designer. Crumpled chip bags and soda cans in the trashcan, a half-full cup of coffee sporting tiny islands of green and white mold, random sketches of the battlefield simulation taped to the walls.

"OK," I mutter, sliding around the desk. "Let's see what you've got, other Peter."

I jostle the mouse, waking the computer, and fiddle with the bracelet while I wait for the dual screens to brighten. My gaze strays around the cluttered desktop, lands on a framed picture, and freeze.

It's of me and Alana. We're a couple years younger and standing on a stone bridge overlooking an ice-choked river. Behind us, red-tile rooftops carpeted in snow stretch as far as the eye can see, interrupted here and there by black tram lines and, higher up, the fairytale spires of old churches that sparkle and shine in the midmorning sunlight.

We've never been to Prague, but I'd recognize it anywhere. It's always been at the top of my bucket list of places to travel, but money's always been tight, game development has always come first until it didn't and then visiting alternate realities filled that void, the girls are still too young to appreciate it, and so on and so forth. Of course, the one time we mentioned it around them, Cassie and Evie immediately began researching the best pancake joints in Europe. By the time they were done they'd amassed a list of twenty-seven restaurants in fifteen countries.

This Peter and Alana, though, have obviously made the transatlantic trek. A spark of jealousy ignites, threatening to inundate my mind with its favorite game in the world.

What if.

What if this was my life?

You've seen plenty of other Peters' lives. Rich and poor, married to other people, with or without kids. You've never wanted to trade with them before. You always want to go home because it's your *home,* your *Alana,* your *kids. No other place, no other family, can fit the puzzle piece of you.*

What if I had the chance to travel like this Peter and Alana?

You literally travel between realities. Who needs Prague when you've got an infinity of dimensions? Not to mention you'd be forever indebted to the military-industrial complex.

What if I–

What if you stop acting like a selfish asshole and get the fuck home to the family that loves you, dickweed?

Right.

Touching my bracelet for luck, I focus on the computer. This Peter hasn't bothered to set up a password on the login screen. It's a minor break, almost too good to be true, but at this point I have no choice but to take it.

I scan the files littering the desktop. One of them is marked SF2. I don't have to open it to know what the initials stand for, to know that the file will be full of rambling thoughts: fragments of a plot, thin character sketches, ideas for puzzles and combat systems, everything that goes into designing a game.

Peter's making a sequel to *Scorchfell.*

Just like that, all the old emotions I thought were long dead and buried crawl out of their graves like a horde of hungry ghouls.

It's tempting. So damn tempting. But I've been down that road before. Spent those late interminable nights staring in bleary-eyed frustration at a fictional world that won't cooperate no matter how I attempt to manipulate it, all the while outside my studio the real world passes me by.

I leave the file unopened, its secrets forever in the dark.

Thankfully, it only takes a few minutes to dig up the

battlefield dev kit I'm looking for. It's an early version, barely above rudimentary in terms of graphics, but it will have to do.

X-ing out of the program, I rifle through Peter's desk drawers until I find a flash drive, then plug it into the USB port and download the dev kit.

That done, I pocket the drive, allow myself one last glance at the file and the photograph, and then take my leave of Peter's office.

I hurry down the corridors, shove the fire extinguisher back into the elevator, and press the button for sublevel four.

With a convulsive rattle and clank, the doors slide closed.

Down I go, the flash drive in my pocket, the first thrumming hints of adrenaline kick-starting my heart.

I'm going home.

The elevator reaches the bottom and shudders to a grinding, geriatric stop. Once again I leverage the fire extinguisher between the half-open doors, mostly for Reggie's benefit so that once I'm gone she's not stuck down here. It's a small courtesy for the huge favors she's done for me, but it's all I've got.

There's practically a bounce to my step as I hurry down the corridors toward the Deep Dive chamber. I'm nervous as hell about using the submersion tanks. So much could go wrong.

Baby steps, dude, I tell myself as I duck my head and step over the threshold. *First get the dev kit loaded, then worry about the–*

From my left comes the soft shuffle of boots. I twitch, start to pivot, but freeze as the cold, unwelcome kiss of a gun presses into my temple.

"This probably goes without saying," Finn proclaims, "but if you so much as even act like you're about to make a run for it, I will blow your fucking head off."

CHAPTER TWENTY-ONE

The lightness that carried me down the corridor vanishes in a debilitating rush. In its place is a world-weary numbness that seizes hold of my entire body, robbing me of momentum and hope.

"When I tell you to march, you march, got it?" Finn's close enough that his breath tickles my ear, propelling the sharp tang of mustard into my nose.

I don't move. Don't even nod. All I do is choke out a "Yes" as empty of life as death.

"Good. Then march."

Across the room I plod, my feet weighted down by the sheer enormity of my complete and utter fuck up, the pressure of Finn's gun against my back a constant threat urging me toward where Shepard stands behind a still-seated Reggie.

The anger radiating from Reggie's face is hot enough to melt the ice in my veins and replace it with a shame far greater than anything I felt in the wake of *Scorchfell's* fiasco.

I should have seen this coming. Hell, Reggie even bandied it as a possibility. *I'm pretty sure Shepard has a way down here that only she and O'Laughlin know about.* But in my haste, in all the turmoil of my recovered memories, I forgot.

And now we're about to pay the price for my negligence.

"Stop," Finn barks as we reach Shepard.

I stop.

Shepard regards me with a sad expression. "Oh, Peter. I really hoped it wouldn't come to this. You understand what's about to happen to Alana, right?"

"Fuck off, you lunatic."

Finn slaps me across the back of my head. "What'd I tell you about talking?"

Wincing as much from pain as humiliation, I dig my fingernails into my palms hard enough to bring tears to my eyes.

"Where you see lunacy," Shepard says, her eyebrows creasing in consternation, "I see pragmatism."

Her words call to mind the moment earlier, when she and Finn argued about the continued stasis of the soldiers in the submersion tanks – Shepard ostensibly unconcerned, Finn demonstrating that he might actually have a heart after all.

"So everyone is expendable," I say. "Alana, Doran, those people in the tank."

Shepard shrugs. "Casualties are an unfortunate part of war."

Behind me, Finn exhales sharply, a bull expelling steam.

"I didn't realize we were at war," I say.

Shepard nods as if I've just confirmed a long-held suspicion. "Which is why you lost, and I won."

"You've got a broken machine and another version of me, not to mention five of Finn's soldiers, trapped in suspension pods where they're all likely going to die. How exactly is that winning?"

Finn's feet shift. The gun digging into my lower back drifts sideways an inch.

"Because until you arrived, we didn't really know what we were dealing with." Shepard lays her hands on Reggie's shoulders and looks down at the pregnant woman. "Thank goodness I was able to remote access the camera and mic on the computer you were using, Peter, otherwise I would've never overheard your astounding confession to Dr Manasa about trips through realities and the endovascular stent that's implanted in your brain."

"I– I'm sorry, Shepard," Reggie quivers, shifting personalities like coats. "I just wanted to discuss some of the MRI findings with Mr Banuk, and then he threatened m– my b– baby and I…"

She sniffles, and I swear to God there are actual tears in her eyes.

Damn, she's good.

"Cut the crap, Regina. Edward told me all about how the two of you conspired to help this Peter escape."

Reggie stops sniveling. Her forehead furrows, tugging her eyebrows closer together. "That rat-bastard little bitch. You tell him the next time I see him I'm gonna put his head through one of his stupid fucking tinted windows."

Holy shit, the hatchback is Edward's? What a rat-bastard little bitch.

"I'm sure you and Edward will have plenty of time to chat once business returns to normal," Shepard says. "Until then, I need you to focus on the task at hand."

"Eat a dick, Shepard," Reggie says, shrugging off Shepard's hands as she scoots the chair away. "I'm through helping you."

Back arched, she presses out of the chair.

"Where exactly do you think you're going?" Shepard says.

"Home. I quit." With that, Reggie turns and trundles toward the door, mouthing a *Sorry* as she passes me.

I shake my head, *Don't worry about it.*

"Tell me," Shepard calls out. "Have you talked to your wife today?"

Reggie's steps slow, then stop altogether. One hand on her lower back, she spins slowly until she's once again facing Shepard. "What the fuck did you say?"

"I only ask because I'm sure she'd tell you that all this stress is unhealthy for the baby."

Reggie stomps toward Shepard, hands clenched, death in her eyes. "So help me fucking God, you bitch, if you've so much as laid one crooked eye on Kellye I will rip your intestines out through your belly button and strangle you with them."

The gun disappears from my back.

"Stand down, Dr Manasa," Finn barks, training the weapon on Reggie.

Reggie halts, throws a disbelieving stink-eye at Finn. "Seriously? I always knew you were an asshole, but shooting a pregnant woman seems a bit extreme even for you."

Her tone is sincere bravado, but I've been around her long enough now to see the worry creeping in.

Shepard raises her hands. "Everyone calm down. Finn, please stop waving your dick at women who aren't interested in it. Reggie, I have no intention of harming your wife. I simply asked about her to illustrate a point."

Finn mutters something under his breath but lowers his gun.

Reggie squares off to Shepard. "Unless your *point* involves pointing me to the exit and leaving Kellye the fuck alone, then I'm not interested."

"I need you to think this through."

Reggie sighs. "I'm tired, Shepard. Not only am I tired, my back hurts and I need to fucking pee. Unless you want me to drop a bladder bomb right here, for once in your messed up life just say what you goddamn mean."

"Fine. I'll leave you and your wife to your suburban life if you do one last job for me."

"And what's that?"

Shepard finally returns her attention to me. "Remove his stent."

I blink rapidly, not wanting to believe I heard Shepard correctly. The stent is my way home. My *only* way home. Without it, I might as well be playing Russian roulette with a six-shot revolver packing all its bullets.

"Come the fuck again?" Reggie says, her eyes flicking to me and back to Shepard in the space of one of my now-stuttering heartbeats.

"What was the term you used?" Shepard says to me. "Oh right, a tether. Why should we spend months, maybe years, developing one of our own when we have a working model right at our fingertips?"

"Ignoring for a moment just how royally messed up that is," Reggie says, crossing her arms and laying them atop her stomach, "I'm not a neurosurgeon."

"You went to medical school, right?"

"That's like saying people who know how to read can write a novel."

"Um." I clear my throat. "I don't suppose I get any say in this."

"You had your chance, Peter," Shepard says. "You blew it. So shut it. As for you, Reggie, didn't you study the brain?"

Reggie shakes her head. "There's a whole fucking world of difference between studying a brain and cutting into one. Not to mention, even if I knew what I was doing, which I don't, I'm pretty sure the procedure would kill him. Also, I'm not doing it."

Shepard sighs. "Then it appears we're at an impasse." She flicks a finger at Finn. "Take Peter back to his cell. Reggie and I have some things to sort out."

"Wait!" I move toward Shepard, but Finn grabs my arm and jabs the barrel of his gun into the side of my ribs.

"March, Banuk."

"Don't do this, Shepard." My mind grasps at paper straws, desperate for something to sway her. "I'll tell you everything I know about the stent. Just let Reggie go."

"I'm afraid it's too late for second chances, Mr Banuk."

"What about them?" I say, gesturing at the soldiers and Peter 2 floating in their tanks. "Don't they deserve a second chance?"

Finn's grip tightens on my arm. "What are you talking about, Banuk?"

"Ignore him," Shepard says. "He's talking nonsense."

I turn to face Finn and find myself staring at his gun. Gulping, I lift my eyes so I'm not sighting down the barrel and use my most persuasive voice – the one that charms Cassie at her most pig-headed – to say, "James and his team got lost on my side of the Nexus. When I found them, I tried to lead them out, but something happened. Maybe the door to this reality closed before they made it through. Regardless, I'm pretty sure they're still in the Nexus, trapped because of whatever corrupted the software. Let me upload a new simulation. I'll go into the Nexus, find them, and show them the way home."

"He's lying," Shepard says, more of an edge to her voice than I've heard before. "Sad as it is, their minds are gone. There's no use worrying about them anymore. Take him to his cell, Finn."

"No man left behind," I say to Finn. "Isn't that the Ranger motto?"

His expression darkens. I inch toward him. He doesn't lower the gun, but he also doesn't yell at me to stop moving.

"If you let Shepard take out my stent, you'll never get them back," I say softly. "They'll just be more casualties of her war. They don't deserve that."

"I said that's *enough*!" Shepard draws her pistol and aims it at my head. "One more word and Dr Manasa won't have to worry about accidentally killing you when she removes the stent."

Even though I'm as close to peeing my pants as Reggie is, I ignore Shepard and tap my head. "Once I visit a reality, the tether is forever synced to its location in the Nexus. Same with any minds I encounter. So long as they're in the Nexus, the tether can ping their location. I can bring them back."

"How do I know you're not bullshitting me?" Finn says.

"A better question is, why doesn't Shepard want you to let me try?"

"I warned you, Peter," Shepard says, cocking her gun.

"No!" Reggie shouts.

I clench my eyes shut, send out a silent *I'm sorry* to Cassie and Evie, and prepare to die.

But I don't die.

Instead of the supersonic crack of a bullet ripping through

the air, what I hear is, "What the hell are you doing, Finn?"

My eyes pop open, fully expecting to find Finn's gun still trained on me.

It's not.

It's trained on Shepard.

"Why won't you let him try?" Finn asks.

"Oh, for the love of... I told you, he's lying!" Shepard says, her gun still pointed at me. "Peter only wants access to the Nexus so that he can go home. He has no interest in saving your precious Rangers. Now lower your gun and take him to his goddamn cell!"

But Finn doesn't lower his gun. With steel in his eyes he says, "I've about had it with your fucking orders, Shepard. So here's what's going to happen. First–"

Quick as thought, Shepard turns her gun on Finn and pulls the trigger.

Finn lets out a startled grunt as the bullet punches into him with a sickening wet *squerch*, spinning him around so forcefully he trips over his own feet and tumbles to the ground. Warm blood splatters across my face. The retort reverberates around the room like thunder, the fading sound intercut by Reggie's strident cursing and the percussive thump of my heart trying its damnedest to smash its way through my ribcage.

"I cannot stand insubordination." Shepard turns her gun back on me. "Now, where were we? Ah yes. You were just about to–"

Unlike the single, concussive burst from Shepard's gun, Finn's assault rifle produces more of a furious *rat-a-tat-tat*. A dozen bullets scream past my face faster than the speed of sound, creating a brief, hot tailwind that lingers on my face like a summer heatwave.

Half the rounds slam into Shepard's chest, shredding shirt and skin and bone. The rest of the bullets strafe the wall screen behind her, turning it into a fractal pattern of shattered glass that showers onto the ground like a razor-edged ice storm.

Somehow, Shepard's still standing. She blinks. The gun

falls from her hand, clattering to the floor like a bone. Blood saturates the front of her shirt, spreading rapidly until every inch of fabric is stained red.

Slow as molasses, she tilts her head down, a confused look on her face like she's not entirely sure what's happened. She touches her shirt, lifts her bloodstained fingertips, blinks again once, twice, and then her eyes roll back in her head and she crumples lifelessly to the ground.

I stand there, stunned, my ears ringing with the rumbling echo of Finn's counteroffensive, the image of Shepard's dead body superimposed over the top of Doran's corpse.

It's Reggie who sets the world in motion again. "What. The. Actual. FUCK?"

She goes on like this for about ten seconds, only stopping when Finn, using his assault rifle as leverage, props himself up. His left arm dangles uselessly at his side, a tributary of red trickling down his ropy muscles.

"Shepard… was always… a shitty… shot," Finn rasps.

The gun slips, goes clacking across the floor as Finn goes down again. The back of his skull thuds against the ground, and he goes still.

Reggie and I exchange startled glances.

"Is he dead?" she whispers loudly enough to be heard all around the room.

"How should I know?"

"Psst. Finn, you dead?" He croaks out a low, protracted groan. "Close enough." Reggie looks at me again, her eyes widening. "Holy shit. Did that just happen?"

"I think so?"

"Should we be doing first aid on him or something?" Reggie asks.

Both of us regard the injured man. Finn defended me. OK, fine, he was defending his team, and Shepard did shoot him first, so really he was exacting revenge. Still. He might be borderline murderous, but he stepped up when it mattered.

That doesn't mean I trust him, but it does mean he doesn't deserve to bleed out while we watch.

Cursing silently, I take off my shirt and kneel beside him.

"Um, what are you doing?" Reggie says.

Gently as I can, I turn Finn over, searching for the bullet wound. "I need something to staunch the bleeding." There. A bloody, black-rimmed hole right below his left collarbone. Tugging Finn's shirt to the side, I wad up my own and press it to the burbling wound. "Do you have anything I can tie around him to keep this in place?"

"That asshole threatened to shoot me and Elijah and you want me to help him?"

"I thought you were a doctor. Aren't you supposed to try and save everyone no matter the circumstances?"

"Motherfuckers watch a couple of medical dramas on TV and think they know everything," Reggie mutters. She takes off her cardigan and, while I prop up Finn, ties it as best she can around his upper body. "I don't see an exit wound."

"Is that bad?"

"Eventually, yes."

"So what do we do?"

She pats Finn's head. "For now? Nothing. I'll get you home, and then I'll go for help."

"All right." Joints creaking, I stand and pull out the flash drive, examining it for damage. Thankfully, it seems to have survived.

"Were you lying?" Reggie asks. "About saving his team?"

I shake my head. "I'm not saying I can pull it off, but the theory's sound." I rub my face. "Were you lying? About not cracking open my skull?"

She dismisses my question with a shrug and a flippant wave but doesn't come out and directly answer me. I decide not to push it – at this point, I'm in no position to judge someone else for trying to keep a loved one safe.

"So what now?" she says.

I hold up the flash drive. "Now I upload this to Deep Dive."

"And that's going to work?"

"Guess we'll find out in a few minutes."

Moving stiffly, I make my way over to the computer. Somehow, despite the damage done to the wall screen above it, the computer survived Finn's barrage unscathed.

Into the USB port goes the flash drive. Opening it, I drag the dev kit file onto the desktop. A download meter appears. If it's right, I have ten minutes until the simulation's ready.

Ten minutes until I can go home.

Trying to keep my nerves under control, I walk up to the submersion tank where Peter 2 floats. Even now, part of my brain balks at the sight of this other me.

"That will never not be weird," Reggie says, joining me.

"How do these things work?" I ask.

"Do you want the egghead explanation or Deep Dive for Dummies?"

"What do you think?"

"Dummies it is." Reggie taps the side of the tank with a bright pink fingernail. "Basically, the goopy pink lemonade shit is a breathable, neuro-conductive fluid that supplies all the oxygen the body needs while amplifying your brain waves. Also it's great for your skin."

"How do you access the simulation?"

"Have you ever worn contacts?"

"No."

"Oh good, this ought to be fun. Follow me."

We circle Peter 2's tank and make our way toward the central cylinder, where, of all things, curtained changing stations stand behind each pod. Reggie picks up a small plastic container and pops it open, exposing a pair of contact lenses.

"Unlike your fancy-schmancy brain stent, we designed contacts with built-in Wi-Fi and neural interfaces. The signal from the simulation is beamed directly to your eyeballs."

I take the case from her. I'm not overly excited about stuffing shit into my eyes, but Bradley is going to love them.

"OK. So what now?"

"Now, you strip to your skivvies, put in the contacts, and crawl into the tank. I'll take care of the rest."

There's an awkward moment where I debate hugging Reggie. She saves me from embarrassing myself by clapping me on the shoulder.

"Give your girls a hug for me when you get home."

"I will. If you're still stuck on a middle name for Elijah, I hear Peter's pretty biblical."

"No offense, but two Peters in my life is more than enough."

"Fair enough."

She moves past me, then pauses. "Also, try to relax when you get in the tank. It's going to feel like you're drowning at first."

"Awesome."

She grins. "See you around, Peter."

"Thanks, Reggie. For everything."

Flapping her hand at me, she disappears around the submersion pods.

It takes me a couple of tries to get the contacts in. That done, I take off the rest of my clothes, leaving only my boxer-briefs in place, and climb the ladder attached to the pod next to Peter 2's. There's a round opening at the top.

"Here goes nothing," I mutter, and lower myself into the tank.

I stretch out on the bottom, doing my best to relax. Above me, the hatch seals, and pink goop begins to fill the pod.

It's warm, and has the consistency of snot.

As it rises up my body, I start to feel the first twinges of anxiety. Not only for myself, but for the mess I'm leaving behind.

"Reggie?"

Like in the MRI, her disembodied voice echoes from speakers embedded in the frame. "Chill, Pete. You're almost there."

"What happens when O'Laughlin finds out?"

She chuckles. "Funny story, after I saw you in his office I decided to hack into his personal files. Let's just say that shitstain will do whatever I tell him if he wants to keep his sorry ass out of jail. Now shut the fuck up and relax."

Her cyber sleuthing is one more useful bit of happenstance I don't have time to ponder, because the goop reaches the top of my shoulders, tickling the base of my neck.

"I don't think I can do this," I say, starting to sit up.

"If you don't, you'll never see your kids again."

Shit. Fuck. OK.

I lay back down. The goop is up to my chin now.

"Hey Pete?" Reggie says.

"Yeah?"

"Catch you on the flipside."

The trickle becomes a deluge, and before I know it the entire tank is full. My body goes weightless. I close my mouth instinctively.

Ten seconds pass.

Twenty.

Thirty.

My lungs are burning, desperate for air, but I keep my lips clamped shut, refusing to give in. You can't breathe liquid. You just can't.

Eyes wide, I slap at the sides of the tank.

Let me out, Reggie! Let me out, let me out, let me

"Out!" I gurgle, and in rushes the goop.

I swallow involuntarily. My throat fills with fluid. There's a faint taste of antiseptic. I feel my gorge rising even as I start to choke. I try to spit it out, but there's nowhere for it to go.

I start to drown.

My lungs catch fire. Adrenaline rockets through my nerves. My vision blurs. My chest is about to burst.

I'm sorry, girls. I tried, I really did.

But just when I think I can't take it anymore, something changes.

My throat stops seizing. The fire in my lungs abates, replaced by a cool sensation that spreads from my chest out to the rest of my body.

I'm not drowning.

I can breathe.

All around me, pink goop sparkles like unicorn vomit.

As amazing as this is, one thing's for certain: there is no way, no fucking way I'm recommending this method of immersion to Bradley.

I don't have much time to relax, though. A strange glimmer spreads across my vision. It takes me a second to understand it's the contacts receiving the wireless signal.

Taking a deep, calming breath of liquid oxygen, I slowly flip myself over until I'm facing the bottom of the tank. A weak electric prickle crawls across my skull.

I have about a second to wonder when the simulation will fully kick in before the world implodes.

CHAPTER TWENTY-TWO

My brain is matter dragged into the heart of a black hole, crushed and mangled and spun about like it's been shoved inside a galaxy-sized garbage disposal. Down the pipe goes my mind, racing this way and that until without warning it's spit out into open air.

Gasping, I bend over and prop my hands on my knees. That was nothing like Bradley's headset. That was more like having my brain sucked out through my nose and crammed into someone else's much smaller skull.

I am decidedly not a fan.

I give myself another couple of seconds to let my mind settle, then stand up and take in my surroundings.

I'm standing in the middle of a wide, square-shaped pavilion. Tall, bright white windowless buildings line every side. Darkened street entrances lurk in the angles. Beneath my feet are smooth flagstones as white as the buildings. Above me, a gray sky stretches in every direction.

It's all rendered well enough, if a little *Nier: Automata* for my tastes, but the texture of everything is slightly off – if I squint just right I can almost make out individual pixels, and the edges of everything look almost fuzzy, like they've been etched by pencils.

"You son of a bitch," a familiar voice growls from behind me.

I whirl around, fists up and ready after the lesson Reggie's sucker-punch taught me, and come face to face with myself.

Oh shit.

Anger flushing his cheeks, Peter 2 advances toward me. "What the hell did you do to me?"

I open my fists, palms placating even as I back up several steps. "Whoa. Relax, buddy. Remember what happened last time?"

I don't know if the same rules of paradox apply in a virtual world, but I'm none too eager to find out. I've had my fill of memory loss, thank you very much.

"Oh, I remember." Peter 2 keeps moving toward me. "You attacked me."

"Um, I think you've got that backwards." I retreat across another section of flagstones. "I'm pretty sure you're the one who came at me. Also, dude. Stop. Stop!"

My voice bounces off the white-walled buildings like a chorus of me yelling at myself. It's disconcerting enough to halt Peter 2's advance.

He frowns, finally looks around. Recognition dawns.

"This is one of my dev kits."

"Bingo."

"How?"

"Your *Metal Gear Solid* knockoff broke. I had to upload a new one."

"Fuck you, knockoff." He scratches his face. "Wait, so I'm in a submersion pod?"

"Yeah, about that. I'd highly recommend going back to a headset, because that breathable liquid shit sucks."

"Why am I in a submersion pod?" Peter 2 kicks the flagstone beneath him with his heel. "Jesus, I haven't looked at this in over a year."

"Look," I say, glancing toward the corner of the pavilion nearest me. "I realize this whole thing is weird bordering on downright ludicrous, but can we walk and talk? I really need to find a door."

Peter 2 scrunches his face, then his eyes go game disc-wide. In a quiet voice he asks, "You really are another me, aren't you?"

"I really am."

The clop of our footsteps echoes all around us as we head for the exit, our strides evenly matched. While we walk I explain the past few days as best I can, starting with a condensed version of why I showed up in his reality, what happened when we met, and the days I spent questioning my mental health until I met Doran.

"They really shot him?" Peter 2 says as we duck into the shadowy passageway.

"Don't worry," I say. "Shepard and Finn got theirs."

Buildings loom on either side of us, their walls flat and featureless. By the time we reach the end of the passageway I've brought Peter 2 up to speed but haven't spotted a single door.

We step out into the corner of another pavilion that's an exact replica of the one we just left. Bright white windowless walls span the length and breadth of the square. My chest constricts as panic's greedy claws begin to scratch at the underside of my ribs.

"Let me get this straight," Peter 2 says, crossing his arms. "Not only did you pretend to be me for nearly a week, you also almost got my wife killed? And yet you're telling me everything is fine?"

"In my defense, I didn't completely know that I wasn't you. Not at first, at least. And hey, Alana's safe now." *I think.* "Look, not to be insensitive, but where are all the doors?"

"Hey!" He snaps his fingers in my face. "You can't just drop that kind of bombshell on me."

Sighing, I devote my full attention to my doppelgänger. "I get that this is a lot to take in, honestly I do. But the longer this takes, the more likely it is that O'Laughlin's going to start wondering where Shepard and Finn disappeared to. If I'm not gone by then, I'm never getting home. Whereas all you need to do is log off and you've got your life back."

Granted, his married life is in turmoil, he's most definitely lost his job, and there's a very good chance O'Laughlin will blame him for everything that's happened. Still, I'm the one who has to find the Nexus. But without a door I'm screwed. In theory I could log off and upload another simulation, but again, there's no time.

I blink back to virtual reality to find that Peter's giving me a funny look.

"What?" I say.

"It's not just me, right? This is the most surreal thing you've ever experienced."

"Talking to you?"

He nods.

"Yeah, it's pretty much the Picasso of buddy comedies, only without any of the humor."

We regard each other like identical twins meeting for the first time.

"What's it like?" he says. "Having kids? Alana and I have talked about it a few times but we're both so busy we decided it wouldn't be fair."

The question catches me totally off guard. "Honestly? It's the most frustrating, wonderful, stressful, mind-boggling thing I've ever experienced." I choke down the lump in my throat. "Can I ask you a question?"

"Shoot."

"What was it like, winning Game of the Year for *Scorchfell*?"

"Honestly? The most frustrating, wonderful, stressful, mind-boggling thing I've ever experienced." He grins. "By the time it released I'd put on, like, thirty pounds and been spending so much time at work that Alana was barely speaking to me. I'm happy I pulled it off, but glad it's over."

Bittersweet pangs roil through me. I obviously don't know if he approached designing the game the same as I did, but the fact that he succeeded where I failed is still, after so much time, incredibly hard to swallow. But this isn't the time for maudlin reminiscing.

"So working for the government is your way of relaxing?"

"Until you showed up, yeah."

"Look," I say. "Finn's a prick, but I promised him I'd try to find his team. But I can't do that without a door, just like I can't get home without a door. So for the love of God, will you please tell me how to find one?"

"I can't."

"Why not?"

"Because there aren't any."

He might as well have kicked my legs out from underneath me. "What do you mean, there aren't any?"

"This was an early demo. I was just getting a feel for the basic geography and architecture. I couldn't decide on what kind of doors to use, plus you know how much of a bitch they are to get right, so I skipped them." He looks around at the bright monochromatic buildings. "Honestly, I might have been drunk when I designed this. I scrapped the design when Shepard told me they wanted something less futuristic, something more in line with modern urban settings, so I..."

He keeps talking, but I've already stopped listening.

So I skipped them.

There aren't doors.

Without a door I can't reach the Nexus.

If I can't reach the Nexus, I can't go home.

In theory I could log off and search Peter 2's computer for another simulation, but then I'm not only dealing with the risk of O'Laughlin coming to his senses and checking on us, I'll also be dealing with the Peter paradox. Two of us in real life, each with his own incompatible realities. My memories on the chopping block yet again. The only reason I can think of that things haven't gone to shit right now is because we're in a virtual environment where, in theory, anything is possible so long as you think to design it, which is why virtual reality is the natural stepping stone between the fixed real world and the quantum infinity of the Nexus.

Problem is, Peter 2 designed this place with practically nothing. I mean, I get it. That's what you do when you embark on a new project: scratch out the bare bones, add some flesh here, some hair there, and then delete the whole thing in a fit of mania because you're convinced nothing you ever do will be good enough. Then you start over.

Except, nothing is ever really deleted, is it? This dev kit simulation wasn't. It was just dumped into the bowels of Peter 2's computer. Developers are notorious for never throwing anything away. Sometimes you know you're on the wrong path, but you want to test out some feature or another anyway. Other times, you'll realize, way down the road, that what you thought was a wrong turn was actually your subconscious tossing out a totally workable idea your brain wasn't fully ready to deal with yet.

So you save it, tucking it away for posterity or potential later use inside a debug room.

A room hidden somewhere within a game.

A room whose location is only known by the game developer, locked behind a door that requires a specific key code in order to access it.

I stab a finger at Peter 2, interrupting him. "Where's the debug room?"

"Why do you want—"

Understanding dawns.

"It's got a door, right? Some sort of entrance?"

He scrunches his face. "Yeah, but it's been so long since I messed around with this place I'm not sure I remember the code to get past the lock."

"Try. And while you try, walk."

So we walk. Through darkened passageways, across empty ice-white courtyards, beneath a gunmetal sky. Each pavilion we enter looks the same as those we've left behind, a lifeless city of neo-noir monotony.

All the while Peter 2 mumbles to himself, second-guessing and backtracking and pausing at random and spinning in place like an excited compass needle unable to locate true north.

The longer we walk, the more frustrated I become, until, as we trudge into yet another pavilion, I finally lose it.

"Jesus Christ, how many of these fucking places did you copy and paste in here?"

He ignores me, turning a slow one-eighty as he taps the air with his finger.

"Hey!" I grab his arm, jerking him around so that we're face to face. "I'm talking to you."

Scowling, he wrenches free of my grasp. "And I'm trying to count, shithead, so leave off!"

He goes back to tapping the air while I stew and consider throttling him. I've never been much of a scrapper, but I'm ninety-five percent certain I can take myself.

Right when I decide I can't take it anymore, he pivots to the left, points at the passageway we just exited, and says, "We went one too far."

Off he goes, back down the featureless alley.

I never used to understand what Alana meant when she said talking to me was like talking to her own ass, but I do now.

Grumbling to myself, I follow.

When I catch up to Peter 2, he's busy smacking at a wall on the side of a building that looks exactly like every other damn wall we've passed.

"It's got to be here somewh… Ahah!"

Pressing both hands to the wall, he puts all his weight behind himself and pushes.

To my surprise, the outline of a door appears. In the center, where a faceplate would be, is a glossy black rectangle. Peter 2 taps it, and a command prompt appears with a keypad beneath it.

"Please tell me you remember the password."

"Shh." He bites his lower lip, fingertip hovering above the

screen, then inputs a string of numbers and letters at least twenty-four characters long. The panel flashes, and the outline of the door solidifies into an actual door replete with an old-school doorknob. Grinning, he sweeps his arm at the entrance to the debug room. "Et voilà."

"Lucky guess," I say, unable to stop myself from grinning back at him.

But as we each regard the other, our smiles slip.

"So this is it, huh?" He rubs the back of his neck.

"I know I already apologized," I say, forcibly resisting the urge to rub my own neck, "but I really am sorry about all the shit that's happened."

He shrugs. "Too bad about the whole paradox thing. It might've been cool to actually hang out for a while."

"It's probably better this way. I hope your Alana's OK. Tell her I said thanks for everything."

"I will. I hope you find your kids."

"Me too."

We stare at each other, two too many, then nod in unison.

"Safe travels," he says.

"You too."

Peter 2 looks up at the gunmetal sky. "All right, Reggie. I'm ready."

IT'S ABOUT GODDAMN TIME, a voice from the heavens booms. YOUR WEIRD LITTLE BROMANCE WAS STARTING TO GET ON MY LAST DAMN NERVE.

I let out a startled curse, jumping two feet into the air. I'd totally forgotten Reggie was watching from the computer.

Her laughter booms across the sky like peals of thunder. Peter 2 grins, shimmers, and then disappears.

I smile at the sky. "Thanks for everything, Reggie. Have fun being a mom. You're going to be great at it."

GET GOING, LOSER. MAKE SURE YOU HUG THE CRAP OUT OF THOSE GIRLS FOR ME.

"Will do."

I face the door, take a deep breath of virtual air, and channel all my disparate emotions into one singular sentiment.

Need.

In the end, that's what it's all about. The first time I entered the Nexus was an accident, a moment of technological happenstance combined with a fair amount of mental distress. It wasn't until the second time, when I stood before the open door in the labyrinth and stared in confusion not at the silvery sea of infinity but at a room full of dust and cobwebs, that I realized how much desire played into it.

Deep Dive will get you to the brink, but it's your own mind, your own need, that allows you to make the transition.

I *need* to see Cassie and Evie.

I *need* to see Alana.

I *need* to go home.

With their faces firmly in my mind, I grasp the knob, twist, and open the door onto a sea of silver light.

CHAPTER TWENTY-THREE

I lie still, willing my heart to slow. Even though I can feel the firm seal of the headset and the comforting stiffness of the ergonomic chair cradling my body, I can't quite bring myself to open my eyes for fear that something's gone wrong, that I've wound up in the wrong reality.

But then a sound reaches my good ear, and I smile.

Arms shaking, I reach up and gingerly take off the headset.

Soft fluorescent lighting illuminates the Reality Room.

I expel an exhausted sigh of relief, place the headset at my side, and sit up.

I'm back.

Across the room, Bradley is horizontal on the couch, snoring loudly. A full pitcher of water and a half-empty bottle of Lagavulin 25 sit next to an empty heavy-bottomed glass on the coffee table in front of the couch.

Shaking my head, I lower my legs, set my feet on the floor, and stand.

It's like stepping off a ship after half a year at sea. My knees wobble, my body tilts precariously. Stifling a curse, I grab hold of the chair to steady myself.

Bradley snorts, smacks his lips, briefly opens his eyes, and then shuts them again.

One, two, three…

Bradley's eyes slam open. He shoots upright, almost kicking over the bottle of scotch as he lurches to his feet only to plop back down on the couch.

"Peter?" He blinks rapidly as if not quite trusting what he's seeing, which, considering the amount of scotch missing from the bottle, makes sense. "Is that you?"

"Unless you convinced some other fool to investigate alternate realities, yeah, it's me."

"Fucking A, what time is it?" He picks up his phone, wincing at the light emanating from its screen. "Jesus, it's after two am. What took you so long?"

"It's nice to see you, too," I say, pushing off the chair. "Is it really that late?"

What I didn't tell Shepard and the rest of them was that not only is the tether synced to my reality spatially, it's also synced temporally. Meaning when I arrive home, hardly any time has passed in my reality. At least, that's what's supposed to happen.

"Guess the tether's glitching. I'll look at it in the morning." Bradley leans forward, pours himself a finger of scotch, and slugs it back, then pours another and offers it to me. "So how was it?"

I shake my head at the scotch. "The other reality?"

"No, Tsushima." He tosses back the booze. "Yes, the other reality."

"That," I say, "is a very, very long story that will have to wait until tomorrow. Did Alana call?"

"A couple hours ago."

"What'd you tell her?"

"That you were in the lab and would call when you could."

I make a point of not pulling complete all-nighters, but Bradley and I have spent enough late nights diving into alternate branches of realities that two am isn't an unreasonable hour.

At least, that's what I'd been telling myself before this latest dive. Before I realized I'd started falling back into my *Scorchfell* ways, when I spent more time at work than I did at home.

I glance at the Deep Dive headset. "Don't hate me for saying this, but I think I need a break."

Bradley leans back and throws his arms across the back of the couch. "No shit. Really? I've only been telling you that for months now."

"You're OK with it?"

"Dude, I have an entire tech empire to run. The other realities aren't going anywhere. Take a vacation, get some rest. Hang out with your family. Deep Dive will be here when you're ready."

The way he's all encouraging makes me think that he, despite his other business concerns, has no intention of taking a similar break.

"Just be careful, all right?"

Bradley frowns. "Seriously, though. You look more like hell than you usually do. What happened over there? Did you find the ghosts?"

Strangely, I didn't have to search for Finn's missing team. The moment I strode through the door, their minds swarmed past me in a rush of nebulous shadows. I waited until the last of them were through and their virtual avatars were on solid ground, then shut the door in front of their mystified faces. The simulation disappeared. In its place was an infinity of realities. I floated in the silver sea, giving myself a moment to reacclimatize, then activated the tether. Immediately, the black islands of other worlds whirled around me in a furious maelstrom, dragging me toward its center where a single pulsing sphere awaited.

"The ghosts are good." I raise my hand to forestall any further questions. "Like I said, we can talk tomorrow. I need to go home."

"Fair enough." Bradley pours another finger, pauses, then fills half the glass. "Have a good night, Peter."

"You too, buddy."

Bradley raises his glass as I walk past him, leaving the Reality Room behind for what might be the final time. I know it will be hard to resist, but if the past four days have taught me anything, it's that some things are far more important than an infinity of what ifs.

My truck's right where I parked it. Before I crank the ignition, I send a quick text to Alana.

On my way. Sorry it's so late.

I don't expect an answer, but a second later my phone vibrates. I glance down and see a single heart-shaped emoji.

My own heart fit to burst, I put the truck in gear, pull out of the parking lot, and leave Boundless behind.

The porch light winks on when I pull into the driveway.

I sit there, the truck idling, and utter a silent prayer that I'm not about to experience a repeat of the last time I walked into my house.

Taking a deep, steadying breath that only speeds up my already racing pulse, I turn off the truck and climb out.

The air is humid and smells sweetly of azaleas and freshly cut grass. Somewhere nearby, a nightjar trills. High above, the full moon casts its silvery light on my front door.

Palms sweaty, I step into my house, close the door behind me, and take a moment to let my eyes adjust to the shadowy interior. When I can see, I tiptoe into the living room, bracing myself for what I'll find.

On the floor in front of the fireplace, a group of Barbie dolls sits around a table strewn with tiny tea cups and saucers. A dog-eared copy of *The Lion, the Witch and the Wardrobe* lies on the coffee table.

My throat tightens. My eyes threaten tears. It's all I can do not to charge up the stairs and wake everyone up, but I force myself to take each step one at a time, avoiding the creaky one at the last second.

To the right, the sound of Alana's white noise app rumbles gently from our bedroom.

To the left, the glow from Evie's galaxy globe fills the hallway, painting her sister's door with a slowly whirling sky of green and purple stars.

The tears come freely now, trickling down my cheeks as I make my way along the hall. Despite all the evidence to the contrary, part of my brain is still convinced I'm going to walk into Evie's bedroom and discover her gone.

But that's not what happens.

What happens is, I reach her doorway, steady myself against the doorframe, and look inside.

There, asleep in her bed with the covers kicked down around her feet, is Evie.

The room goes prismatic as a deluge of tears overwhelms my eyes. Tiptoeing in, I pull the sheets up to her chin, then lean down and plant a trembling kiss on her forehead.

"I love you," I whisper.

Evie smiles, mumbles something indecipherable, and rolls onto her side.

Kissing her again, I tuck her stuffed elephant Peanut into her arms, then tiptoe back out of the room.

As soon as I reach the hallway, I burst into tears.

Sobbing into my hands, I slide down the wall, my entire body shaking.

There's a quiet click across from me, the sound of a door gliding open, and then:

"Daddy?"

The sound of Cassie's concerned, groggy voice is the most amazing thing I've ever heard.

Wiping my nose, I lift my head, smile, and open my arms.

Still half-asleep, Cassie topples into my lap, snuggling in as I hug her with all my might.

"Are you OK?" she whispers.

I almost break down again. "I'm fine, baby girl. It's just been a long day is all."

"We missed you," she says, drawing her spindly knees to her chest.

"I missed you, too."

"Evie got in trouble."

"Did she?"

"Uh huh. She threw an olive at me. Mommy was mad."

I laugh. "I bet she was."

Cassie tilts her head, looking up at me. "Do you have to work tomorrow?"

"No, sweetie. I'm going to stay home."

"Good." She glances into Evie's room, then whispers as though we're conspiring against her sister: "Will you make chocolate crepes for breakfast?"

I snort-cry as I press my lips to her forehead. "Absolutely."

"Thanks. I love you, Daddy."

"I love you too, Cass."

She snuggles closer, lays her head against my chest, and I hug her tighter, inhaling the coconut scent of her hair.

I should tuck her back into bed, but I make no move to get up. Not yet. It's too soon. I'm afraid if I let her go, she'll disappear forever.

So I sit there, Cassie clasped in my arms, Evie snoring gently in her bed, and watch the stars from the nightlight dance silently across the wall while two words repeat themselves over and over in my mind.

I'm home.

I'm home.

I'm home.

ACKNOWLEDGMENTS

Deep Dive would not be the book it is, and I would not be the writer I am, without the support of so many amazing people.

Huge thanks go out to the entire team at Angry Robot for making my publishing dreams come true, especially Eleanor Teasdale, for being the best editor a debut author could ask for; Kieryn Tyler, for designing an absolutely stunning cover; Paul Simpson, for indispensable copy edits; Amanda Rutter, for masterful proofreading chops; Gemma Creffield, for the email that marks the moment my writing life changed; and Sam McQueen, for all the patient behind-the-scenes help and for feeling as sad as I do that whoa is not spelled woah.

I am forever indebted to David Dunton, agent extraordinaire, for taking a chance on an excited, frazzled writer. Your insight and advice have been utterly invaluable, and I cannot wait to see where our partnership takes us next.

Outside of words, if there's one thing a writer needs above all else, it's other writers who will cheer your successes and offer to burn down the world anytime you find bad news in your inbox. Eva Gibson and Jill Corddry are experts at both. You two have sat next to me on this rollercoaster for longer than anyone else. You've read every book I've ever written and made each one better than I ever could've managed on my own. There is no way I would've gotten this far without you.

Ditto goes for Kristin Wright, Mary Ann Marlowe, Elly Blake, Jen Marie Hawkins, Kelly Siskind, and Summer Spence, who have been my daily dose of sanity for over seven years now. I would've quit long ago if it hadn't been for your sympathetic shoulders and side-splitting snark, and I thank the writing gods every day that Pitch Wars brought you into my life.

Deep Dive isn't the first novel I've written, and it certainly won't be the last. No matter the book, though, a writer needs readers who can point out what does and doesn't work. Eternal thanks go out to Meredith Tate (whose presence in my time zone is greatly missed), Marisa Hopkins (whose presence in a time zone adjacent to mine is greatly appreciated), Donna Muñoz, Julie Abe, Meredith McCardle, and Julie Hutchings for supremely spot-on critiques.

Finally, while *Deep Dive* is fiction, the struggle Peter faces to balance his professional creative life with his personal family life is very, very real. I cannot begin to express how much it means to me that my wife, Liz, and my daughters, Charlotte and Caroline, love me enough to let me disappear into my words for months at a time. The three of you anchor me to the reality of us no matter how far I drift into my imaginary worlds. I hope I've made you proud, not only as a writer but, most importantly, as a husband and a father.

Fancy some more thrilling science fantasy? Check out Swashbucklers by Dan Hanks

Read the first few chapters here

PROLOGUE

Gerald heard the whispering on the baby monitor five minutes before he died.

He dismissed it instantly, of course, and kept drinking as he watched the evening match. The little flash of red, blinking from the box on the shelf, was just another twinkling light in their very festive living room. Barely even noticeable against the glowing Christmas tree and all the flickering fake candles. It was probably picking up interference from another wireless contraption on their street, the signals cutting into the sweet sound of his daughter gurgling happily to herself as she fought sleep.

Certainly nothing to get him off the couch to check on her. Even if the sound had made his heart race that little bit faster and his hands grow clammy.

Then it happened again.

"Shhhhhhh."

The light seemed to flash more urgently, as if in warning.

He frowned and hit mute on the remote. The football continued silently, as he fixed his gaze at the bookshelf where the monitor sat, waiting for confirmation he'd heard what he'd heard. For a second, nothing happened.

Then the red light flashed permanently.

"...tubby little..."

Not only had something just shushed in his daughter's room, but the musical mobile over her cot had started playing.

The mobile his daughter definitely couldn't reach to turn on.

"...stuffed with fluff..."

The cushions fell aside as he leapt up and scrambled up the stairs, beer spilling all over the carpet, leaving a trail his wife would later find when she returned from Pilates to discover his eviscerated corpse.

"Sarah!" he cried out, despite knowing full well his four-month old wasn't going to respond to him. "Sarah, don't worry, I'm–"

He never got to finish his sentence.

Sliding into the nursery, he ran face first into a wall of fur. Half-cursing, half-spitting it out, he collapsed backwards and landed on his bum, as the life-sized toy he had bought only last week loomed over him. The soft toy of Sarah's favourite children's TV show.

"Let's see what they stuffed *you* with," Daphne the Disco Duck squawked.

He screamed as the thing fell on him and ate.

In the cot on the other side of the room, his daughter gurgled like her daddy was now doing, before she finally drifted off to sleep as the blood rained down around her and the mobile continued to spin and play.

CHAPTER ONE
Sequels

Dark Peak hadn't changed in thirty-two years.

Cisco wasn't sure if he had expected that. Ever since deciding to come back, he'd been playing the scene over and over in his mind, like repeats of his favourite show.

Most of the time the fantasy consisted of a slow summer drive through the high street. He'd stare with distaste at the new buildings where old stone terraces had once stood. He'd shake his head at the high rises going up in what used to be little parks or fields around the town. He'd probably frown as he saw the bustling new bars vomiting up tables and chairs into what had once been quiet countryside streets.

Of course, like a goddamn pro he would take all this newness in and say nothing. He'd channel his unflappable weird-kid-returns-home-as-awesome-adult *Grosse Point Blank* composure, pull up to the pavement and get out. Heads would turn his way as he slammed the door. Childhood friends who'd never left the town would recognise him and run over and slap his shoulder as though he was some kind of soothing ointment to their tired lives. Old jokes about what had once happened… well, they'd be long forgotten, surely? There would be nothing but respect.

"Cisco Collins!" they'd say. "Great to see you again, mate. Welcome home!"

Maybe they'd go for a beer and catch up. Or he'd just give them a cursory nod and slip on past as enigmatically as possible.

Of course, that wasn't how things ever went in reality. And in this reality especially, it was clear the timeline's dial had been knocked from "pretty normal" to "perpetually ridiculous". Which meant he should actually have been relieved his wintry return to Dark Peak was initially met with no more fanfare than the harsh December squall whipping around the town square and a swaying Christmas tree that was spooking the pigeons.

In fact, as he stood there, back in the location where everything had changed – the site of the infamous 1989 Halloween gas leak that had left most Dark Peak residents seeing monsters and several people dead – he felt a strange sense of happy nostalgia warm his insides.

Because after all this time, nothing had changed.

Same old buildings.

Same old people.

It was almost like stepping back into a cosy memory or returning to a treasured world in a sequel.

Except that sequels were never quite as good, were they?

"Oi, Gasbuster!" a balding man in a bright yellow puffer jacket yelled across the gardens, as his three screaming kids chased each other around the grass and muddy flowerbeds. Cisco shouldn't have turned at the name. But there's a sadistic instinct in humans that makes you do things when you know you really shouldn't, and he had already locked eyes with the man before he realised his mistake. The man grinned like a fisherman who'd just hooked his first idiot of the day. "Yeahhhhh, I knew it was you! The kid from the gas leak!"

Cisco swore under his breath and let the wind carry it away, as the man grabbed his eldest daughter and pointed as if Cisco was some kind of festive attraction.

"Look, honey, that's the bloke from the bedtime stories your mum tells you. The gas leak boy. I told you he was real!"

The girl laughed joyously and waved to him. Grim-faced, Cisco waved back.

A hand tugged at his jeans.

"Who's that?"

Cisco reached down and gently squeezed the mittened hand of his eight year-old son. "I've no idea, George."

The boy's flushed face, squashed in between his knitted beanie and the scarf around his neck, tilted up at him with a puzzled expression. "Then why are you waving to her?"

"That's what you do when kids wave to you. It's the law."

"There's a law about waving?"

"Uh-huh, a parent's law." Why did he often find himself lying to his son to get out of answering a perfectly reasonable question. *I don't have the energy for the technicalities of a discussion that could spawn a thousand more questions and last forever*, came the well-worn reply from his brain. "When you become a parent, George, you absolutely have to wave when kids wave at you. I would expect the same if you did it to someone else."

Of course, George instantly began waving to the man. Cisco thought he recognised him now. He fumbled in the closet of his mind where he'd shoved a lot of past trauma. Dean someone?

Most-likely-Dean laughed again nastily and didn't bother waving back to George.

"OK, not everyone knows the law, I guess," Cisco said, gently putting the boy's hand down.

George seemed to mull that over for a moment. "What did he mean by Gasbuster? Shouldn't it be Ghostbuster?"

"It should have been," Cisco admitted, unable to help the regret seep into his voice. "But that's not what everyone ended up remembering."

"Why?"

"Oh, it's a long story."

"But why?"

Cisco sighed, not fancying that conversation right now. He

looked around for a distraction. Distraction and lying, that was his parenting style.

There was a little café on the north side of the square, its windows finely decorated with colourful festive scenes and golden angels and falling snow. A cosy, beckoning light shone through the steamy glass. The Pepino Deli sign above the door had been draped with colourful lights that were blinking on and off.

"Need a wee?" Cisco asked, pulling George in that direction.

His son resisted. "No, I'm OK."

"How about a cake?"

"Let's go faster!" George said, leading the way.

They headed up the uneven flagstones, trying not to slip on the wet brown leaves and fighting the sleet that was now beginning. Cisco could hear the name again, "Gasbuster!", carried through the squall, but couldn't tell if it was the man or his own brain gleefully playing tricks on him.

The trouble wasn't so much the name, he reminded himself, following quickly after George who was now suggesting that maybe he'd like a hot chocolate with his cake. Yes, living with the humiliating moniker had been annoying in the aftermath of that particular Halloween night. Having it haunt him like a particularly irritating poltergeist. Hearing it in whispers behind him in class or in assembly or in the dinner line. At least until he'd been able to convince both his mothers that maybe, *maybe*, they might want a change of scenery for his final year at school? A change that was as far away from his childhood home as possible.

But, really, the name was just that. A name. He'd been called far worse.

What really bugged him about the whole thing was that the name implied his heroic efforts had been for nothing. It suggested something very mundane had actually happened back then. That the monsters everyone remembered for weeks and years afterwards were some kind of mass hallucination brought on by some ridiculously implausible gas leak – when they had been very real indeed.

Real enough he could still feel the manifestations pouring through him, after his body had been turned into a gateway to hell. Real enough to have driven him out of his beloved hometown so he could attempt to live a half-decent life away from the whispers and stares and rumours. Real enough to have given him scars on multiple levels.

All those classic 80s movies had led him wrong for so long. Saving the day wasn't always met with a happy, heroic ending for the teenagers, before the credits played out to some great power ballad. Sometimes the grown-ups just didn't understand what sacrifices you'd made to protect everyone from the supernatural. Sometimes it was easier for them to make up some more plausible explanation for what had happened, blame *you* for the chaos, and then leave you to deal with the fallout. And even though you waited for those damn credits to roll, just to end your suffering, you were left with the horrible realisation that they never roll in real life. The treadmill just keeps going. And if it's smeared with crap you don't get a chance to step off for a moment and clean everything up… you just have to keep running, getting messier and messier, until you are only age and shit, and there is nothing else left of the person you used to be.

"Happy Christmas!" the hand-painted sign on the café door read, not picking up on his mood at all.

Cisco let his son lead him in. The boy saw the cakes on the counter and slipped out of his grasp, leaving him alone to search for a table.

At which point he saw her.

A blast from the past. His very best friend in forever. Until he'd left her behind like he'd left everyone else.

Doc saw him. Her eyes widened. And not for the first time in his life, Cisco wondered if adulthood would be easier all round if the hell portal he had once helped close would open up again and swallow him whole.

I should have told her I was coming back, he thought, far too late.

"Cisco?" Doc said, removing her headphones and sitting back from her table as if needing more room to take in the unkempt mess he knew he'd become. "Now there's a sight I didn't expect to see blowing in on the winter winds like some scruffy, middle-aged Mary Poppins."

Maybe it was the instant warmth of the café after being outside in the winter chill, but Cisco's cheeks were burning.

"Hey, Doc," he mumbled.

Dorothy Constance Forbes, Doc to her friends, stood up and walked between the tables, continuing to look him up and down, still wearing that enigmatic smile of hers.

"I know in these situations it's usually polite to lie and say you haven't aged a bit, but man, you *got old*!" She touched his hair. "Look at those streaks of grey. And some kind of beard, too. I have to say it suits you. The age *and* the beard."

Standing face to face for the first time in a long time, he realised with secret joy that just like the town Doc had held onto all these years, she hadn't changed much at all either. Still an inch taller than him, vibrant dark curls framing her glowing black skin and mischievous eyes. And there was still a presence to her, an energy that only a few people you ever meet in life have.

They leaned in awkwardly for a hug, before he was immediately pushed back by the point of her finger as she jabbed it in his chest.

"Now, what the hell are you doing here?"

"Huh?"

"We haven't talked in forever, haven't seen each other in longer, and now you just show up? Waltzing into my favourite café without a bloody word of advance notice, even after all the invitations I sent your way to come and see us. Why?"

He glanced around to make sure George wasn't in earshot. The boy knew a little about what was going on with his mum, but again the warning *no energy for questions* flashed repeatedly in his head. "It's complicated," he said, dropping his voice. "This seemed as good a place as any for George and I to squirrel ourselves away for the winter to survive the transition back home."

"Like the nuts that you are," Doc replied good-naturedly. She took the hint though, as he knew she would. Any time *it's complicated* reared its ugly head, it was a good bet to nod sympathetically and back the hell away from whatever the real details were – which in this case was Cisco's soon-to-be-ex absconding with her gym instructor. A cliché, sure, but there was a reason clichés were clichés. They were prone to happening. Especially in gyms with so much spandex and adrenaline.

Thankfully he hadn't really been all that bothered by what she'd done. There was a part of him that had always known it wasn't right. They wanted different things, saw the world in different ways. She liked being fit and active, he really didn't. She liked going out with her friends all the time, he preferred binge-watching TV shows on Netflix. All the usual stuff you discover far too late, before realising you should have been listening to that gut feeling that kept nagging you all that time – even if that gut feeling had always been searching for someone it wasn't even sure existed. A love just beyond touching distance, as though maybe it might just have been from a dream or some movie he saw once or a forgotten friendship from childhood.

He wondered suddenly if maybe he could open up, now he was safely back home. To spill everything out to his best friend as he'd done as a kid. Doc was always the first person he told when anything remotely interesting happened: getting his first games console, that time he was shoved into the boiler room at school as a prank, the night Rebecca Miller finally accosted him and shoved her tongue into his mouth, whirling it like a washing machine and causing him to gag.

And now he'd returned home because interesting things were happening again, weren't they? Not the divorce, that was almost mundane in comparison. No, it was more the recurring dreams of a familiar woman trying to give him a message. The unshakeable anxiety of a threat on the horizon, like dangerous clouds threatening an unrelenting snow.

The murder.

Yet as quickly as the urge came over him to spill his thoughts and feelings out to her, the responsible adult part of him pushed it back. Now wasn't the time and this definitely wasn't the place. So he didn't offer any more details, only a tired smile.

"Where are you staying?" she asked, never one to press for more information than she needed. He loved her for that. "We have room with us if you need a place to crash for a while? You know Michelle would love to see you. Cecilia, too."

"Oh, thanks, but Jake offered–"

"That little shit knew you were back before me!?"

Cisco couldn't help his smile growing wider at the stirrings of that old animosity. He'd missed that. "I might have grown old in all the worst ways, Doc," he said, "but it's nice to see *you* haven't changed a bit. Yes, I told Jake I was coming back. We're going to be staying at his place with his family. But it was a last-minute thing and… well, I asked him not to tell you or Michelle."

Doc glowered and turned on her heels to return to her table. She hadn't punched him out though and he took that as an invitation to join her. He whistled to George, gesturing for him to stop prodding the cakes, and pulled the seat out opposite her.

"Look, I'm sorry. I should have told you, but I just figured you were busy with work and everything."

She frowned. "Did you just whistle at your son like a dog?"

As George came running over, Cisco kicked aside the chair next to his and gestured for him to sit.

"It's the only thing that cuts through the excitement in the circus of his mind and I'm at the stage of being a dad where I do whatever gets the job done. Judge all you want."

She picked up her drink and eyed him over the rim. "Oh, I am." Then she took a sip, put it down again and turned to George. It was like switching on a light. Suddenly she was all warmth and a beaming smile and those twinkling eyes again. She reached out a hand and they shook.

"You must be George, nice to finally meet you. I'm betting you're here to learn all about the place where your Daddy grew up, huh?"

"I guess."

"Find out anything fun so far?"

The boy shrugged. "He used to have a lot of gas."

As Doc began laughing, Cisco joined in. A long, loud laugh of letting everything go that turned everybody's heads and had his son shrinking into his coat with embarrassment beside him. Yet it felt good. As though he hadn't laughed in years. Which come to think of it he probably hadn't. He hadn't found anything this funny in a good long time.

"Ah, that's fantastic," Doc groaned, wiping her eyes. She put her hand on George's arm and leaned in. "Yes, your dad had a lot of gas. You heard the name then? Gasbuster. Like a Ghostbuster, but with more farts."

George giggled.

"Doc, you're not helping."

She grinned over the small table. "Then tell me the truth, Cisco. Why didn't you want me and Michelle to know you were coming back? We love you, you silly oaf. And you would have given us something to get excited about! Not that married life isn't exciting, of course. That girl still gives me chills in all the right places, if you know what I mean."

George frowned. "What are chills?"

"Why don't you go and have a look at the cakes again and pick all three of us something nice?" Cisco replied, giving his son some money as he scowled at his friend.

Doc just laughed again as the boy ran off.

"Sorry, I'm usually a little more subtle but yeah. It's just that, you know, it's *you*, Cisco. You're back in Dark Peak! We honestly never thought we'd see you here again after everything that happened. With the…"

Her voice trailed off.

"Gas leakage incident?" he offered.

She held up her hands in immediate surrender.

"Let's not get into that again. Whatever it was we went through back then – and thankfully I've been able to forget the entire charade for the most part – it's just good to see you back here where you belong. You fancy joining us for dinner one night, to regale us with tales of your lives and the real reason you've returned?"

Cisco dropped his eyes away, a little taken aback she'd seen through him that clearly. But before he could reply, the person at the next table got up, folded their copy of the *Manchester Evening News*, and left it on the table as they made their way out of the coffee shop. And there, on the front page, was the real reason he had come back to Dark Peak. The beacon of darkness that had lured him here, instead of going to literally any other place on Earth where he might have been safer for a while longer.

Baby monitor murder, the headline screamed. *Costumed attacker at large.*

Steeling his jaw, Cisco's gaze dropped to the artist's reconstruction attached to the story. A terrifying drawing of a giant fluffy duck with glowing red eyes that witnesses described fleeing the scene after murdering some poor father in the village just down the road.

Dressed as a popular children's television character, they'd said.

Cisco didn't think it was a costume at all.

Looking away from the story, he regarded the woman opposite. The woman who had once saved him from a similar fate at the hands of a two hundred year-old pirate and all manner of wretched fictional monsters only he seemed to remember.

"Sure," he replied, wondering how Doc, Jake and Michelle were going to take being told they were all in mortal danger once again. "Dinner sounds good."

For more great title recommendations, check out the Angry Robot website and social channels

www.angryrobotbooks.com
@angryrobotbooks

ANGRY
ROBOT

We are Angry Robot

angryrobotbooks.com

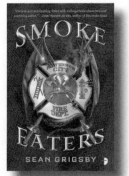

We are Angry Robot

angryrobotbooks.com

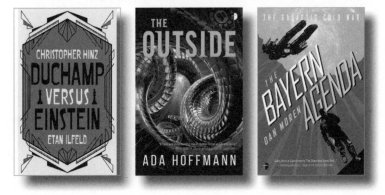

We are Angry Robot

angryrobotbooks.com

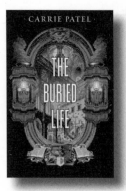
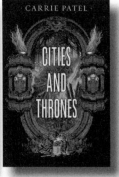

We are Angry Robot

angryrobotbooks.com